SCAMPER'S

F

C000000757

By this author

The Lucy Trilogy

Call Mama
Scamper's Find
The Leci Legacy

Short Stories

A Tale or Two and A Few More (First edition)

Children's books

The Clock That Lost Its Tick and other tales

Novella

A Case for Julie

SCAMPER'S FIND

TERRY H. WATSON

Ramoan
Press

This edition published in 2018 by Ramoan Press

Originally published in 2016 by Matador

Copyright © Terry H. Watson 2016

Terry H. Watson has asserted her right to be identified
as the author of this Work in accordance with the
Copyright, Designs and Patents Act 1988

ISBN Paperback: 978-1-9996502-0-9
Ebook: 978-1-9996502-1-6

All rights reserved. No part of this publication
may be reproduced, stored in a retrieval system, or
transmitted in any form or by any means, electronic,
mechanical, photocopying, recording or otherwise,
without the prior permission of the copyright owner.

All characters and events in this publication, other
than those clearly in the public domain, are fictitious
and any resemblance to real persons, living or dead, is
purely coincidental.

A CIP catalogue copy of this book can be
found in the British Library.

Published with the help of Indie Authors World

IndieAuthors
World

For my nieces and nephews.
You have brought so much joy into my life.
Thank you.

ACKNOWLEDGEMENTS

Sincere thanks to my readers who so enthusiastically welcomed CALL MAMA and encouraged me to continue writing. Scamper's Find is the result of their encouragement, comments for the proposed storyline, and enthusiasm from family and friends as well as the many total strangers who were eager for this sequel to be published.

My thanks to Glenboig Neighbourhood House Digital Inclusion Group for assistance with IT; to my first-draft proofreaders, Drew, Robert and Marie Sweeney for comments and corrections; to my mentor, Rebecca Forster, for her honesty, inspirational advice and friendship; to Kim and Sinclair Macleod of Indie Authors World for professional assistance, and finally,to Drew, my constant and long-suffering supporter throughout this process whose enthusiasm and tea-making skills contributed immeasurably to the completion of SCAMPER'S FIND.

CHAPTER 1

Not many people noticed the bloodstain. It was as if time had forgotten the heinous murder. A crime that reverberated throughout history, a volatile history at that. People in their hundreds walked by the spot where David Rizzio, musician and secretary to Mary, Queen of Scots, was brutally murdered in her presence; a stabbing that her husband, Lord Darnley, demanded she witness as vicious revenge for what he thought was Rizzio's apparent closeness to Mary.The ruthless, devious, scheming lord hoped that she would miscarry her child. The blood-spattered floor from the explosion of blood remains to this day a reminder, a sacred relic almost, of the brutal deed normally unobserved by all but the most observant tourist to the tragic Queen's tiny chamber high up in what was then a cold, dingy, forlorn part of the Palace of Holyroodhouse. The brownish stain, protected from the elements, preserved and soaked into the wooden floor, conjures up the haunting ghost of David Rizzio.

***

Julie Sinclair sighed as she signed off her computer, removed her half-moon specs, stretched her long, toned limbs, and called to her three lively pets to follow her outside. She wrapped up well as the early evening often concealed a deceivingly chilly wind. Her well-worn fleece jacket, which she referred to as her doggy coat, would keep her warm and cosy as she trekked along at a spritely pace, breathing the fresh reviving air. A tall, fit woman, she covered a few miles in almost record time. She had been writing for several hours that day and desperately needed a break; her head, shoulders and indeed every muscle seemed to ache.

The writer walked through the countryside, deep in thought as she mulled over ideas for her latest novel. The balmy October evening walk was a regular event for her. An unexpected Indian summer had left a welcome warmth in the air. *I love this time of year in Scotland*, Julie thought as she scrunched her way through piles of stunning autumn leaves, a favourite caper of hers taking her back to her childhood, evoking memories of carefree, heavenly days, when time seemed to stretch to infinity and holidays lasted forever.

She had been indoors all day and now relished the sights and smells of an autumn that clung onto its season, as if reluctant to give way to the approaching winter. From its high vantage point, a lone blackbird sang its evening chorus, lifting the writer out of her reverie as she listened to its melodic tone. She laughed at the antics of her dogs as they rolled and frolicked, chasing each other like the puppies they still believed themselves to be, pausing to sniff the air before periodically returning to check on her.

Early evening walks calmed her spirit, cleared her head for the inspiration she so badly needed for the next chapter of her book. She was at a crossroads with it. How was she to proceed when she was experiencing writers' block? Panic was setting in. Pressure from her publisher heightened the already stressful situation. *Where am I going with this character?* As she deliberated, the dogs returned ready for home and dinner. The sun was beginning to set: it cast a silvery sheen through gaps in the almost leafless trees, highlighting the unique shape of each species before they became invisible when dimness took hold of the night sky.

"Come on boys, time to head back. Dinnertime! Scamper, come on boy."

Scamper, well named for his penchant for taking off on his explorations, was nowhere in sight. The light was slowly fading. Julie wanted to be out of the dark, wooded area before total darkness descended. She called incessantly for the tardy mutt.

"Oh come on, Scamper! Biscuits!"

The latter normally brought the wily canine to heel, but on this occasion he appeared to ignore all her commands. He often appeared home before the others. *I bet he is sitting by the door demanding food.*

"Right, boys, home!"

Scamper was not, as expected, waiting by the door, nor was he in the vicinity of the neighbourhood, nor in Julie's overgrown, unkempt garden. Fully expecting him to return soon, she fed the others. Her phone rang as she did so.

"Where have you been? I thought you'd be home ages ago."

Julie related the tale of the overdue dog to her fiancé.

***

The dogs were an issue for Craig to the point that it hindered the development of their relationship. A horrendous childhood incident with a stray dog resulted not only in physical, but mental scars; the skin graft to his thigh a constant reminder of the trauma. He had almost, but not quite, issued an ultimatum to Julie: *the dogs or me, your choice!* His love for her prevented him saying something he might regret. Sensing his unease, the animals would leave him alone when he stayed over, and much to his relief, take themselves off to their own area of the house.

"They really only want to be friends with you," said Julie, bemused as to why he was so reluctant to overcome his anxieties, while she herself was completely oblivious to the lasting emotional effect of his boyhood shock.

"If Scamper hasn't turned up by morning, I'll come over and help you search. Where was he last sighted?"

"Oh, on my usual route, over the wooden style onto the path leading to the copse, and back by the bluebell wood. It's not strange territory to him. He'll probably limp home when he's finished chasing rabbits or whatever else he gets up to. It's pitch black now and I've no intention of chasing after him tonight."

Julie let the shower cascade over her tired limbs. She had read somewhere that hot water hitting the head helped trigger brain synapse. *I could do with some clear thinking right now.*

***

Next morning, she and Craig trekked through the wood, following her regular path and calling out to the lost pooch as they went along. A gentle rain shower during the night had left a freshness in the air which the two were oblivious to, so intent were they on their mission to allow themselves to be distracted by anything that nature had to offer. After more than an hour Craig stopped.

"Quiet! Listen! Stop scrunching the leaves; move over here and listen; I'm sure I heard something."

In the silence, broken only by their own breathing, they both heard whimpering.

"Don't move!" hollered Craig. "I can see where he is. Stay back!"

A hole had opened in the ground almost beneath where they stood. The area was riddled with old mine shafts from the heyday of a thriving coal industry. Several pit seams had been operational then. Sadly, the decline in coal stock and political interference caused the industry to nosedive. It was not unknown in mining areas for the weakened ground to open to reveal a water-filled pit similar to a sinkhole.

In such a shaft, Craig located the terrified dog, whimpering and stuck on a narrow ledge of rock, caught in some kind of chain.

"Don't move Scamper buddy, keep calm."

This was the first time in his life Craig had shown any concern for a dog. He was typical of his Celtic race, polite and chivalrous and with a tendency to fight for all unjust causes, his love of music and art in sharp contrast to his rough manner, which to those who knew him was a front to conceal a deep sensitivity.

He lay prone and took stock of what he saw. Julie, frantic by now, lay on the ground, peered into the crevice and was horrified at the scene below.

"Oh, Craig, if he moves an inch... "

"Stay with him, there's no clear phone signal up here. I'll run for help. Derek lives nearby. I'll be as quick as I can. Keep talking quietly to Scamper and don't make any sudden moves and don't go too near the edge."

Water-filled pits and mines can hide rock ledges such as the one Scamper lay on. Abandoned mines can be hundreds of feet deep and filled with all kinds of rusted machinery and rubbish. Julie edged as near as she could; spoke quietly to her pet while trying to keep her voice from rising an octave or two from sheer terror. She could see into the murky darkness and was horrified at the depth of the water. Her own fear of tumbling headlong into the crater, like someone drawn by the hypnotic force of the water, took second place to her concern that Scamper might make a move to reach her and plunge into the abyss. Her imagination ran riot as she lay on the fragile ground, trying hard not to think of it moving under the weight of her body. Her breathing became almost uncontrollable and just as she feared she would experience a panic attack, Craig returned with his friend.

Derek owned a building firm and brought with him various pieces of equipment. He lay on the ground and assessed the situation. His agility contradicted his stature. His over-abundance of food and alcohol made him almost obese, but he lay there like a cat stalking its prey, planning his next move.

"Keep talking quietly to him, Julie, while I figure out what to do here. One false move…"

Julie did not wish to hear of any worsening dangers.

"Craig, shine the torch, just there. I might be able to hook him up by the collar with this long pole. He seems entangled in some sort of chain. These old shafts could have all kinds of metal and corroded materials in them."

He worked quickly, made a few attempts to secure a hook around Scamper's collar, which had loosened slightly, and eventually succeeded in hoisting the bedraggled mutt out of its prison and into the arms of its relieved owner.

"Quick everyone, move back from the area!" shouted Derek. "The ground around has weakened by the cave-in. It's not safe."

Snuggled into Julie's jacket, the terrified animal was examined for injuries.

"I can't see any obvious breaks or signs of injury, but we better get him to the vet as soon as we can."

As Julie climbed into the truck holding onto the whimpering dog, Derek took Craig aside.

"Scamper wasn't alone down there. He was hooked onto a chain and the chain had another occupant. We best get the authorities here to secure the area and remove a body."

CHAPTER 2

The authorities moved quickly to secure the scene. Coal Board officials, police, forensic scientists and various other agencies swooped on the area. Vehicles, sirens roaring and lights flashing, seldom seen in such numbers, followed each other like worker ants foraging and protecting their community. They quickly set up their headquarters in the nearby village community hall, which became a hive of activity, awakening the caretaker into a frenzy of action last seen when the village dance was in full swing. The residents of the sleepy village were curious at the disruption to their normally quiet, uneventful lives. Door-to-door enquiries did not reveal any concerns about missing people from the district. Initial investigation began in an attempt to identify the body. Police records of missing persons were summoned from dusty basement files and re-examined. Coal Board records too, were collected and checked for past mining disasters where lost miners were unaccounted for.

"The problem is," began Doctor Brody Cameron, a renowned and prominent forensic scientist, "as yet we are unable to give much information until tests are complete, so we can't say how long the body has been in the pit shaft nor can we identify the deceased by simple visual means. Dental records and possible DNA samples from nails, bones and hair follicles are all we have to go on at present. It's a gruesome task to be faced with first thing on a working day," he concluded as he tapped his tobacco pipe on his trouser leg, emitting dust, more of which came from his well-worn clothing than from his ancient rusticated pipe. His colleagues held him in high esteem. His sharp mind and ability to solve the most difficult of cases never failed to amaze them.

He was a commanding figure, tall and straight as a ramrod; his grubby Belstaff jacket told of many hours of outdoor activities. Removing his specs from his pocket caused a spillage of its contents. Every imaginable essential tool for the trade shared its space with his lopsided specs and smelly pipe. With his battered deerstalker hat totally out of place with his attire, he had the look of a rather eccentric and scruffy Sherlock Holmes stand-in.

"Can't you even tell from the state of decomposition how long the guy's been down there?" questioned Detective Inspector Rab McKenzie, inspector in charge of police involvement. It had been established that the corpse was male.

"Not so easy, Rab. The water temperature has a significant bearing on decomposition, and water in that mine would have been colder than an Eskimo's nose."

What had not been revealed to the public were the gruesome details of the discovery made by Derek when he rescued Scamper; that the body had been chained to an iron bar, its arms raised above head height and secured by handcuffs. Only officials Derek and Craig knew those details at present.

DI McKenzie continued, "Can we establish if the man drowned or was he alive when submerged? From the little we know based on the chaining, we are talking serious crime here which will involve calling in the guys from our special unit."

"Our forensic team will pull out all the stops to establish the nature of this death. It will not be an easy task but my boys like a challenge. Unfortunately, there won't be much in the way of fingerprints to help identification," added the forensic expert. He and Detective Inspector McKenzie had worked together on many occasions and had complete trust in each other's skills and in the competence of their respective squads.

The scene was photographed as well as could be achieved in the murky, dark, dangerous waters using highly sophisticated underwater cameras. It was deemed too dangerous for divers to venture into the flooded shaft. Eric Quigley, the police photographer, using a state-of-the-art digital camera secured in waterproof housing, took charge of the camera work and later reported to the waiting team:

"From what I can see, there's a mountain of old machinery there. The depth is difficult to estimate but the blackness indicates hundreds of feet. No one in their right mind would go down there, or be allowed to with our strict health and safety rules. This camera is connected to a monitor here on the surface. It will collect whatever evidence is there. We'll just have to depend on it for as much data as we can gather. At least we will have a permanent record of what I find."

Recovery of the body was a challenging task. Highly specialised cutting equipment was used to release the iron bar with the body still attached to it. Those who released the corpse needed strong stomachs. Foul smells assailed the nostrils of the rescuers, and in spite of wearing face masks, they could not escape the stench which caught in their throats. Once the scene had been photographed and all possible evidence collected from the surrounding area, the shaft was sealed over and cordoned off, hopefully for ever.

"Too many of these damn things in the area," said the young constable sent to guard the crime scene as he stamped his feet to keep circulation going. He blew on his hands to emit some form of heat as the cold air, in keeping with the grisly find, seemed to mock him like a sadistic jester on an unsuspecting audience.

"My grandfather was a miner," he continued. "He told me these underground tunnels stretch for miles. The body could have floated from miles away."

"Not our stiff though," replied his equally chilled partner. "He didn't float from anywhere; he was well anchored."

Media descended on the area in force like bees round a honey pot. Speculation was rife. What they didn't know, they surmised. Unable to obtain much information from even the most inquisitive of the rural community, they concentrated instead on Scamper who had become an overnight star. Tabloid newspapers carried the headline: *The Mystery of Scamper's Find* and other similar mishmash captions. Scamper was indeed famous.

Julie, jaded by constant phone calls and requests for pictures and interviews, became more irritated at each passing day. Finally, with more interruptions than she could cope with, she locked up, piled the dogs into her car, and headed to a friend's house.

Liz, her bohemian and slightly quirky friend, owned boarding kennels and happily agreed to take the animals to allow Julie time to concentrate on her writing.

"You know I love your boys and they can have a clean up while they are here," smiled Liz with a friendly dig at her friend's reluctance to tackle the messy job. Julie was oblivious to the state of the dogs. She loved them as they were, and seldom took time to notice their unkempt appearance.

"They will only get messed up again," she would reply. "Why put all that energy into something that won't last ten minutes?"

Julie arrived at the kennels, parked up, and located her friend sitting on the grass surrounded by dogs of all breeds. Liz's long auburn hair and the full-length dress she favoured were a tangled mess of dog hair. Her pockets bulged with dog treats. She was unconcerned about her appearance, and to anyone who met her for the first time, she gave the impression of being a flower power, 1960's hippy.

As her three dogs romped around the enclosure, chasing each other and enjoying the various toys there, Julie discussed her book's progress with her friend who was an avid reader. The pair often had brainstorming sessions when Julie felt the need for fresh thinking.

"This incident has set me back so much. My editor is biting my ear for a projected date for completion of the manuscript. I'm off to Craig's place for peace and quiet. He is back at work so I'll have his house to myself. Trust Scamper to cause this fuss."

Craig worked offshore in the oil industry. He normally worked two weeks on and two off. With him safely out of the way and with no distractions, Julie concentrated on her writing.

Sitting at her fiancé's large kitchen table, she continued to write:

Mary, the enigmatic, tragic monarch, had her claim to be heir to the English throne cunningly thwarted by her cousin Elizabeth 1, who insisted she marry someone chosen by her. The Scottish Queen was to cease referring to herself as Queen of England and agree to the terms of the Treaty of Edinburgh...

What tragic, confusing times these cousins lived in, Julie thought as her fingers moved swiftly over the keyboard.

***

Doctor Brody Cameron's team of forensic scientists worked endlessly. Minute DNA samples from ribs, teeth, bone and hair follicles were deemed enough to assist in identification. After some time, reporters and other interested parties gathered outside the village hall to hear Brody Cameron make his initial report:

"We have established male Caucasian, aged forty to forty-five. He has been in the water ten months or more, perhaps even more than a year. Human remains from water over this period are normally badly decomposed or incomplete, but our victim, by being chained up, had part of his torso intact and hanging just above the waterline.

"Our guy was alive when submerged. The marks on his wrists showed he struggled to loosen the chains. His mouth was taped, he had chewed away part of the tape, and water had eroded most of it. It was common duct tape available worldwide. The most probable cause of death was cardiac arrest. We have tapped into our own bank of DNA information. You all know that we have the largest collection in the world right here in the UK of which I'm mighty proud. The DNA international data section is working alongside us on identification as we speak. I fully expect a result before too long."

He smiled as he spotted a newbie reporter turn chalk white and run from hearing any more gruesome details.

As he answered questions from the assembled reporters, he lit his pipe, slowly and deliberately, savouring the moment like a skill crafted over the years, and after a few draws on the device, smiled as one by one, the crowd overpowered by the fumes, left the scene. *Works every time,* thought the crafty man as he headed back to headquarters. Smoke 'em out. One thing he detested was wasting time answering questions from impatient reporters, when there were no possible answers to be given.

CHAPTER 3

Thirty miles from the scene of the macabre find, Tommy Graham had not returned from his daily cycle run. He was training for an upcoming rally and covered the same route each day. He normally finished his routine at his parents' cottage, before heading to his own home. His wife, Ann, contacted her in-laws when her husband was uncommonly late.

"He hasn't been here, Ann, and we are beginning to worry. It's gone dark. He's normally like clockwork," said the frantic mother.

"That's what concerns me. We know he times himself to the last second. He wants to improve on his personal best. I'm worried in case he's had an accident. It's such a remote area out there and there's no phone signal. His mobile phone is ringing out."

Much later, the distraught cyclist arrived at his parents' home, having limped several miles in the dark over rough ground. His cycling outfit was torn; blood poured from his arm, his ankle was swollen to twice its normal size. His disheveled appearance was in stark contrast to the normally spruce athlete who prided himself on his image. He was fully aware of his striking good looks, a man happy in his own skin and proud of his physique.

"What happened son? You're in some state!"

"Phone Ann, please. Tell her I'm okay. The bike hit a chunk of concrete and veered to the left into water, throwing me off to the right. I've damaged my ankle. I think it's broken. The pain is almost unbearable. I don't know how I managed to make it here. My flashlight was smashed in the chaos and then I fell over a tree trunk and lost my phone somewhere along the track and couldn't see to find it.

"When I tried to retrieve the bike, only the back wheel was visible. It was stuck in an old pit shaft. I tried to pull the bike out by the wheel but it caught in some metal structure or other. But that's not all, Mum; my hand touched a human head. There's a body in there, chained to a metal bar. I've never been so scared in all my life."

With that, Tommy struggled to the bathroom where he emptied the contents of his stomach.

***

Once more, a team comprised of the same officials gathered at the crime scene, secured the area and proceeded to obtain evidence by means similar to the previous incident. Yet again, Eric Quigley was called to record the scene with his hi-tech underwater camera. In the dark, murky waters he discovered that part of an iron bar had loosened, leaving the body dangling by one wrist that was handcuffed to the remaining fragile structure. The entire weight of the body hung in a precarious position.

"Best get this body out ASAP!" he hollered to the waiting cops.

"The bike seemed to have dislodged a weak bar so it could come away at any moment and the body will be lost. We have to get this corpse out of here."

Once more the onerous task of removing a body from a water-filled mine shaft was undertaken by a specialised team.

"I hope we don't have any more of these. I couldn't eat for days after the last one," said a stoical officer.

Similarities between the two crime scenes were noted and discussed while the team, once again, awaited DNA outcome. For decades, scientists have successfully used hair follicles to obtain DNA results for identification purposes.

Brody Cameron explained: "As long as our forensic guys have samples of hair roots, that's the bit underneath that we can't see and not just a cut sample, they have something to go on. This victim's DNA will be identified fairly soon, I'm sure of that. My guys should be well on their way to putting a name to the poor fellow from the other shaft before too long."

"What's the connection here? Until we have positive identification we are left with a hell of a mystery," said DI McKenzie scratching his head as he attempted to puzzle out the link, silently hoping there were no more corpses to rescue from old mine shafts. He walked around the crime scene, his astute detective mind alert for any minute piece of evidence that might hold a clue, any clue to the bewildering find which must surely be inexplicably linked to the previous corpse.

Police officers retrieved the body from the pit, but in doing so sent Tommy's bike into the abyss. Tommy was given the news he had been expecting.

"We tried to save your bike," reported one of the detectives to the anxious cyclist, "but it was tangled in the metal and all sorts of discarded machinery. Our priority was to get the body out intact if possible, a difficult job, and the bike plunged deeper into the water. These old pit shafts are hundreds of feet deep and there was just no way of retrieving your bike. Sorry! I'm afraid it's lost... And now if you feel up to talking we need to log details of it for our report."

"Thanks for trying, Officer. I didn't expect you'd rescue it. When I looked into that shaft it was hellish dark. I knew it was deep. One wheel was above water level, but only just, with the rest well and truly submerged. When I tried to pull the wheel I knew it was caught in something. Then... then I felt something under my hand... man, I nearly passed out when I realised it was a body. I don't mind telling you I was petrified. At first I thought it was a rat, and then I saw a face like something from a zombie movie, staring at me as if I were invading his space."

He took a deep breath as if trying to shake the image from his mind. He continued, "That bike was my pride and joy, only had it six months. I had a cheap second-hand mountain bike to start with which was okay, but when I got serious about cycling I saved hard and bought the hybrid, a Hoy Shizuoka, cost me over £500, a great ride, so efficient, it suited my range of different riding conditions. The hydraulic brakes are reliable..."

He tailed off, as if in mourning for the lost machine. The detectives knew he was still in shock from the experience and let him chat on about cycling which was obviously a passionate hobby of his.

"I'm sure your insurance will cover your losses, enough to get you a replacement, and maybe some compensation money. Would you buy the same make of bike?"

"Hey, I hope that happens! I dream of owning a Colnago 3x zero some day. It's not cheap. It comes in about £3K. It's a carbon filtered racer, eleven-speed, but man, that's only a dream!"

"You never know, Sir; get on to your insurance. They'll contact us for our report which will be ready fairly soon. Best of luck with it. Hope you recover well from your injuries."

"Thanks. I won't be riding for a while until this ankle has healed. It's broken in two places. When I improve on my personal best score I qualify to train at the new Sir Chris Hoy stadium in Glasgow, and to think how near I was to that before this happened."

CHAPTER 4

On the other side of the Atlantic a party was in full swing: wine, food, and conversation were all in plentiful supply. Noise levels increased as the evening wore on and the participants renewed acquaintances with former friends and colleagues.

Superintendent Benson's leaving party was well attended. He strutted around the room making conversation with colleagues to whom, in the past, he had hardly given the time of day. He roared with delight at his own attempts at wit, which was met with polite laughter. When she became aware of the discomfort caused by her tiresome husband, especially when he had overindulged in alcohol, his long-suffering wife moved in, suggesting he speak to another group. Her petite frame and outwardly demure appearance hid a toughness that anyone crossing her path was sure to encounter. There was no doubt who wore the trousers in the Benson household. Superintendent Benson may have ruled supreme in his place of work, but within the confines of his home, he came under the strict regime of his wife, who ceaselessly attempted to control his diet and alcohol consumption.

"I worry about you honey, and want you to enjoy the retirement you have been looking forward to, but if you go on like you're doing, you'll lessen the precious time we have to travel and do all the things we've planned to do with the grandkids."

Her concern fell on deaf ears.

"I'll turn over a new leaf, honey, once I retire. I might even go to the gym or take up golf. Plenty of time to think of stuff like that, but for the moment I'm sure gonna enjoy what's on offer."

As he moved around the room, glass in hand, she shook her head knowing that for the time being at least, she was speaking to a brick wall.

The master of ceremonies called for silence for Mayor Carson who spoke at length and extolled the virtues of the retiring superintendent.

"Gerry Benson has been an inspirational leader of the police department in our great city of Chicago. He ran his squad with a rod of iron, but fairly and compassionately. He coped honourably with a monumental corruption crisis within our force. I'm sure you will all be familiar with the details of that. He saw off a corrupt cop and thanks to Gerry here and his team, the crook has been dismissed from the force and will languish in jail for a long time. Gerry deserves his time now. I just hope he gets out from under Elspeth's feet and goes fishing! We wish you well, Gerry, and sincere thanks for the years you gave to CPD."

Obligatory applause broke out among the guests.

Tony Harvey, chief of the Bureau of Detectives, glanced at his deputy chief, Carole Carr, and raised an eyebrow at the mayor's interpretation of the incident where they were unfairly and wrongly suspended from duty, suspected of leaking sensitive information to the media and almost lost their careers and pensions.

The newly retired Gerry Benson thanked the mayor for his kind words and assured him he would take his advice about fishing.

He continued, "Before you all return to the revelries, I've been asked by Mayor Carson to announce tonight the city's choice for my successor."

A hush fell over the gathering. Speculation had been rife that an unknown chief from outside the state had been appointed and staff were keen to know who their new boss would be.

Benson continued, "It's my pleasant duty to announce the name of my successor, and all hell will break out if he doesn't come up to my high standards!"

Once more, polite laughter followed his remark.

"Get on with it," hollered a rather inebriated young cop, much to the amusement of the partygoers.

"Raise your glasses in a gesture of approval as I present to you, the new Superintendent of Chicago Police Department, Tony Harvey."

A cheer went up, a roar of which any baseball scorer would have been proud. The appointment was enthusiastically approved. Tony Harvey was a popular choice. He was a hard-working detective known for his fairness to his squad and attention to detail in solving the city's crimes. Glasses clinked in approval at the news.

"Cheers, Tony. Cheers!"

"Tony, you brute, you kept that quiet from me," remonstrated Carole, his trusted deputy for many years.

"It was hard to keep it under wraps Carole, but I wanted to see the look on your face tonight. Believe me, I so wanted to tell you."

"Tony, Tony," chanted the crowd, "come on, give us a speech!"

Feigning shyness, Tony allowed himself to be dragged to the podium. Once there, he became serious.

"I'm humbled by your reception of the news and grateful for the trust placed in me by the mayor's office. I intend building on the foundation set by Gerry, and work you guys to the bone to clean up crime in this city. No mercy will be shown to citizens who flaunt the law and, may I add, no mercy will be shown to corrupt cops on my watch. They will be weeded out of the force."

This was greeted with genuine, enthusiastic applause; everyone there knew he referred to the bent cop, Kip O'Rourke, whose betrayal almost cost him and Carole their careers, four years previously.

"Finally," continued Tony, "we wish Gerry a long and happy retirement and on behalf of the squad, we would like him to accept this gift which we trust will keep both him and Elspeth happy."

A junior officer stepped up to present a state-of-the-art fishing rod and tackle to the delighted retiree who beamed with delight at what he thought was his adoring squad. Just as he was about to launch into yet another speech, a basket of fresh flowers was presented to Elspeth, thus taking the attention from the tipsy retiree. Now officially retired and with his successor announced, Gerry Benson took himself off to the bar with some buddies from his early days as a rookie cop, who had come along to support their former workmate.

"This is my round guys; we have a lot of catching up to do."

From a distance his wife spotted him with his friends and resigned herself to several hours of patient waiting for her spouse. *Have your last fling*, she thought to herself, *a new regime starts tomorrow, honey.*

As the new superintendent, Tony Harvey, circled the room accepting sincere, raucous congratulations, Carole Carr breathed a sigh of relief and remembered the conversation she had with him not many months previous.

"I need a change, Carole," said Tony as they had lunch together in the staff restaurant. "I'm in a rut. That suspension back there gave me a jolt. It was cruel and demeaning and made me doubt my own ability to do the job. I want to move on. I've applied for a job with the Los Angeles Police and if I'm successful, I'll be off soon."

"I understand where you're coming from Tony, but, boy, will I miss you. I can't imagine ever settling to work alongside anyone else. If it's what you really want, then go for it! I wish you all the luck in the world."

Deep down, she felt as if she had been handed a bombshell. She had never given a thought to life without her trusted partner. She shared her fears with her husband who knew the bond between the two was so strong that they could almost read each other's minds when it came to solving crimes on their patch. Their work relationship was stronger than with any other of their work colleagues. They trusted each other implicitly and in dangerous situations with their very lives.

"I'd hate to see him move away from CPD too, Carole, but he's such a skilled and experienced detective who deserves to go for promotion. LA isn't the end of the world and I'm sure we'll visit. Let's wait and see what pans out with his application before you get yourself any more upset. You've cried non-stop since Tony broke the news to you. The kids came to me and asked why mom was upset. They thought Walt had died on his visit to the vet and that you didn't want to break the news to them."

He laughed as he tried to cheer his forlorn wife. At the mention of his name, Walt, the family pet, bounced onto Carole's lap almost toppling her from her chair and succeeded in bringing her out of her miserable mood.

That was some months ago. Tony was unsuccessful in his application for promotion to the LA police force. Mayor Carson encouraged him to apply for Benson's job.

"You would be a hell of an asset to CPD. This city needs you to stay on and clean up the place. It was unfortunate about your suspension over that political fiasco. I must say, you handled it stoically. Any other guy would have caved in under the pressure. You have my unreserved admiration and support Tony, go for it!"

Tony did indeed submit his application for the post of Chicago's superintendent of police but kept the news to himself. He even joined in the speculation as to who the new boss might be.

"I hear it's to be a guy from New York," commented one cop. "My cousin is with NYPD and says the guy in mind is a real smart ass, doesn't miss a trick and gives his squad a tough time."

"No. It's some tough guy from Boston. Everyone knows the job is his," chipped in another.

"Well, let's hope the city chooses someone sweet and cuddly," commented Tony while attempting to keep a straight face.

When he was called for interview, he almost lost his resolve to remain silent. So excited was he that he desperately wanted to share the news with Carole, knowing her kind wishes would send good vibes and dispel the nervousness he felt in the pit of his stomach.

CHAPTER 5

Previously in Rio de Janeiro, 'Les's Bar' on Copacabana beach-promenade had been exceptionally busy with training in full swing in the area for the Beach Soccer World Cup that took place every two years. The district buzzed with excitement as the imminent tournament drew near. Everyone, it seemed, had an opinion on the fitness and otherwise of each team aiming for gold. Bars and clubs benefited from the extra clientele, with 'Les's Bar' showing an increase in sales.

"Fred, more beer barrels down this end," said B-J, the owner.

"Coming up, boss."

The head barman smiled to himself. The word 'boss' brought back memories of a previous clandestine period in his life.

Loud steel-drum music assailed the ears. Locals talked incessantly about the upcoming games. They were vocal in their encouragement of their team. The noise level increased as the evening wore on, and to the bar owners, the tills rang out like church bells celebrating a festive day.

"B-J, will you be supporting your England team then and watch them crash out in the first round?" teased one customer.

"Yeah," said another, "they've only been in one final. But us, we've got the most powerful team, been in every world cup final. Beat that, B-J!"

"Best change your allegiance to Brazil, buddy, got more chance of success... give up following losers!" said another drinker to the seemingly good-natured Englishman who owned the popular bar.

"Our guys have the skill. Hey, you should see how they play. It's fast moving, they can score from anywhere on the sand."

"Yeah, and the goals come fast and furious."

B-J roared with laughter as the banter continued, drinks were demolished and the tills rang out like music to his ears.

***

"You ever think of going home to your England?" asked Fred as they sipped a beer during a lull in business. After-noon temperatures drove most people indoors and gave bar staff a well-earned rest before the evening mayhem began.

"Sometimes I think it would be nice to see dear old London Town again... have to say, I do miss the place, but I've been away so long..." B-J continued with his reverie.

"I'd sure as heck like to visit England, see all them places you've told me about. Maybe get me a nice English gal to settle down with. I don't seem to have much luck here."

"You're right. You've no chance pal, not with them scars. You scare the pretty girls away. Even with that plastic work we forked out big bucks for, you still look like a Halloween monster," chuckled his friend, knowing the remark would be accepted with good humour.

That night the oppressive heat kept B-J awake. He mulled over the idea in his mind. *It might be nice to see the old place again.* He lay awake thinking of his early life and upbringing in a rough area of east London and of his criminal career, which to him was the norm for his generation, where poverty and deprivation was rife. *Me mam did her best, I suppose, given the little we had and the extras I managed to acquire helped her out. Miss you old gal. You died too young.*

In the morning he spoke to Fred about their conversation the previous evening.

"Do you really think we could visit England, Fred? I've been mulling it over and have a notion to go back to Blighty."

"Blighty? Where's that?"

"Sorry, buddy… it's a slang term for England. It got me thinking of the old place where I grew up; memories came flooding back, not all good ones, but it was my home, and where I learned the trade."

"Trade? You mean the criminal kind?"

"Hey, keep your voice down," implored B-J as he looked around. "It's been good to us, buddy. Just look how far we've come; we own our own bar here, and we get a good living from it, don't we? We are almost respectable now."

"Us? Respectable!" laughed Fred. "Look at you with that ponytail thing you insist on having hanging down your back, and where's your hair gone from the top of your head then? You ain't no beau, my friend."

Good-natured humour kept the two friends grounded and helped cement their friendship. They reminisced about how fate had brought them together in a Chicago prison many years ago where they established a friendship built on trust and unequivocal loyalty, and very firmly grounded on the code of honour among thieves.

A shoddy money-lending business which they established in New York had a detrimental effect on their unfortunate clients, but led the pair to a lucrative financial deal in aiding and abetting a heinous crime that resulted in tragedy and deceit, sending shockwaves around the political world and putting an end to the career of a potential president.

"And look at us now! Anna's money has set us up for life. She was a generous employer, a real nice lady," said B-J as he let his mind wander to that episode in his colourful life of crime.

"Yeah, but we did work for it and gave her what she wanted in the last months of her life. It was only right for her to award us so generously. Hey, I've never admitted this to anyone, but she sure scared me to death. Me! Scared of a broad?"

B-J laughed at his friend's discomfort and secretly wondered why his best buddy showed such nervousness at the mention of the name of Anna Leci. He didn't think of him as someone who ever felt guilty or had a troublesome conscience and he never questioned his best buddy's unease.

"That's how she was able to control those guys and get them to carry out her plan to abduct the kid; fear and terror, Fred, fear and terror."

"Shame Les never got to spend his share of the money!" smirked Fred. "Hey, I'm sure he'd be happy for us to keep hold of it. After all, he broke our sacred code of honour. We can't forget that. He was a wimp was Les, no backbone."

Fred smiled nervously as he thought of the ruthless way they had made use of their ex-prison cell mate. His brows furrowed at some long gone memory, suppressed, but never quite leaving him in peace. At times he shook with terror as he recalled past activities. He never mentioned the nightmares that crept up on him, unforgiving and unrelenting, tearing his soul apart at times, disturbing the casual life he now lived and menacingly threatening his comfortable existence.

"Sure, but he'd be pleased we've called our business after him; kinda forgave him, gave him respect like."

Both men turned to the neon light above their heads, lifted their drinks, and in unison said, "Cheers, Les."

"Shame about the others on that plane, though. Sure didn't expect such a disaster. Hey, I was real sure the passengers would be okay. It was Les I was hoping to injure, not kill; just meant him to suffer a bit. I must have set the device too far back… it must have been too powerful," mulled a slightly downcast Fred who almost nightly suffered flashbacks to the airplane crash, guilt oozing from every pore of his being. He did not share his fears with B-J.

B-J attempted to console his friend. "Fred, what's done can't be undone. Sure it was a shame about that kid, but don't dwell on it. So, what do you think? Could we safely make it to England without being caught? We'd need new passports and stuff, and would have to travel separately with several days between us. You know the authorities will be on the lookout for us. Look on it as an adventure, a bit like Bonnie and Clyde – you know; the outlaws who travelled around Central America with their gang. Sure gave the cops a hell of a headache! We would have to change our names again."

"Do you think they're still after us, after all these years?"

"Fred, they'll never give up, not after all those deaths, and as for the kid's pa, that politician guy, that was big-time news, they'll be after us forever and a day, sure as I sit here. We must be on every wanted list there is. The FBI will have us on theirs for ever. We must be public enemy number one. Hey, we've already outsmarted them for years, what with my cunning planning and superior intelligence! We can still give the authorities a run for their money."

"Okay, B-J, you know me, fearless and always up for a challenge. Let's see if we can rub their noses in it and get ourselves to your Blighty place. Now, I just happen to know a guy who can turn out perfect documents."

"Fred, I knew you would come up with the goods, and money is no object. I'm sure Les wouldn't mind us having a road trip on him. We'll drink to his memory in dear old London Town. I know a real good East End pub where we'll down a few pints of English beer. You ain't lived, Fred, until you've tasted English beer. We could ask Dan to take charge of the bar. He's a cool guy and real honest."

"Imagine us having honest friends," roared Fred.

As they watched the beach area come to life with sun-seekers settling themselves to catch the endless heat for their already bronzed bodies, and surfers riding the foamy waves to hone their skills, B-J continued:

"Sure glad you got that bit of plastic work done on your ugly mug; changes your whole appearance. You look real cute like! You look a heck of a different person now from those years ago when even the cops were scared to look at you!"

"Yeah, well at least we've put our honest earnings to good use!"

"Honest earnings? Well, I'm not sure how honest our earnings were, but it was sure nice of Anna to reward us with mega bucks."

The normally jovial Fred paled at the memories stored in his heart, memories he was unable to share with his best friend.

"You okay, buddy?" asked a concerned B-J. "You look a bit pale."

"Yeah, I'm good. I think that chicken korma has upset me. Yeah, I'm okay."

"Well, I guess I'll need to teach you the language before we go!" said B-J laughing at the expression on his mate's face.

"What do you mean? Don't they speak English over there?" he screeched.

"Sure, of course they do, they invented it! I'm talking about London's very own language, cockney slang. It's like, special to Londoners, real Londoners that is, ones like me, born in earshot of Bow Bells, that's the bells of St Mary-le-Bow Church, just up the road from where me mam gave birth to me.

Listen up Fred, here's your first lesson: 'we're having a giraffe' means 'we're having a laugh'; laugh rhymes with giraffe; 'finger and thumb' is 'mum', got it?

"Another one, Fred, is, 'having a butcher', which means 'having a look' and 'play the old Joanna' means 'piano'... you following all this?"

Fred nodded, totally confused as to why they had to change words which to him were self-explanatory. Their hilarity ended abruptly when the first of the day's customers arrived at 'Les's Bar' to quench their thirst.

CHAPTER 6

Results from DNA testing were faxed from Brody Cameron's forensic team to Detective Inspector Rab McKenzie. McKenzie read the report and immediately called Cameron to discuss the findings.

"Great work Brody, you always come up trumps. So, we now have a positive identification of our first victim from the pit shaft. Poor chap, what a death. Who could have done that to a fellow human being? He must have been absolutely terrified to have been thrown in there alive knowing there was to be nothing for him but death; makes me shiver to think of the poor guy."

"Save your sympathy, Rab, for the victims of your so-called tragic pit-man. Are you ready to hear our guy's exploits? Do you recall the chaos in Washington a few years back when a presidential nominee had to stand down shortly before the elections?"

"Aye, who can forget that? It caused chaos over there, and then it was followed shortly by that mysterious plane crash carrying his daughter; aye, I do remember it well."

"It's an ongoing investigation in the USA. It has gone international, as two of the suspects behind it were still at large, at least until now. We have identified our boy in

42

the shaft as Alfred Wysoki from Chicago, one of the prime movers behind that crime where all those people on the plane with the girl were killed. We suspect the second body to be that of his mate, Barry Jones, a London man who had been in the States for several years. Over there he went by the name of Barclay Ellis-Jones. We're hoping to have results of his DNA in a few hours. I'm about to phone some high official in Chicago. As gruesome as their deaths were, part of me has little sympathy for them, not after what they did."

"Well I never took you for 'an eye for an eye man'," said Rab, "but, you know, some cases make us grow a hard shell, don't they? And this seems to be one of them. I understand how you feel about those guys. The human race hasn't evolved too well, has it? There's still that primitive need to kill. But, man, that's big news. But how did the two suspects from the USA end up down mine shafts in Scotland? And thirty miles apart, at that?"

"That's for detectives like you, Rab, to solve! I've done my bit," laughed the forensic scientist preparing for another smoke of his pipe. "You know of course we're on hand to help where we can. I'll keep in touch with the the big boys from America when they have the forensic results, then no doubt they will contact you and your squad and link up with your team. It's been a good day's work; nasty, but we got a result."

Brody Cameron mulled over Rab's comment as he lit his pipe, satisfied when the smoke finally emerged like an old steam engine struggling to power up. *Maybe I am a bit too thick-skinned now and have neglected to see the person behind the mounds of evidence. Hmm, food for thought, even at my age. An eye for an eye? Hmm.*

The new superintendent of CPD, Tony Harvey, busy moving furniture around, had hardly settled into his new office when he had a call from Scotland from Doctor Brody Cameron with news his police force had long been awaiting. After preliminary introductions and congratulations to Harvey on his new post, Cameron got to the crux of his call.

"We have found someone here we believe you've been trying to trace in relation to the tragic disaster you guys had four years ago concerning Lucy Mears, the child who was abducted: Alfred Wysoki."

"What? That is amazing news! Tell me more. We've been searching for that guy for years. Where is he and what's he saying?"

"He's not saying a word now."

Cameron went on to relate the grim discovery of Wysoki in the disused pit and the subsequent discovery of a second body.

"We fully expect DNA to show the second body to be your other guy, Barry Jones, known to you guys there as Barclay Ellis-Jones, who also went by the name of Barclay Jones. Our forensic tests are almost complete."

The two officials continued to converse at length, and questioned how the two fugitives got to the UK without detection.

"They went off the radar after the tragic airplane crash and we heard they had gone underground in Mexico but we had no definite sightings of them. No one knew if they were together or not," explained the Chicago chief.

"Hey, but this is big, big news. We've been at our wit's end trying to trace those villains. Even offering a huge reward didn't flush them out. Your guys are great." Superintendent Harvey agreed to liaise with DI McKenzie in a few hours when he had time to impart the news to his colleagues. His first call was to the mayor.

"Tony," the mayor said, "I knew you'd be the man for the job. I just knew you would bring this sorry tale to a conclusion. Now tell me all."

Harvey's squad was occupied in various offices scattered around HQ, busy with their own particular tasks, when an excited rookie officer sent to fetch them and hardly able to draw breath, announced with some pride at having been chosen for the important task:

"The Super wants you in the incident room, ASAP or even sooner. He says you have to drop what you're doing and get your asses over here. His words, not mine," he added quickly when he saw the face of one particularly stern detective who looked as if he could turn him to stone with one crushing glance in his direction.

The assembled squad waited patiently for the arrival of their boss.

"This better be important," muttered one. "I've got a caseload that's gonna keep me here for hours."

"And me. I'm in court tomorrow and have to prepare for it."

"It must be something big. I hope he doesn't take too long. When did the Super gather us together like this before? All of us and not just the big boys in the squad?" said another whose comments were cut short at the entrance of the imposing figure of the Superintendent.

Harvey commanded immediate attention and silence as his curious team waited to hear the cause of such unusual activity. Never one to procrastinate, Harvey got to the point of the meeting.

"Many of you worked with me on the case of Lucy Mears. I have to inform you of the death of Alfred Wysoki, one of our most wanted criminals from that incident."

Several people in the room with him had been involved in the lengthy case of the abduction of Lucy Mears and were keen to learn details of the fugitives they had been trying to bring to justice for several years. There was muttering from the assembled gathering, ranging from relief that the man had been located, to curiosity as to where the information had come from.

"What happened, sir?" asked an impatient officer. "Can we have details?"

"We have been chasing this suspect now for four years and built up a profile of the guy. His folks came over here from Poland, from Krakow, for a better life and settled in Chicago. From what we know, they were hard-working, good people. How they came to have a son like him is beyond me. He probably got in with the wrong crowd, and then ended up in prison where he teamed up with Barclay Ellis-Jones, who used the names Barry Jones and Barclay Jones."

Several of the squad nodded as they remembered the various names used by the fugitive.

"Our missing man, Wysoki, has been found dead, murdered, and dumped in an old mine shaft, thousands of miles from here, in Scotland, UK. We're waiting for confirmation that the second guy to be pulled out of another mine shaft there is our old friend, Jones. The forensic guys are working flat out to finalise a result."

The team was astounded at the news; voices rose, reaching a crescendo as they debated and questioned the unfolding news. They were brought to heel by their boss calling for silence.

"What we have to figure out is how the heck they got to the UK, to Scotland, when every force in our country was on the lookout for them. How did they slip by? I'm taking a team with me to the UK to work alongside our Scottish buddies. Together we'll get this mystery solved. At last we may be able to put the Lucy Mears case to bed, but there's some work yet to be done before that happens. Now I have to visit Brenda Mears to detail her on these developments, not that it will bring her kid back, but it might help with closure when she hears the criminals will no longer harm anyone else ever again. I've called a press meeting for five o'clock. No one has to breathe a word before then. We want no more Kip O'Rourke's in this department."

Murmurs of agreement filled the room and as the team filed out all thoughts of their own workload were temporarily forgotten as they discussed the astonishing news.

CHAPTER 7

A difficult task lay ahead for Harvey in speaking with Brenda Mears whose daughter's abduction led to a tragic end for Lucy and the others travelling with her in the airplane. He asked Carole Carr to accompany him to the mansion. As they drove up the long drive that curved around an ornate water feature, Carole said, "All this wealth and so much tragedy. Guess she'd trade every cent to turn the clock back. What's the point of wealth if there's no happiness? The garden looks unkempt now. It was never like that, ever. There are signs of neglect all around and look at the paint peeling off that door."

"Yeah, Carole, a lot of water has gone under the bridge since we first set eyes on this monstrous place. It was a difficult time for us all, one of the most stressful cases I've worked on in my entire career. Let's hope we can have it rubber-stamped soon, as done and dusted."

They sat in the car for a few moments, neither of them relishing the thought of what lay behind those giant oak doors. It was as if they were reluctant to reawaken the deep sorrow felt when young Lucy was lost to them forever. They were not looking forward to an encounter with Brenda Mears. Without speaking, the two detectives nodded to each other, signalling that it was time to move.

Brenda Mears, sitting in semi-darkness listening to music, was alerted to the detectives' visit by a young housemaid who, in awe of her employer and fearful of her mood changes, knocked gently and waited with bated breath for a response. She was nervous and unsure of what to expect. She announced the arrival of the two people whom Brenda Mears had hoped she need never encounter again.

Brenda received the news from Superintendent Harvey with quiet resignation. The past years had been extremely harrowing for her. She had to come to terms not only with the loss of her daughter, but with the knowledge that her own aunt, her own flesh and blood had perpetrated a heinous crime in order to seek revenge, and for what? She firmly believed Anna had been mad, a madness that drove her to inflict terror and consequent death on her own young relative.

Brenda had to adjust to life without Lucy. The guilt she felt over her daughter's apparent feelings of being unloved by her, her own mother, cut her to the quick. She spent many hours in her darkened room and mulled over where she had gone wrong in the child's upbringing, blaming herself for being too immersed in business matters, resulting in the emotional neglect of her child. Her life had now turned upside down. She had aged considerably. Gone was the confident, formidable, sophisticated businesswoman, once a force to be reckoned with, to be replaced by a broken shell of a woman who had all but given up on life. Her casual clothes, lank hair and lack of make-up spoke of a neglect brought on by tiredness and a certain amount of apathy. Her business empire continued to flourish as her loyal executive team kept it on track, albeit with a little less enthusiasm. They continued to run Mears Empire almost on autopilot. The business prospered, but the same commitment was no longer there. They, too, felt the loss of the child they had known well. They knew their employer had lost interest in any development of Mears Empire and that she trusted them implicitly to keep the firm progressing and competitive, hoping that she would emerge some day from her dark cocoon into the light.

"Thank you both for bringing me the news personally. I have little reaction to it. I'm numb."

She shook her head and continued: "Nothing will shake off my despair and I live with the consequences of my past life. So many people have suffered because of me. Molly will never recover from Lucy's death, nor will Nora; all those innocent victims. And you, yourselves. How could I ever think you were involved with that corrupt cop, Kip O'Rourke and his unscrupulous reporter friend? You were truly, totally professional throughout the investigation. My mind was in such turmoil then, I knew I wasn't thinking straight, but to turn on you two good people was unacceptable."

She was assured that they harboured no ill feelings towards her.

"It was a stressful time for us all," replied Carole, attempting to defuse the situation, "and emotions sometimes got in the way of clear thinking. We were able to find the source of the leak fairly quickly and dealt promptly with the culprits. Please don't let it prey on your mind; we have long forgotten it."

They spoke at length about life after the tragedy. Sensing that the wistful lady wished to be alone, they declined her offer of coffee, thinking it was a gesture made out of politeness. They were aware of her relief when they stood up to leave.

"I have to let Molly know of these developments. She has suffered so much and I look at her now and no longer see my vibrant fun-loving friend. I'm quite concerned about her health."

Brenda showed the detectives out before returning to her morose existence.

She asked Molly, her housekeeper and life-long friend and mentor, to bring some coffee and sit with her awhile as she related the reason for the detectives' visit. The two had become extremely close, finding comfort in each other's understanding of loss. They often sat in silence while Molly knitted furiously to keep herself occupied, dropping stitches and venting her anger on her work. "Damn cheap wool," she would mutter, her fingers gnarled from years of hard work and unable to hold the knitting needles as firmly as she thought she should. Her mind moved from scene to scene over past events and always, always finished with the tragic airplane crash. She, with others, had watched as the plane exploded in a ball of flames that lit up the evening sky and ended their hopes of any reunion with Lucy.

Brenda could not put her mind to anything constructive and sat in guilty silence.

Inevitably, sobbing from one would rise up and engulf both women. Molly had all but retired from household duties. Two 'town girls', as they referred to their cleaning helpers, kept the place reasonably respectable. Neither Brenda nor Molly cared much about the state of things. The once pristine mansion showed signs of neglect; layers of dust lay on the once highly polished furniture, which at one time was Molly's pride and joy. 'Get a shine on that surface, Nora,' she would say if the sheen did not meet her high standards. 'I want to see my face in it. Get to it gal.'

Now, Lucy's rooms were locked and strictly out of bounds to all but the two inconsolable women. Brenda found solace in sitting among her daughter's possessions where she felt a sense of connection with her lost child. She had not altered anything in the girl's suite of rooms. Only when she fingered Lucy's baby grand piano and thought of the times her child had played so beautifully, and cast her eye over the empty cello stand, did the enormity of her loss overwhelm her.

Oh, why could I not see how passionate she felt about music instead of insisting that she follow a business career?

Many changes had taken place in the last four years. Nora, Molly's daughter, unable to come to terms with either the loss of Lucy or her beloved fiancé, George, no longer lived with her mother. She had moved to the Florida Keys and obtained employment in the hotel business. She kept in regular touch with Molly, but felt unable to visit the place where so much sadness engulfed its occupants and memories lingered in every corner, like ghostly apparitions lurking to reawaken terror and sadness in tortured souls. Molly missed the presence of her daughter with a pain manifesting almost like another bereavement, but she would not stand in the way of Nora's future.

"I hate to leave you, Mom, I truly do. We've never been apart, ever. Will you re-consider? Please come with me to Florida; we can start afresh and try to forget this horrid place. I hate it here now."

"Honey, I'm too old to be uprooted. I'll miss you too, but, hey, we can call each day and keep in touch. No, you go, make a new life for yourself while you are still young. I'll be fine here with Brenda. We've gotten kind of closer now, and she needs me with her. I fear for her mental state at times and would rather be near her."

***

Others too, shared a deep loss at the demise of young Lucy. Ken Farmer, Lucy's rather eccentric music tutor, no longer taught music. He also found it difficult to sing in his choir as certain pieces moved him to tears, tears for the loss of his talented pupil, tears for her lost promising career, tears for a world deprived of a gifted cellist. He became a recluse, spending his days in restoration of his beloved musical instruments. He seldom visited the library now, preferring to purchase books online. His librarian friend who adored the kindly man had long retired and moved from the area.

***

Some time after the tragedy, a memorial service attended by those closest to Lucy and her family had been held in her school. Fellow students from the school orchestra played poignant music which included some of Lucy's favourite pieces. Many of Lucy's fellow students who had finished school and had moved on with their lives returned to attend the service. Gina and her daughter Abigail, Lucy's best friend, held each other closely, human contact helping in some way to ease their grief. Quiet sobbing was extensive, muted, private and personal. Brenda's executive staff, as well as workers from all branches of Mears Empire gave their support both emotionally and by their presence. Representatives from CPD were also in attendance.

As the service concluded with a rendering of Taube's gentle nocturne for cello, Brenda, overcome with such emotion, held onto Molly and whispered through tears, "Don't ever leave me Molly, please don't ever leave me."

A scholarship had been established in Lucy's memory, to encourage young people to study music and help fund the purchase of instruments and to provide expert tutors. Funding also helped furnish a state-of-the-art music studio, adding to the already flourishing music department, and helped too, with cost of travel to various venues for the school orchestra. It was a fitting tribute to a talented student. A seraphic painting of Lucy adorned the wall of the music department. It had been commissioned by her mother, the artist being Lucy's friend Abigail who had captured the spirit of the well-loved student with a talent and professionalism well beyond her years.

"A stunning portrayal of my daughter. Thank you, Abigail. It is precious. You have such talent, just like Lucy. Follow your dream, and don't let anyone stand in your way."

Brenda's voice trailed off as she studied the image captured by the young artist and wished, oh how she wished, her daughter was alive to follow her own dream.

CHAPTER 8

Such was the gravity of the macabre finds and the positive identification of his country's most wanted evildoers, that the newly appointed Superintendent Tony Harvey gathered an experienced team of trusted detectives and headed for Scotland. Before leaving, he told the rest of his squad: "I can't sit here engrossed in paper work while there is a gruesome mystery to solve. Those of you who worked with me and Detective Carr during the time of young Lucy's disappearance have, as of now, been relieved of all other duties to concentrate on figuring out how the two scumbags got themselves killed in Scotland. Your specific tasks will be given to you before I leave for the UK. Other cops will take over your routine work until such times as we bring this mess to a close. Regardless of our feelings towards Barclay Ellis-Jones and Alfred Wysoki, a crime has been committed resulting in their deaths and we have a duty to bring the perps to justice."

During the long flight, Tony and Carole mused over events of the past few years that had taken over their lives.

"Was there anything else we could have done to save young Lucy?" Carole pondered, more to herself. The question never really left her mind, as she often privately mulled over the case, questioning her own and her colleague's skills in tracing the elusive abductors.

"Carole, seldom does a day go by that I don't ask myself that question. We did all we humanly could, and truly have nothing to beat ourselves up about. Fate led us too late to figure out that Anna Leci was the kidnapper. She didn't enter the equation until it was impossible for us to act. Those two, whose deaths we are travelling to the UK to attempt to shed light on, are the real villains. We have to put aside our opinion of them, and however ironic it might seem, we need to bring their killers to justice.

"Anna Leci wanted her niece returned home safely, but those two criminals who wanted to settle a score with their former buddy, Les Soubry, thwarted the plan. Why the hell didn't they just deal with him without taking those poor people with him? That will probably never be known now. Heck, Carole, we could mull over this forever and never find answers. Let's get some shut-eye or we'll arrive in Scotland looking like two wet rags. The rest of our team seems to have nodded off."

A squad from Police Scotland greeted him and his team warmly, drove them to their hotel and after a reasonable rest met to tackle the investigation that had drawn them together. Barry Jones, who as they all now knew, used the alias of Barclay Ellis-Jones and Barclay Jones had, like his fellow criminal, died from cardiac arrest in another murky pit shaft. Harvey told his opposite number in rank that US intelligence had traced the two to Mexico shortly after the airplane deaths, but they had lost track of the villains after that.

"They went off the radar after Mexico and probably used it as a stepping stone to South America where they went underground. How they got to the UK remains a mystery."

"That is what we hope we can solve together," replied Rab McKenzie. "We are presently checking out all UK airports' CCTV, ports and harbours around the country. We may look a small island but we have over 19,000 miles of coastland. Scotland itself has over 6,000 and, if you count the many islands, we have over 10,000 miles of coastlands, so your guys could have entered the UK by any number of ways, legal or otherwise. We'll check back as far as we can with the recordings; there's no guarantee of them being still in existence. They are usually overwritten after a relatively short period."

The Chicago contingent moved on and viewed the two crime scenes.

"We would like to see where the crimes were committed. Let's start from there."

"Gruesome!" exclaimed Carole, as they studied the area around the pit shafts. "But why so many miles apart? I've heard of these sinkholes back home, but, hey, how scary is that, that they can open up so easily?"

"Mine shafts are slightly different," explained one of the Scottish detectives. "The ground has been disturbed by blasting during the working in the mines, to the extent that the ground is weak and the torrential rain we can have here upsets it even more. Mine shafts are man-made and can cave in if there's been a poorly supported mine roof. Sinkholes are usually the result of extreme rainfall in an area built on chalk; the water seeps through and dissolves the chalk. Whatever we call them, they cause massive problems."

After examining what they could of the grim sites and the video recording captured by the police photographer, the detectives visited the cyclist, Tommy Graham, who was nursing his broken ankle. After polite enquiries into the young man's injuries and commiserating with him on the loss of his treasured cycle, the detectives brought the conversation around to the task in hand. ·

"Just so we get the feel of things," said Harvey to the nervous Tommy who was in awe of the American cops, "we know you've made your statement, but run it past us again."

Tommy recounted the traumatic events but had nothing new to add to his previous account.

"To tell you the truth, I want to forget the whole thing, but I can't seem to shake it off, especially when I try to sleep. I relive it all. Touching that dead guy's head freaked me out, man. I've never been back to that place since. It was a great route for my cycle practice, but all the money in the world won't get me to ride there again. I keep thinking about how different it would have been if I'd fallen to the left instead of to the right of that pit shaft. I'd be the one in that shaft and it would have been curtains for me."

They left to contact the writer whose dog was responsible for the initial horrific discovery. As they drove along, Carole commented on the visit to Tommy.

"That guy sure needs counselling. Don't you offer it to folks like him who have had such a traumatic experience?"

DI McKenzie smiled to himself, raised his eyes to heaven and quietly replied, "He's a Scot, Carole, we're hardy folks. We just get on with things. No disrespect Detective, but that's the way we do it up here. Of course, if the lad asks for counselling, it would be arranged."

Julie, now back living in her own home with her three rescue pets, invited the detectives indoors and recounted her version of events.

"I wasn't told about the body in the pit shaft, not at first anyway, Craig and Derek thought I'd been upset enough.

I feared I'd lost Scamper forever. He had settled in so well here with the other two. He'd had a rough life before he came to me and I feared the pit experience would set him back, but he's a tough wee guy."

"And which of these cute dogs is Scamper," asked Carole, "the one who was responsible for that awful find?"

On hearing his name, the infamous mutt made his introduction by tail wagging and general exuberance. Carole, the dog lover, fussed over him. Julie talked through the horrific events but had little to add.

"How did that guy get there?" she asked the assembled officials. "And a second body was found too, so I'm led to believe. What's going on in this neck of the woods? It's normally very quiet. That's why I chose to live here, I usually get peace to write," she said as she playfully shook her finger at the lively animal.

"The last bit of excitement was when some money went missing from the church collection box and the whole village was put on alert to a potential thief in their midst. The excitement died down once the minister remembered he had put it safely in a kitchen cupboard when he went off to answer the phone."

"That's the big question. At the moment we don't know how those two guys got here," replied Harvey, "but we won't stop until we find out why our most wanted American criminals ended up traumatising you Scots, not to mention scaring your lovable pet."

They chatted to Julie about her forthcoming book.

"What's your book about?"

Julie explained her genre was historical novels.

"I love history. I took a history degree at Edinburgh University and became interested in the Stuart and Tudor periods. That's what I mostly concentrate on; fiction, with a historical bias. I'm writing about the conflict between Mary, Queen of Scots, and her cousin, Queen Elizabeth 1. I'm attempting to portray a more human side to the two women, rather than simply stating facts about their lives."

"I'd sure like to read your book when it's finished. Hey, maybe you could write about all of this some day," suggested Harvey, waving his hand in the direction of the lively dog as they stood up to take their leave of her.

"I would certainly not have far to look for inspiration," she replied with a sigh, "not after Scamper's find. That dog of mine doesn't know what he has got us all involved in."

"Yeah, but if it wasn't for him we would still be searching for two wanted criminals. Scamper has done us all a great favour."

Scamper, excited at hearing his name yet again, entertained the visitors with his liveliness and fetched his favourite toy in the hope that someone would take up the offer to spend time frolicking with him.

Her fiancé, Craig, was unavailable for face-to-face interview.

"Unless," smiled Rab McKenzie to his guests, "you fancy a trip north to Aberdeen and a fifty-minute helicopter ride out to Shetland and landing on an oil rig in high winds? That's where the guy will be for another two weeks. He works in the oil industry."

"Shetland sounds idyllic," replied Carole. "I read up about it when we first got your report, and about the re-enactment of burning a Viking boat. You guys sure know how to keep history alive. But I'll pass on 'copter rides in this wind. Can we call him?"

Rab arranged for Harvey to call Craig Coyle at Sullom Voe Terminal on mainland Shetland. Craig recounted his horror when he and Derek rescued the bedraggled dog and discovered a body.

"Derek spotted the guy first. We didn't want to scare Julie any more than necessary. I had a discreet look at the body when she was engrossed in seeing to Scamper. I don't mind telling you, I've a strong stomach, but, man, when I saw that guy hanging there, eyes bulging and staring right at me, it took me all my time not to throw up. His arms were above his head, handcuffed to an iron pole or something similar, his face distorted and black like a mask. I've never been back to that area since that night and don't intend to. And I hear there was another body found. What's going on? Is there a mass murderer on the loose?"

"That's why we've teamed up to investigate this mess. We'll solve it. We're all focused on bringing it to a quick conclusion," he was informed.

After some more questions, Tony Harvey ended the call, knowing nothing new had been added to the investigation.

"I didn't really expect these witnesses to have anything more to tell us, but we had to check things out, if only to see if these folks have recovered. Sometimes after a bit of space and time to reflect, they remember more detail. Seeing the two crime scenes was pretty horrific. We must have a sadistic killer out there and he's got to be caught. Makes me wonder if there are any more bodies lurking in those pit things?

"One thing that's certain is that the crime couldn't have been committed by one man. Those bodies would have been deadweights, pardon the pun, so it would have taken two people to do the deed. The shafts would need to be levered open and the bodies handcuffed to those iron bars. It would take the strength of Hercules to do that alone."

Brody Cameron, puffing on his pipe and blowing smoke rings around him, commented on that.

"My forensic boys looked at the part of the iron bar that one of the unfortunates was still attached to and wasn't convinced it was part of the structure of the pit shaft, but there was no way anyone was going to look in there again. Eric's camera shots were too dark to be any clearer, so where the iron bar came from is anyone's guess."

Carole said, "It seems that Scamper is the only one not fazed by the experience. He's a great dog. Hey, I'd love to take him home with me; he'd be great company for my old mutt."

"Forget it," laughed her Scottish colleague. "Scamper stays here, he's our prime witness! We might have to put him in our witness protection scheme if you have your sights on him."

Derek Reid's account did not add anything to his original statement, but like the others, he recalled the horror of the scene as it opened up in front of him.

"It was nerve-wracking trying to prevent Scamper from slipping and trying to ignore the grisly head only two inches from my face. I don't mind telling you how sick I was when I got home but had to keep it together for Julie's sake. It was a horror movie in the making. I thought the ground was going to open up even more and I'd be a goner. It was the most stressful experience of my life. I feared we might have to let Scamper go, but after a few attempts I managed to hook him up. It was as if he trusted me to help him; he didn't panic or make any sudden moves, he just looked at me with those big doggy eyes; he never took his eyes off me. I knew I had to save him."

Derek, like the other witnesses, had been informed of events leading to the search for Barclay Ellis-Jones and Alfred Wysoki.

"Sounds to me, and I'm an amateur, as if they had been traced by someone affected by their crimes back in the USA, someone who wanted revenge; but why here? What's that all about?"

"What we have to establish is how these guys got over here," said Rab, "and when."

"Fishing boat, maybe?"

"Pardon, Derek? Fishing boat?"

"Aye. There's plenty fisher folk and guys with private vessels who would drop your boys off at a quiet location if the price was right. Just a thought, you know. Every inch of our border can't be manned."

"Before we head off, Derek, you were nearer to the scene than any of us. Did you notice anything about the metal bar the guy was hanging from? Any observation on that?"

"I didn't stick around to study anything. Just wanted to get the dog out and get away from the place... but now you mention it and from the image in my head that won't leave me, I don't think it was part of anything in the pit. I would say at a guess that the guy was handcuffed to it before he was shoved into the pit and the metal bar caught on something and stuck there."

"That's given me food for thought," replied Brody Cameron as he thanked the young man for his observation.

On the drive back, Harvey discussed the possibility of the criminals entering the country illegally in a small fishing vessel or something similar.

"It's not outwith the realm of possibility, I suppose," mused Rab, deep in thought. "Leave it with me. I have pals in the fishing industry. I'll sound them out; not that they would be involved in covert games, but they might just know of others who would not turn down a bit of extra cash. It's worth investigating but I would doubt your guys arrived here that way. Mind you, I was hearing the other day that the authorities are bringing reinforcements to the Isles of Scilly in an attempt to ward off illegal entry to the UK by that route. I'll get our border control guys onto this. We'll explore every avenue to get to the bottom of this."

CHAPTER 9

The lawyers acting for Anna Leci, Brenda Mears' aunt, spent considerable time dealing with the complexities of her estate and her vast wealth. Once a respectable time had passed, the senior partner contacted Brenda who was at first reluctant to have him in her home, but relented in the hope of perhaps discovering more about what happened to Lucy during her abduction. She asked Molly to be present.

"Molly, I really don't want to hear anything about my aunt, but I cling to the hope that we can learn some more about my darling's last few weeks. Stay by my side during his visit."

An unusually nervous Brenda indicated where the lawyer was to sit, and waited. The palms of her hands were clammy. She felt faint and stressed. *I don't need this hassle*, she thought as she waited for the elderly man to begin, hoping the meeting would be brief.

"As Anna Leci's only surviving relative, there are some issues which have to be resolved regarding the disposal of her properties and personal effects," began Jordan Garnett, the elderly, senior partner of his family firm as he adjusted his glasses and shuffled large envelopes around before selecting the documents he required. He was equally nervous, having heard of the formidable Brenda Mears and did not relish meeting with her.

Brenda interrupted him sharply.

"I have to say at the outset I want nothing, repeat nothing, belonging to that woman. I only allowed you here to shed more light on my daughter's tragic death." The lawyer was taken aback at this but surmised that there must have been no love lost between aunt and niece.

Wishing to avoid confrontation, he suggested, "I understand you are upset and I don't wish to add to your pain. I have been Anna Leci's lawyer for many years. I knew her well and advised her in the final draft of her will. Would you prefer, rather than discuss things here, that I leave some sealed documents with you and perhaps contact you when you have had time to digest their contents? One is a letter written for your daughter describing some family history which Anna wanted her to have. Anna left it for Lucy in case she passed on before meeting the child. She was so looking forward to Lucy's visit. She had terminal cancer and knew her time was limited. Lucy read this document and had it explained to her by her great-aunt. Anna informed me of this just a few days prior to her death when I called to have our last brief conversation. I knew I would never see the dear lady again."

The elderly gent removed his handkerchief, wiped his eyes, blew his nose noisily and said, "Excuse me; I fear I may have the beginnings of a nasty cold."

Once composed, he continued, "This second sealed document, rather confusingly, was drawn up putting sole blame on herself and exonerating those involved in delivering Lucy to her, giving reasons why they had no choice but to follow her bizarre instructions regarding travel arrangements that she had made with you. I honestly have no idea what this is about. She instructed my junior partner to draw up the document for her to sign during my enforced absence. She had become more and more confused towards the end. It has taken many years of working on her will after the dreadful tragedy involving your young daughter and the staff members who were on the plane with her, which is why I have only now been able to contact you.

"I think they will go some way to ease your confusion as to what happened to your daughter and why your aunt arranged for her to be away from you much longer than planned. She wanted her to visit her cabin in Montana. She fully intended her to return safely to you after the agreed time. The plane crash was so tragic. At least dear Anna was spared the knowledge of the horror of it. She had passed away days before."

Brenda looked at Molly to confirm that she too was baffled by what he had related. Neither woman had the energy or presence of mind to question the lawyer on anything he had said. He excused himself, gathered up his belongings, and departed rather abruptly, stating his health was not good and he must leave at once. He appeared to have been overcome emotionally as he spoke of Anna Leci.

"Well," declared Molly as they attempted to recover their composure, "did you ever hear the likes of that? What's gotten into that man? 'Dear Anna', my foot! Oh, honey, don't cry, don't let him upset you so, he's a confused old man, ought to have retired years ago, in my opinion."

Through tears, Brenda, clinging onto her dear friend, mumbled, "Has he no idea of the reality of Lucy's abduction? Surely he knew that Anna abducted Lucy. What did he mean by Anna having arranged Lucy's trip with me? And Lucy looking forward to it? What is going on, Molly? I don't understand any of this. Oh, I have more to think about than worry about an old man's memory loss. You are right; he should have retired long ago."

In disgust, Brenda tossed the envelopes carelessly onto a table.

"They can stay there until I decide what to do with them. Molly, I'm going to rest, I have a migraine coming on."

Some weeks after the visit from Jordan Garnett, Molly suggested they peruse the documents.

"It might give us an insight into what gibberish that man was talking about. If things are not any clearer we can trash them. But at least let's look over them."

The two pored over the documents, taking time to digest the contents. As they read, silently at first, tears streamed down their cheeks. They looked at each other and then gave vent to their emotions. It was difficult for them to comprehend such deliberate evil inflicted on people by one sad, mad woman.

"How could she blame me for my mother's death and seek revenge? How could she even reason that out?"

Brenda was stunned to read that her own birth, and her mother's death in childbirth, was the cause of her aunt's misery.

"She wasn't a reasonable person, honey. No normal person would have acted as she did. Obviously she loved her sister with a devotion that coloured everything else in her life and she had to find someone to blame when her sister died giving birth to you. Grief seemed to have over-whelmed her and she could never accept her sister's death so she focused her resentment on you."

"But, it was such a long, involved trip to put a child through, Molly. How could she do that? And those people travelling with her; hadn't they the guts to call the authorities and take some responsibility for their actions? I'm sure they would have been safe from Anna's threats to have them deported. The authorities would have looked favourably on them for ending Lucy's nightmare. I'm sure of that. And as for that old lawyer, he has a lot of questions still to answer. I could not follow his garbled story. I need to speak with him and clarify a few things.

"Beats me how any one person could control and manipulate others to do such evil. Anna was wicked, or mad, or both."

Closing the documents, Brenda said, "I'm sure glad I never really knew my Aunt Anna. She never visited or called, and as far as I know, she never sent gifts for me, *her only niece*! My father never spoke of her for reasons unbeknown to me. She turned up here for his funeral, but left in haste before I had an opportunity to talk with her. I thought that was strange, but I was so distressed at the time and was trying to hold it together and found it hard to to speak to people. She had gone before I noticed."

Jordan Garnett called some time later to arrange to visit Brenda. She was reluctant to enter into conversation with the elderly gentleman and was about to request a call from a younger partner in the firm, when Jordan Garnett launched into a spiel: "I expect you have some questions to ask me about the documents. Perhaps we could arrange for me to call by?"

"I most certainly have; several questions in fact, Mr. Garnett."

"Oh, please, call me Jordan. Mr. Garnett is too formal."

"Goodbye, Mr. Garnett," said Brenda. "I will arrange a time for you to visit."

As the call ended, the elderly gent thought to himself, *what a strange lady, so abrupt, not a bit like dear Anna.*

***

He arrived at Brenda's home at an appointed time, unsure of the reception facing him; I might as well get this over with and escape from that odd woman.

He began by saying, "I was thinking you might like to visit your aunt's cabin in Montana. I say this to reassure you that Lucy spent time in beautiful surroundings. It might help your healing to see the area where she spent her last days, before we dispose of the property. For all we know there may be some of her belongings there. I can arrange with the elderly couple who look after it, to have it prepared for your stay and arrange for you to collect keys to the property. Anna so wanted her great-niece to visit there."

"I'm not sure about that at the moment. You have given me much to ponder over, including your part in Lucy's trauma which I am determined to get to the bottom of, but right now I do not have the energy to pursue your involvement with my wicked aunt."

The elderly man looked totally bemused but Brenda had neither time nor patience to have him in her home any longer than necessary. She agreed to give the suggestion some consideration and curtly ended his visit.

A most odd lady indeed; most odd, he thought as he drove off to find sanctuary in his office.

Brenda was unsure if she could cope with the emotional roller coaster that such a visit might add to her already exhausted mind and body. She was concerned too, that

Molly, now much frailer, might not be fit for such a trip. The events of the past four years had taken their toll on the once exuberant woman. They discussed it at length and eventually decided on a course of action. They would visit in early summer. Brenda contacted Jordan Garnett for him to arrange the visit to Montana.

CHAPTER 10

Before his gruesome death, Barry Jones, the organiser, the schemer, planned the trip to London with precision. He made sure Fred, formerly known as Alfred Wysoki, knew exactly what he had to do regarding travel arrangements, and cautioned him to merge in with the crowd. Alfred hated his full name, preferring 'Alf" or 'Fred' to 'Alfred'. He always worried when he had to have a name change in case he messed up.

"Okay, so kinda try to remember your new name for this trip. That is what is on your documents, so if anyone asks, remember who you are. We travel separately, five days apart. It's gonna take a hell of a long time to get there cos we ain't taking a direct route to Europe, but it will work out just fine if you stick to the plan. We'll be going by different routes. We should avoid detection that way. Anyone looking for us will probably be watching for two guys travelling together. You're gonna dress up to look like a suave businessman. The documents look great by the way."

"Yeah, yeah, got it B-J! You've told me this a million times."

"We gotta make sure we don't mess up!"

The evening before he was due to leave on his travels, Fred spent a restless night going over in his mind the route he was to take to reach London. He was used to having B-J's company from the time they were released from prison until now, and was panic-stricken at the thought of travelling alone.

An apprehensive Fred set off on his epic journey. His smart appearance, change of hairstyle and previously treated facial scars, made him almost unrecognisable as the scruffy Alfred Wysoki formerly from Chicago. He flew from Rio to Uruguay and spent an anxious time before finally boarding a flight from Carrasco International Airport for a sixteen-hour journey to Brussels.

Sleep evaded him. Every unfamiliar noise startled him, causing a concerned flight attendant to ask if he felt unwell. She was used to nervous passengers, but this one seemed to her to be particularly stressed.

"I'm okay. I hate flying. Never used to, but I sure hate it now. How much longer are we on this darn aircraft?"

"Sir, we have a long flight ahead. We aren't even halfway yet. Why don't you try to sleep? It will help shorten the journey for you."

Try as he might, the reluctant flyer could not sleep. Each time he closed his eyes he imagined he was on the doomed flight that claimed the lives of five people, some four years earlier. As the plane prepared to land he clenched his fists tightly, closed his eyes, and tried not to imagine what it must have been like for those travellers.

I must be getting soft in the head to even let it bother me, he thought as the plane touched down safely.

Arriving in Brussels, exhausted and dishevelled, he followed directions from B-J and located his hotel. For the next few days he posed as a tourist and joined a guided tour of the capital, visiting the magnificent St Michael's

Cathedral, the Royal Palace, the Chinese Pavilion and Japanese Tower, none of which held any interest for the disorientated man. He avoided conversation with his fellow travellers by sniffing into his handkerchief, feigning a severe cold in an attempt to ward off unwelcome attention.

Completely out of his comfort zone with jet lag, language, strange food and loneliness, he spent three miserable days there before boarding a ferry, as instructed, to Newcastle in north-east England.

Once there, he took a train to London and arrived at a hotel which B-J had booked for him under his false name. En route, his documents passed inspection. He was exhausted from travel and for the first time in his life he felt out of control of life's events.

Wish B-J was here.

B-J set off five days after his associate. His fresh appearance disguised the normally casual style associated with the beach bar owner. He flew by Air France to Charles de Gaulle Airport in Paris, where he too spent time as a tourist. Being more confident than Fred, he merged into the tourist scene with ease and, with phrasebook in hand and oozing confidence, enjoyed the delights of the capital. Had he not had a prearranged date to meet his ally, he would have revelled in a few more days of sightseeing, with an opportunity too of satisfying his taste buds in several of the gourmet French bistros. *I'm sure gonna spend more time here on the return journey.*

From Paris, he travelled by Eurostar train to Ashford in Kent in order to avoid arrival at the central London hub where he suspected security would be tighter. After two nights there, he boarded a coach to the capital and checked into his chosen hotel, a few streets from Fred.

On a prearranged date and time, the two met up and began a relaxing vacation in and around the capital. A much-relieved Fred, now less fearful since he was no longer alone and had his friend to act as guide and companion, settled in to life as a tourist. Never having had much experience of travelling, he felt completely out of place in this strange country. From the top deck of a city tour bus, B-J pointed out places of interest. He was elated at being in home territory.

"I hardly recognise some of the old places," he told his mate; "Big, big improvements, most of them for the better. So what do think of London, Fred, I mean what do you really think?"

"Gee! B-J, hey it's awesome! I'm sure glad we came, but hey, I haven't heard any of that slang talk yet; seems to me the place is full of all foreign accents just like that Belgium place."

"Tomorrow, buddy, you'll hear cockney slang. We'll head for the real London, the East End, and go visit a real East End pub."

Next day, they walked through street markets off Mile End Road. The place was alive with stallholders, voices reaching fever pitch as they tried to outdo fellow merchants in attracting customers. Good-natured banter filled the area. B-J revelled in the exciting atmosphere.

"Just listen to the chat as we go along and you'll hear some of the lingo."

"Hey, they talk so fast! I can't understand a word they're saying."

They spent a few hours there and soaked up the atmosphere of this strange new world for the bemused traveller. B-J took him to see the area of his old home and school that had been demolished during the development of the city docklands. He stood in awe as he looked at the transformation of the area. The dockland area was unrecognisable to him.

Gone were the old dilapidated warehouses, rusted machinery and cranes which, as a boy, he remembered reaching out their menacing arms over the grim East End as if mocking the poverty-stricken area and its inhabitants. All the paraphernalia associated with that long-gone industry had now been replaced by a city of glass; a thriving, modern business and up market district and home to the many up-and-coming young people whose careers centred on the capital.

They took a ride on the Docklands Light Railway. Fred was in fear of his life on discovering that a computer controlled the train, and that no driver occupied the front seat. B-J ignored his protestation that they were going to crash at any moment, and absorbed the splendour of this new space age world. He was so engrossed in his return to his homeland that he was unaware of the stress from his companion.

They exited at Island Gardens and walked for fifteen minutes through the Greenwich Foot Tunnel under the River Thames to visit the Cutty Sark, a tea clipper built in the latter part of the 1800s.

There, Fred was given a history lesson from his exuberant companion on the stunning ship and its adventures.

"Have you ever seen such an elegant vessel, Fred?" as he climbed aboard to the visitors' galley.

"Sure is awesome, B-J."

Scared out of his wits at the idea of tons of water from the mighty Thames having been just feet above his head in the foot tunnel, the now reluctant tourist insisted they return to London by a more civilised means of transport.

"Oh buddy, you're a wimp! Okay, we'll avoid the foot tunnel. They say it's haunted anyway! I should have told you that! Let's ride a London bus."

They ended the day in a typical East End pub and enjoyed a meal and several pints of beer. Fred, for all his bravado in the world of crime, was showing unusual signs of stress.

"It's either jet lag or homesickness or perhaps the cold. You'll be fine when you've had a few more pints inside you," remarked B-J. "Hey, we still have to drink a few more in honour of our good buddy Les."

***

A customer seated at the opposite end of the bar studied the two men. He discreetly took a mobile picture which he sent to his brother with the message: *Is this Barry Jones?*

CHAPTER 11

As April turned to May, Brenda and Molly prepared for a poignant trip. With everything in place the two flew to Montana and picked up a hire car.

"It hasn't taken us long to get here Molly, but my poor darling Lucy had to endure weeks of winter travel to reach this place. It must have been harrowing for my child."

Following directions from the lawyer, they made their way up the mountain track to their destination where they found the key as arranged. Brenda hesitated before inserting it in the lock.

"Oh Molly, I'm not sure if I want to be here. This is so difficult."

"Let's go in honey, we've come all this way."

In spite of their initial reservation, the women were pleasantly surprised at the decor and lay out of the place. They walked from room to room, examining the various artefacts and acknowledging the significance of the visit. Whatever their feelings towards Anna Leci, they had to admit her taste in art was exquisite.

"I can almost sense Lucy's presence here, Molly. That may sound irrational, but knowing she was here, touching these artefacts, sitting by that woodstove. Oh! Molly, I miss my baby."

Both women dissolved into tears yet again. The passing of time had not healed their pain or soothed it in any way, but reawakened emotions which would haunt them for the rest of their lives.

Through tears, Molly said, "Just when I think I'm all cried out, another deluge comes."

"My daughter was here; my baby was here. This is where she was forced to travel to, all those miles in horrendous winter weather. Only a mad person could have planned that trip, only a mad woman like my aunt."

"Yeah, honey, but look at the spectacular views she had, each window has a very different scene. She must have drawn some solace from the scenery. It can't fail to move the spirit and Lucy had an open spirit; she must have experienced some kind of peace here. There's no doubt this is a spectacular area and to see it in winter must have been amazing."

Their reverie was interrupted by a knock at the door. There stood Ellie Stiller, an elderly neighbour, who along with her husband had looked after the cabin for several years, restocking it with logs and food when requested to do so by Anna Leci. They were forbidden to have any contact with people using the cabin, most of whom wanted to be undisturbed for various reasons.

"Hey, I just wondered if you two needed anything. Me and Gus, that's my man, are going to the grocery store in Polson."

The woman was invited in and after some initial introduction and general chatter Ellie expressed her deep sorrow at the tragic events.

"Did you see my daughter when she was here?" asked Brenda, hoping for any minute detail which might ease her pain.

Ellie told of the sighting of Lucy at the window.

"The weather was far too crazy for her to be outside. She seemed to go from window to window, taking in the different views. This cabin has the best of views in the area. That little shack down there, that's our home, Gus and me. It's not a patch on this and those trees there obstruct our view. Yeah, I saw your little girl most days.

"Gus and me wondered why a kid was up here at that time of year and in such foul weather, but, hey, we were warned never to visit or contact the occupants of the cabin, so we kept to ourselves. Various folks came here, some to paint or write or just to chill. All we had to do was to see that the place was clean and stocked with food and logs. It was Gus who thought the kid might just be your Lucy. We had caught a news item on our old, unreliable radio, we weren't too sure of the facts but he contacted the cops anyhow. I thought he was crazy to let his imagination run riot, but he said he'd never forgive himself if he did nothing about his gut feeling."

The three women talked for some time. Knowing Lucy had been cared for and appeared peaceful helped Brenda to appreciate a little of the beauty of her aunt's place.

***

It was May. The Bigfork Whitewater Festival was in full swing. The two women walked along by the lake and watched in amazement as the competitors rode the rapids.

"My mother watched this event, Molly. According to Anna's letter it was an annual trip for her. I wish I'd known my mother. It pained my father to speak of her. He would only say how beautiful she was and how much she wanted me. Seemingly, they placed me in her arms just before she died. How sad!"

Molly well remembered Brenda's early life when her distraught father entrusted the care of his daughter to her.

"Honey, when I came to Lincoln Park your father was a broken man. He could not cope without his darling Francesca. He hid every picture of her, as if it distressed him to look at her image. She was the love of his life. He was in a bad place then."

Back at the cabin Brenda found a rather worn leather case full of old photographs that she and Molly pored over.

"Look at this! This surely is my mother. My father never showed me any pictures of her; it pained him so. Oh Molly, that could have been Lucy in a few years, look at the resemblance. If only she hadn't been…"

Brenda continued to sob as she picked her way through the photographs. She laid aside those of her parents and burnt those of her aunt.

"I've seen all I want to see here. I'll never return. Jordan Garnett can arrange for the cabin to be given to those old folks. They can move in or let it out, whatever they wish. My emotions are in turmoil Molly, but I'm glad I came here; I felt close to Lucy."

"Me too, honey, me too. Let's go home."

After some days they locked up the cabin and headed home. They returned to their Lincoln Park home more at ease within themselves and with hope in their hearts that some day they might find some semblance of peace.

"Molly," said Brenda as they sat together in the kitchen some months later, "how would you like to have a vacation? I'm planning a trip and would love you to come along. I'm sure it would lift our spirits. I have to admit I did not think that reading Anna's documents and visiting her cabin in Montana would have helped, but in a kind of way, they have."

"Awesome! Yes indeed, a proper vacation would be good for us. I'd love that. The Montana trip wasn't a vacation for either of us. What are you planning; a Caribbean cruise?"

"No, not a cruise; I would like to do Europe and visit places my parents visited on their honeymoon. Their photographs are amazing! I look at them regularly now, and wish so much to replicate that tour. When I was clearing out my father's personal documents after his death I came across a holiday diary and pictures which I didn't place much importance on at the time. I laid them aside to look at later and forgot about them until recently. It was a holiday diary of places that my parents visited on their European honeymoon with details of hotels, restaurants, places of interest. Seemingly, my mother adored Paris. I'd love to visit Paris. I've been looking on the Web. We can begin our tour at the end of next month. I have to go to the office, speak to Myra and the others, and fix some business stuff which I've been neglecting, and then we can go see Europe! Molly, do you think you are up to the travel?"

"I'm so excited! You try stopping me! I might be getting on a bit honey, but a change of scene will bring a new lease of life for me. But, hey, I have to get this house clean before we lock up. Those two girls! Never seen such sloppy work in all my born days! I'll take charge of them and have this place spotless in no time. We can't leave it in a mess. Every corner will be cleaned and locked up before we leave. Oh, I'm so excited!"

Brenda smiled to herself, knowing the two young helpers were in for a shock.

Poor kids! She chuckled as she pictured their reaction to the sudden change in Molly, who attacked the chores vigorously with renewed energy and fearsome zeal. They worked unrelentingly, fearing Molly's sharp tongue, knowing no stone would be left unturned by the formidable housekeeper. Each area was cleaned, dust covers put in place, and the rooms locked for the duration of the vacation.

"What's gotten into her?" whispered one of the helpers. "She sure scares me with her, 'do this, do that'..."

***

Brenda arranged with Anna's lawyer for the Montana cabin and contents to be given to Gus and Ellie Stiller to use as they wished. The couple were overcome at the generosity of the kind person who had suffered so much herself with the loss of her child and who had selflessly gifted the cabin to them.

"After all," said Gus, "we were handsomely paid for the work we did, and it was never strenuous, but to be given the cabin. Wow! Such kindness. I had been thinking, Ellie, that now the old lady has died, our little bit of extra income would dry up. Not that we really needed it, but it did get a few luxuries."

"Luxuries?" laughed his wife. "You mean extra baccy for that old smelly pipe of yours?"

***

From the sale of the estate Brenda instructed the lawyer to give substantial money to the gullible victims, the innocent people, who, when down on their luck had the misfortune to meet Barclay Ellis-Jones and his accomplices and be drawn into his cruel money-lending scheme, consequently becoming unwilling participants in the despicable crime of Lucy's abduction and death. Jordan Garnett appeared unaware of the people mentioned by Brenda, but complied nevertheless with her wishes.

I must talk with young Edward to see if he can shed any light on the confusion around this will, he pondered. *Brenda Mears, it seems to me, has suffered so much from the loss of her daughter that she is not thinking straight and appears quite perplexed. Poor woman.*

***

Clara Blake who struggled daily with her limited income vowed never again to accept a loan regardless of her financial situation. Her wayward son, the cause of her financial dilemma some years earlier and now released from prison, had found employment in a nearby factory. He was determined not to re-offend. He had no wish to be deprived of his freedom again.

"Mom, I ain't never going back to that jail; from now on, I'll be the best kind of son for you. I sure learned my lesson in that hellhole."

His mother, sorely affected by the death of young Lucy, whom she harboured for four days in order to have her debts cleared, often sobbed quietly, lost in her own thoughts.

***

Dale Greer's widow, Cindy, continued to live with her parents. Her growing children put a strain on her income and overcrowding became problematic. The substantial cash gift from Anna's estate helped to compensate in some way for the trauma she had been put through by the evil scheming of Barclay Ellis-Jones, resulting in her husband's deep shame and consequent suicide. His despair at being unable to fend for his family when he lost everything during the banking crisis had tragic results for them all. The once gentle husband and father was reduced to a shadow of his former self and found solace and eventual death, through alcohol.

***

The past four years were for Ross S. Witherspoon fraught with despair. Any hope he had of becoming President of the United States was lost forever. He had been so close to fulfilling a lifelong dream, having been groomed for a high position all his days, culminating in being nominated as his party's choice of candidate for the forthcoming election. He knew he had let everyone down, including the memory of his mentor, his late grandfather. Now his marriage survived only by a thread, the children being the link that held the fragile relationship together. He moved physically and emotionally as far from the political scene as he could, settled in a quiet location, where, after some initial inquisitiveness from neighbours, slowly resumed some kind of semblance of home life. The death of the daughter he never knew had a profound effect on him. The circumstances of her tragic end left an emptiness and deep sorrow in his soul. In an attempt to salve his conscience he wrote to Brenda Mears. She did not reply.

CHAPTER 12

The combined USA and UK squads discussed the gruesome case over lunch. Carole Carr intimated that they most definitely had to consider the deaths of the two men as revenge for the horrific deaths in Chicago four years ago as no other reason could be fathomed for the horror that confronted them.

"Several people could be involved, each with their own reason to seek revenge for their loss," she told the Scottish squad, who as yet were no nearer solving the case that had become a complete mystery. Rab McKenzie asked his visiting colleagues to discuss each possible suspect and bring him up to speed.

"You folks know these people better than we do. Lead on and let's talk about each one in depth. We'll put our heads together and do a bit of brainstorming. You guys may be too close to the situ and my team may possibly see things from a different angle."

Harvey listed everyone he could think of who had been directly affected by the demise of Lucy Mears and those travelling with her. Who could possibly seek retaliation for their loss?

"Carole and I spoke with Lucy's mom and housekeeper some weeks before we left to come here. We can safely discount those two women. They just want to get on with picking up the threads of their shattered lives. In spite of their loss, they would not have the courage or strength to kill anyone. At present they are touring Europe. Brenda gave me her itinerary should I need to contact her. She suffered so much from her aunt's crazy plot based on a revenge scenario. I don't think she would be involved in such evil even though, now here's a thought, she does have enough mega bucks to put out a contract on her daughter's killers."

"We can dismiss that idea," interrupted his deputy. "I'm sure she won't want to open up any more wounds. As for Molly Kelly, the poor woman has aged considerably and doesn't have the best of health. I was surprised to hear she had embarked on such a strenuous tour."

"Are you saying then," asked Rab, "that we discount the notion of the mother putting out a contract? I don't know the person. Is she likely to be so spiteful?"

Harvey assured them that in his opinion, and he was an astute judge of character, Brenda Mears in spite of everything that had happened was not vindictive.

"What about the girlfriend? Didn't George North have a girl he was planning to marry? Would she avenge her lost love?" asked one of the Scottish team.

Carole said, "She certainly had a double loss, her boyfriend, *and* Lucy whom she had known from birth and helped to rear. She was depressed before their loss, and not knowing where they had gone and with the finger of guilt pointing at her fiancé, she was one tense lady. Like the others, she was traumatised after the plane crash, which she witnessed. She never came to terms with what she saw as George's betrayal and took off to work in the Florida Keys. She could no longer live in the apartment they shared, but is it worth chasing her up for interview?"

"Let's not discount anyone at this stage," added Harvey, "although I doubt if she would exact revenge. She doesn't seem the type."

"No such thing, Tony, as a stereotype killer, as you are always telling our squad. Look at Anna Leci. Who would have taken her as a ruthless schemer?"

"Hey, yeah, Carole, but Anna Leci did not plan to kill anyone, did she? She was the mastermind of the abduction plot. From what we know, Lucy was to be returned home the night of the crash. It was our two scumbags who did the killing by sabotaging the plane. Yeah, I agree we don't overlook Nora Kelly. I'll call HQ at CPD and send a couple of our folks to the Florida Keys to speak with her, but I'd be mighty surprised if she was involved in any way in a macabre murder, miles from her home. But, hey, you can never tell. This case has thrown up so many mysteries and twists and turns over the years, so I guess we should be prepared for anything."

Within a few days two CPD detectives flew from Chicago O'Hare to Key West Airport and located Nora Kelly. She had settled to a new life and found love with Peter, one of the hotel receptionists.

"Peter has helped me put the past behind. I'll never forget dear Lucy or George. My mom told me the contents of Anna Leci's letter, explaining his involvement in Lucy's abduction. It sure helped a lot to know he wasn't a bad guy, just weak. Everyone thought he was the abductor but he had just gotten himself caught up in a situation he couldn't get out of. He was too proud to ask for help with his financial troubles and he got caught up in a sordid money-lending scheme which had disastrous results. If only he had confided in me."

Her voice softened, "Now, I have to move on with life. I miss my mom, but talk to her every day. I can't live there in Lincoln Park ever again: Too many ghosts, too many memories."

The detectives spent several hours with Nora Kelly and concluded that she had no part in the gruesome deaths of Alfred Wysoki or Barclay-Ellis Jones. They relayed this information to their superior.

***

George North's sisters were contacted for interview. They were together in Wisconsin celebrating Jessica's birthday, when detectives called at the latter's home.

"This is fortunate to have you both together," said one of the officers as both Jessica and the diminutive Mary-Lou invited them into the house. "I hope we're not disturbing the festivities."

"Not at all Detective; we had the party last week and Mary-Lou decided to stay on a bit. I must say, we were saddened to hear of George's death and stunned to hear details of his part in a kid's abduction. We sure were surprised at that, and then a nice detective lady called to give us some more information about why he did what he did. Seems he was afraid of some rich lady who threatened him, made him keep quiet about some kid's abduction. Poor brother George, and to think we'll never see him again."

"Yeah," chipped in the younger sister, "it sure helped to clear things up for us, but oh, what a tragic end for our brother. My son George, named for my brother, was real angry like when he heard about his Uncle George's involvement with a missing kid and wanted to change his name. 'I won't be named after a man like that,' he told me.

'I'll use my middle name, yeah, and from now on you can call me Jerome after my dad's father, yeah, Jerome.'"

The Chicago detectives explained the reason for the visit. The sisters sat spellbound as they listened to the horrors that took place long after their brother's death. It was obvious to the visiting cops that these two petite ladies had no hand in the Scottish murders. Other than visiting each other, the duo never set foot outside their immediate neighbourhood.

"Well, I hope you find the bad guys, Detectives. I wouldn't like to think they were still out there somewhere, killing folks."

On the return journey, the detectives commented on the visit.

"Such sweet little ladies!"

"Hey, sweet little ladies can be deceiving. Remember the play, and the film, *Arsenic and Old Lace*, the comedy where two sweet little ladies, like the two we have just left, murdered lonely old men by poisoning them with home-made elderberry wine laced with arsenic? You can't always trust sweet little ladies!"

"Well, I sure hope there was nothing in that coffee we drank back there," laughed the detective. "Mind you, you do have a kind of strange paleness about you, Zak."

"That's because of your crazy driving. Slow down man."

***

Clara Blake, grateful to receive a considerable amount of money from Anna Leci's lawyer, moved to a more attractive area. She assured detectives she had no knowledge of the criminals and had certainly played no part in their deaths.

"Can't say I'm sorry to hear they are out of harm's way... When I think what they put me through, and my poor kid when he was in juvie... They had their thug friends beat him to a pulp to get at me. They were evil, pure evil."

Her description of the crooks that came to her door demanding repayment of her debt, and that of the sweet-talking guy whom she met in the pub all those years ago, confirmed the identities of Alfred Wysoki, Les Soubry and Barclay Ellis-Jones and went a long way in helping detectives in their investigations. She had given them their first real lead into the loan-shark business set up by the trio and set the authorities on the right track in gathering evidence against the villains.

"I felt real bad about the kid's death. She was a sweet, pretty kid. I hated what I had to do, but I had no choice but to hide her at my home for a few days until someone collected her. I was supposed to give her some kind of drug from a vial, but I drew the line at that and kept it hidden. When the cops caught up with me, as I knew they would, I handed it over. From what they told me, they were able to trace where it had come from, so I don't feel so bad now. I never knew what it was all about until I read about the airplane crash. Hey, I wish I'd never met those scum moneylenders, they ruined my life. Those thugs were so scary... They've got what they deserve. I can't say I'm sorry for their end. I have nightmares when I think of that poor kid in the plane crash. Her poor mom. What she must have gone through! The money has helped me get on my feet. At first I thought of it as some kind of blood money, but those loan sharks caused me hell on earth and my family deserved better. I can buy my granddaughter designer clothes now without kids questioning her about where she got them from, like they did when I gave her Lucy's stuff. They were too good to burn, like they told me to do, so I had them cleaned real nice like, and gave them to my own little Sara. She had a hard time at school when she turned up in Lucy's cast-offs when the kids there knew how poor her mom and grandma were. We had to make up lies about the stuff coming from a relative who had outgrown them."

***

Dale Greer's widow, Cindy, agreed to talk to the detectives on discovering the reason for their request. She had moved to a spacious house near her parents' home. As she tended her garden, a source of solace to her, officers arrived to speak with her. She wiped the soil from her hands and directed them to a shady part of the garden.

"You don't mind sitting here, do you? It's such a lovely day and it would be a shame to sit indoors."

As she poured cold drinks she spoke of the past few years.

"Things were becoming tense. Living with my folks was stressful for us all. They deserve their privacy at their age. Me and the kids have been grateful for a place to stay these past years, but it was time to move on."

She continued, "The boys need their growing space and I need a place to call home. It was nothing short of a miracle when that cheque arrived from the lawyer. At first I was unsure of accepting money from the woman who indirectly caused my Dale to end his life, but when I looked at my folks and saw the strain on their faces, I thought, what the heck, we all deserve better."

While Cindy Greer loathed the people who caused the desperate situation she and Dale had found themselves in, she had no more desire to kill Barclay Ellis-Jones or Alfred

Wysoki than she had to eliminate the bankers who caused the initial crisis resulting in her and Dale losing every dollar they possessed.

"Why beat yourself up about something you can't change?" she said, parting from the detectives who were satisfied with her interview.

CHAPTER 13

From 3,000 miles away in Scotland, Superintendent Harvey organised his squad in Chicago to interview some other possible suspects and hand-picked various team members for the job, people he trusted to carry out the task that he himself would have preferred to do.

Ross S. Witherspoon was next to be interviewed. He was at first reluctant to be questioned until told of the deaths of the two men who caused his daughter's tragic end. This altered his attitude. He agreed to speak with the detectives. He had aged considerably, no longer having the suave, confident appearance of the aspiring politician of a few years ago. His bearing was that of a broken man. His once chic hairstyle was grey and matted. He was unshaven and looked as if sleep had evaded him for many months. His clothes hung on him, emphasising a considerable weight loss. The detectives were shown to a darkened library where they met with the subdued man, the darkness only serving to highlight the blackness in his soul.

"I have so many regrets. I wish I'd known I had a daughter and been part of her life. She seems to have been an amazing kid. I never knew about her birth," he lied. "That woman, Brenda Mears, her mom, kept it from me. Hey, given the chance, I could have been a terrific dad and my boys would have loved having a sister. How could that woman conceal her from me? My Lucy didn't deserve to die like that."

He rambled on, blaming everyone but himself for his change of fortune. His voice trailed off as he struggled with emotions and memories of the night he discovered he had fathered the missing Lucy Mears; the night when that revelation made in public by a news reporter put paid to his dream of a political life which would probably have taken him to the White House and the power he craved.

"I hope those responsible will burn in hell."

"Do you know anything about how they met their end, sir, or who would want them dead?" asked a detective with a sharp intake of breath, fearing an outburst of rage. "After all, you lost your political future because of them."

"Hey, I do not! But I'd sure like to shake the hand of whoever managed to rid us of that vermin. I only knew they had been traced when one of your detectives called to arrange this interview."

Despite his loathing, it was obvious he had no knowledge of the grisly deaths of the men found in two Scottish mine shafts thousands of miles from the scene of his daughter's death. The detectives left him in his dark world, a world where light would never fully shine again on his tortured soul.

***

Two other detectives interviewed his wife, Linda-Mae, separately. She, too, could shed no light on the Scottish deaths.

"We've suffered so much from all this, so much, Detectives, that life for us will never be the same. My parents struggled to accept Ross back into their lives.

"He and my father had a good relationship before all this, but now, well, my father is so bitter he can hardly stay in the same room as him. He and my mom tolerate him for my sake and for the boys'. The kids, thank God, were too young to understand the scandal surrounding their father, but now as they get older they are asking questions. I had to give up the job I loved in kindergarten and move from the area, as the gossip would have been unbearable. This scandal will never leave us. Ross can never return to politics. He's like a lost soul. He knows nothing else but politics.

"He watches hours of political debates, some current and many from past years. He's attempting to write a political book to keep himself busy. It's heartbreaking to see him so devastated. He spends hours in his depressing library. I have to admit that, at first, I was ashamed that he had fathered and neglected a daughter. He has to live with that guilt for the rest of his days. We go from day to day, hoping that some time in the future we shall all find peace. I don't mind telling you, our marriage was hanging by a thread. If it wasn't for our kids I'd have walked away from Ross. The kids had to endure bullying at school for a time, but things have settled down and they get on with their lives. My boys are strong characters and can stand up for themselves. I'm relieved really that we have been spared life in a goldfish bowl if Ross had ever been the incumbent of the White House. The nightmare we have lived through these past years has shown me that life there would have been too restrictive. I value freedom to bring up my sons. I guess we'll never know what kind of president my husband would have made. Detectives, I can't say I'm sad about the deaths of those two guys who caused Lucy's horrific death, but I assure you neither Ross nor I were remotely involved."

***

Superintendent Harvey was reluctant to sanction re-interviewing Lucy's best friend Abigail and her mother Gina.

"Those two have been through the mill over this. Abigail was in a bad place when Lucy died. Counselling helped, but the kid will never fully recover from the trauma. Her mom has been her rock. We will not gain anything by putting these people through more interviews and having them relive the entire scenario yet again. No. I'm adamant about this; leave these people out of our enquiries."

Carole Carr opened her mouth to protest, but knowing her boss as she did, thought the better of it, trusting his judgement even if it wasn't the road she herself would have taken.

***

Brenda's executive team was interviewed separately. It was obvious that none of them had any dealings with the villains who caused so much heartache to so many people. Justin Palmer, the firm's graphic designer, appeared nervous when interviewed, but the astute detective dealing with him appreciated that the man's demeanour was more from grief than from guilt.

"We can never forget poor Lucy," he told the detective. "This interview is bringing it all back. I'm not a violent man, but I'm sure glad to hear those bad guys will never harm anyone again. It's been so hard for us all, these past four years. Brenda is suffering so much. We try to keep Mears Empire on track as best we can and only hope that some day our boss will take the helm once more."

His partner, Bob Lees, the firm's shipping agent, had similar feelings about the criminals. Dressed in a red linen suit, he cut a fine figure as he entered the office to take part yet again, in questions about young Lucy.

"They seem to have had a gruesome death from what I've been told and I wouldn't wish that on my worst enemy, but they were evil to take poor Lucy from us. I'm not sorry they have gone to face their Maker. It won't do anything to bring sweet Lucy back, but it might bring some consolation to her poor mom."

***

Myra Hill, in charge of finance, had taken on more of the running of Mears Empire with the blessing of her employer. Rushing out to a business meeting she was enraged when detectives arrived early at her office to talk with her.

"I had hoped you would have the courtesy of keeping to the appointed time which is not for another hour. I'm already late for an important meeting."

"Our apologies; we had finished sooner than expected with the other executive staff, and thought we could speak with you and save a return visit, but if you prefer, we'll return later."

"Oh, then let me make a quick call."

She still maintained an impenetrable front for the world, gave nothing away and only revealed her innermost thoughts when asked about the deaths of Lucy's killers.

"In my opinion, they seem to have been taken care of and got what they deserved. The world is free of those two lowlifes. I'll shed no tears for them. Brenda's life has been destroyed. She's heartbroken and nothing anyone can do will help her grief. I fear that she will never totally recover from the devastation of watching her only child die in that plane crash. None of us will really recover. We carry on as best we can here but the spark of enthusiasm has dimmed for all of us at Mears Empire."

The Scotts, Ron, and Olivia, like their colleagues, showed no compassion at the demise of the rogues who ended Lucy's life in such a cruel manner. They too had no knowledge of the Scottish deaths and, like everyone else involved in the case, wondered how the two villains had got to Scotland.

"It seems strange to us, Detective, how those two escaped justice for so long and ended up on foreign soil. I hope the answer will be found soon. How curious!"

***

Harvey's team in Chicago reported to their superior that they were satisfied that all recent interviewees had no part in the Scottish crime.

"No one seemed unduly sympathetic, sir, about the death of those villains. Most commented that the world would now be a safer place without them."

Lucy's music tutor, the eccentric Ken Farmer was dismissed from enquiries after a brief visit from officers.

"The poor man hasn't the strength to lift a pencil, let alone plan a murder."

***

"We have to look elsewhere," said Harvey to the assembled team in Scotland. "Who would want those guys dead? Come on folks, think! It's one thing saying no one cares about their end but a serious crime has been committed and we have a duty to solve it to the best of our ability. I for one would be glad to see it done and dusted."

Carole, unable to sleep, called her husband and kids for a long chat, assuring them that she would find the bad guy and be home soon. Sleep evaded her. Her body clock had not adjusted to the six-hour difference in time zone. She deliberated over past events, on the players involved in Lucy's life; on everyone she could recall who featured in this most horrific of crimes. Her eyes felt heavy. Just as she was drifting off to sleep, she sat bolt upright.

Aha! There is someone we've omitted. Damn, it's too late to call Tony. He'll be snoring by now.

Tony, however, was not asleep. He paced the room, his over-active mind keeping him wide awake as did the difference in time to which his body had not yet adjusted.

There's more to this crime…a hell of a lot more…

CHAPTER 14

Rubbing sleep from her eyes, Carole joined an equally tired-looking Tony at breakfast.

"Hey, Tony! We forgot the very person who might know more about Lucy's death… Rita Hampton! How could we forget that vile woman?"

"Carole, you're a star. I forgot about her, probably because she's safely tucked up in prison."

Tony Harvey, weary from constant transatlantic calls to organise re-interviewing people he thought he would never have to encounter again, and longing to be home, briefed the joint squad on the involvement and trial of Rita Hampton.

"Cops detained her after Anna Leci's funeral in New York. The hearse was pulling out of Anna's outlandish estate when detectives arrived to question the owner, not knowing then that she had died. Sadly, my guys had only just discovered who had arranged the abduction. It is one of the biggest regrets of my career that information came too late for us to save Lucy. Anna Leci's funeral was allowed to proceed and detectives remained in attendance. They detained Rita Hampton immediately after the service. She was Anna's private nurse and was aware of the devious abduction plan devised by her employer. She knew the power Anna had over the others. Anna Leci was mega-rich. She shamelessly exploited people for her own selfish ends. Rita Hampton knew every minute detail of Lucy's abduction, which she could have brought to an end with one phone call to the authorities. I don't buy it that she was afraid of her employer as she maintained in her defence. Anna Leci was dying; she no longer had energy to have a hold over anyone. Rita Hampton feared that her life of luxury within Anna's palatial home would come to an end and she would have to seek employment elsewhere. She is now serving a long sentence in a correctional facility. It's a maximum-security prison for women. I'll interview her personally when I get back home. I can arrange with my opposite number in New York to set up a meeting. She knows more than she has ever told anyone, but I'm sure as hell going to get to the truth of the abduction plot. This case, and now the deaths of the two roughnecks, has coloured my life for many years. I sure as hell won't rest until the loose ends are tied up."

Tony Harvey, as if to emphasis his commitment, thumped the table with a clenched fist. He thumped it as if to reinforce the point. Carole, knowing her boss's every mood, knew he was frustrated at their inability to solve the mystery of the deaths in Scotland of their two most wanted criminals, and feared that tiredness would cloud his judgement and arouse his simmering temper.

***

Over a farewell drink and final meeting they all agreed that coming together had been a productive exercise. Although the Scottish deaths were still unsolved, important steps had been taken to eliminate some suspects. Harvey felt his time with his Police Scotland colleagues had benefited both teams.

"It was good to get the feel of the crime areas," concluded Carole, "and to see how you guys function. I hope we can resolve the mystery of how those two ended up over here. We'll certainly be in touch with any development, especially when Tony speaks with Rita Hampton, and we won't stop until we find their killers, no matter how long it takes. Despite their horrific crimes back home, and whatever thoughts we have about them, we are professional cops and our duty is to bring to justice the perpetrators of the deaths of Alfred Wysoki and Barclay Ellis-Jones."

Harvey and his team took leave of their Scottish peers and headed back to Chicago, satisfied that all that could have been done at that time, had been investigated and that friendships had been forged among like-minded people.

"What lovely people," said Carole as they settled down to the long flight home, "and what spectacular scenery! Someday, I'm going to bring Ted and the kids to Scotland. It's awesome."

She realised she was talking to herself. Her boss had fallen asleep as soon as the aircraft had taken off.

***

Sitting in her drab prison cell, longing for sunshine and freedom, Rita Hampton lifted her head from the book she was struggling to read, turned her face towards the slanting window at the top of her cell, imagining the warmth of sunshine beaming down on her like gentle rays sent to comfort her broken spirit, but facing the reality that no sun ever reached that part of the building. A warden, whom she disliked intensely, hollered at her, disturbing her reverie.

"Get moving, Hampton. You have a visitor. Don't get too excited. It's a cop. Nice looking guy, but, hey, we all know you prefer the gals, don't we, sweetie?"

Rita had long-time learnt not to retaliate and it took every ounce of her willpower not to react as she was prodded along to the interview room.

Tony Harvey wasted no time in setting to interview Rita Hampton. He was taken aback by the change in the woman he first encountered after the events four years ago. Her incarceration had taken its toll; her hair was lank and unkempt and without make-up she had taken on a ghostly look like a lost spirit wandering aimlessly through time and space seeking solace and peace where none could be found. Her general appearance was that of a troubled woman who had given up on a life with no future. The calamitous plane crash so soon after Anna's death shocked her to the core. She found it difficult to come to terms with the death of so many people she had known. Her thoughts often dwelt on those dreadful days. She lived in an isolated unit, as her earlier days in jail had been perilous. Fellow inmates treated her roughly for her involvement in the death of young Lucy Mears, a story avidly followed by them.

"Scum, you could have saved the kid," was a constant comment.

Superintendent Harvey, in agreement with the prison administrator, offered the inmate improved conditions if she provided information to help trace the killers of Barclay Ellis-Jones and Alfred Wysoki.

"We can't reduce your length of sentence, but we'll see you have a few more home comforts and privileges. Tell me, Rita, all you can recall of events at Anna Leci's home, her power over everyone and your own involvement in the tragic death of so many." He kept his eyes firmly on the inmate as he spoke.

Harvey recorded the interview.

Rita spoke of how she had met Anna in a Chicago hospital when the latter was receiving treatment for cancer and she herself was a nurse there.

"It was the worst day of my life, sir, when Anna caught me stealing drugs for my sick father. Our insurance didn't cover the expensive drugs that were keeping him alive. I was desperate. The drugs he needed were there in the hospital, right in front of me. It was so tempting, so easy. From then on she had such a hold over me. I was terrified she would report me to the authorities. I would have lost my job and been jailed. What would happen to my sick father then? How could he cope with his daughter's incarceration at a time when he had most need? I was all he had. I was in a no-win situation."

She went on to relate how, after her father's death, she went to work for, and nurse Anna Leci, an agreement they had come to that fateful day in the hospital.

"I didn't realise how rich she was, how ruthless and scheming one person could possibly be to have total control over the lives of others. They say money talks; well, in my experience it made those of us caught up with her totally silent for fear of reprisals. Her staff was loyal. I never knew what hold she had over the many domestic staff who ran the house, but I reckon there was something in each of their lives that she was aware of. My duties mostly restricted me to her suite of rooms and I rarely saw the housekeeping staff. I had never seen such richness. My own rooms were beyond anything I had ever dreamt of, not that I got to spend my time there; Anna was a demanding boss."

"Tell me now about Barclay Ellis-Jones," prodded Harvey.

Rita paused to compose herself, and continued, "Anna was particularly close to Barclay Ellis-Jones, as he was known then. She'd met him initially at Simon Mears' funeral several years ago when he was employed at Mears Empire. It appears he was a trusted employee, at first that was. Seems he had his finger in the till, so to speak. He was taking money from the firm in small amounts so as not to be noticed, and poor trusting Simon Mears, Brenda's father, was totally unaware of the fraudster in his midst. He trusted the guy. He was such a smooth-talking dude. It looked like Anna and Barclay hit it off and met up again by chance at Lucy's concert in Chicago where I reckon they came up with the abduction plan. Sir, that kid sure had musical talent! What a loss! I heard her play in Anna's house. It was awesome. She played piano with such ease, then the cello. It was almost as if she was part of the instruments; so angelic, so sweet.

"Thankfully, I had little contact with Barclay and his buddies, Alfred Wysoki and Les Soubry. Les seemed to be the nicest of the trio. He would smile and say, 'Hi' when he passed by; the others ignored me, made me feel like scum. It was never meant to end in tragedy, sir. Lucy was to be returned home the evening of the crash. Barclay and Alfred wanted rid of Les Soubry. I was in an anteroom dealing with some of Anna's stuff and overheard them talking. They didn't know I'd heard them. I can tell you I was scared they'd find me. My heart seemed to thump so loud, like it was going to explode; I was real panicky."

"Can you recall what was said?"

"Sure. There was only a thin wall between them and me. They had found out Les had called some cop with details of Lucy's flight home to Chicago. They were furious."

Harvey did not disclose that he himself had taken the call from Les, having arranged with him to do so in return for leniency for his own part in the loan-shark business. The detective arranged for coffee for Rita and himself to give her time to gather her thoughts. His policy at this point was to play the good cop.

Rita thought the coffee was the best she had ever tasted; her taste buds relishing the sweetness denied her for so long.

She continued, "I heard Barclay say, 'That bastard's sold us down the river. He told some cop guy about the flight arrangements. It's what we suspected Alf; he's been going behind our backs, deceiving us.' Alf said, 'Want me to finish him off then?'

"Sir, I was so frightened. There was no doubt that they were going to harm Les, but they'd no right to take sweet Lucy with them, had they?"

She sobbed as she told of the last time she saw the group, and of her conversation with Lucy and Zelda, one of the reluctant captors.

"We spoke for a long time, explained to Lucy about her aunt's hold over everyone, and assured her she would be back in her own home that evening. Little did we know what lay ahead. Lucy was such a trusting kid.

"Anna Leci was mad, sir, not bad. She began a crusade of hatred that got out of hand and worsened as her cancer took hold and she was drugged up. She could no longer think straight. The cancer had reached her brain and she had lost any sense of common decency. In her twisted mind her cruel plan had to run its course."

"What hold did Anna Leci have over the woman you referred to just now as Zelda? Who was she?"

"Zelda told me that she and Kristof, that's her husband, had entered America illegally and somehow Anna Leci found out and threatened to have them deported. Those weren't their real names. I never knew what they were. I don't recall much of the conversation. The past few years in here have played havoc with my mind and I get real mixed up at times."

Superintendent Harvey looked the distraught prisoner in the eye and asked the question he had most puzzled over.

"Rita, at your trial you told how you were afraid of Anna Leci. How could that be when she was so near to death and therefore incapable of harming anyone? Why, at that fortuitous time did you not contact the authorities and put an end to Lucy's ordeal?"

"Sir, I often wish I'd had the courage to stand up to her, but, as I've said, she had such a hold over me. As it is, I've ended up in jail anyway. Lucy's trip went on longer than planned due to the crazy weather that Anna sent them out in, and they all took sick and had to rest up for days. Anna was furious at the delay. That poor, poor kid; she didn't deserve that, and nor did Zelda or Kristof, or kind George North. They were all good people; their only crime was to meet Anna Leci and get caught up in her deviousness."

"Sorry Rita, but that doesn't make sense to me. What could Anna Leci have done at that stage in her life to control you? There's more to this. Don't stonewall me about this; come clean. Were you reluctant to give up the life of apparent luxury that you had in that monstrously lavish place? Did you hope to live there after the death of your employer? Rita, there's much more to this than you're telling me. Isn't that so?"

She lowered her eyes, refused to meet his, fearful that the truth might be released in a torrent of guilt-ridden shame. She sat in silence and waited for the onslaught.

Tony Harvey stood up, pushed his chair away from him with such a clatter that it startled both her and the warden in the room with her.

"I have my answer," he bellowed as he stormed out of the room.

CHAPTER 15

For several days Tony Harvey's mind could focus on nothing but Lucy's end.

Anna Leci's lawyer! He suddenly thought. *He has never been interviewed by us. How did we manage to overlook him?*

He put a call through to Carole to discuss his thoughts.

"He never really came into the picture, Tony. He only came to our attention when we got to read Anna Leci's letter to Lucy. Personally, I never gave a thought to such a professional man being involved in anything covert, but as you so often say, never presume someone is not the criminal type just because of appearance. What's the plan then?"

"Initially, I'll give him a call and sound him out. I'd like to know what he knew of Lucy's abduction. If he had any inkling of it and didn't report it, he's as bad as Rita Hampton and needs to answer for his silence. He must have known about it; perhaps he played a major role in the whole scenario and we've been fooled by him."

The telephone conversation with Jordan Garnett was unproductive; the lawyer claimed to have known nothing of Lucy Mears' disappearance, causing alarm bells to ring for the suspicious superintendent of CPD. Once again he asked Carole Carr to accompany him on a mission to interview the lawyer face-to-face.

"How can he say he knew nothing of Lucy's abduction? Has he been living on another planet? Something is not right here. Has he been involved in the whole sordid mess? We have to do this ourselves, Carole. I won't settle until all avenues of Lucy's death have been covered. We owe it to her. It's the least we can do."

"Tony, you can't forever blame yourself for what happened. We were outwitted by a cunning, crazy woman, but, yeah, okay, let's interview the guy but keep an open mind until we hear what he has to say. Surely you don't suspect him to be the brains behind the abduction. Hey, now, you've got me thinking... "

Once again the duo found themselves flying over 700 miles across the USA.

"At least the mayor has sanctioned this trip. He still feels guilty about how we were treated over the election fiasco and needs to make amends somehow. For the time being at least, he has given us an open cheque book."

***

Jordan Garnett's office in Madison Avenue took the detectives by complete surprise.

"I didn't expect this luxury. Did you, Tony? I got the impression he ran a one-man outfit in a back street, but, hey, look at this! Don't sink into the carpet pile, I might never find you again."

A junior partner escorted them to the penthouse suite where Jordan Garnett warmly welcomed them.

"I appreciate you coming this way. I'm afraid my travelling days are over. I leave that to some of my more able members of staff."

The elderly, dapper gentleman regaled them with the history of the firm, proudly showing portraits of his late grandparents and father, whom he said, built the firm up from practically nothing to be the successful business it had now become.

"I plan to retire at the end of the year and hand over the reins to my talented nephew, my late brother's son. My wife and I never had children so I've been training young Edward to take over the day-to-day running of the firm. He's a capable young man and I have total confidence that it will go from strength to strength under his leadership. I so wish to keep this business in family hands. Now, Detectives, you didn't come all this way to listen to an old man's rant. You want to know about dear Anna. How can I help? And what is this about an abduction?"

Harvey and Carr looked at each other in surprise. Out of earshot, Carole whispered, "'*Dear*' Anna?"

Harvey began to question him. The elderly man was taken aback at the line of questioning and the brusque, perplexing tone from the superintendent. Carole attempted to nudge her colleague to cool it, but Tony, emotions riding high, was on a roll.

"Sir," he addressed the lawyer, "how much did you know of the abduction of Lucy Mears by Anna Leci? I find it abhorrent that you did nothing to stop the suffering of the child."

From the startled look on his face, it was obvious that the poor man was genuinely stunned and taken aback at what he was hearing.

"No, no, you must be mistaken. Anna Leci was a kind, sweet soul who was incapable of harming anyone. I knew her well and helped her compose a letter for her great-niece telling the dear child about the grandmother she never knew. Anna knew her end was near and wanted the girl to have a piece of family history. This is an outrageous suggestion. Abduction? By Anna Leci? The woman was dying!"

He removed a pristine handkerchief, mopped his brow, cleaned his glasses, and stared somewhat unbelievingly at the two senior officials sitting in front of him. He felt as if something sinister was about to enter his otherwise sedate life like a predator ready to pounce on unsuspecting prey.

Harvey passed over the document which purported to have been composed by Anna for Lucy.

"Is this the document you prepared, sir, for Anna Leci?"

Jordan Garnett donned his reading glasses and perused the document in front of him. He paled as he read. He flicked back and forward through the pages, brows furrowing as he read and reread the papers. It seemed an eternity until he spoke. The only sound in the room was that of the rapid breathing of the older gentleman and the irritating, impatient tap-tapping on the desk of Harvey's pen.

"I don't understand this... believe me... this is a mystery. Yes, some parts of the document dealing with Lucy's grandparents and their life together were indeed dictated to me by Anna and written up for her approval. But these pages here... these pages were most certainly not part of the original document. I am stunned to read about the child's abduction and nightmare journey across so many states and Anna's involvement. Detectives, please, please believe me. I am an honest man, too honest it seems. I've been duped. Someone has added to this... look... I did not draw up these pages here... This one here, and these two and this other one... "

The bewildered man wiped his brow of sweat and continued, "Anna Leci told me that her great-niece Lucy was coming to visit and how she was so looking forward to meeting her young relative. She had arranged for some staff to take the child to Montana to visit her beautiful cabin there. I presumed it had all been arranged with the child's mother. I must say I did question the trip taking place in winter, but Anna assured me it was the most spectacular of seasons. 'Jordan,' she said to me, 'I want the dear child to experience the most amazing scenery and I long to hear her recall her impression when she visits me.' I am stunned and totally bemused by this. You have shocked me. I am finding this hard to comprehend."

It was obvious that the elderly man was telling the truth. Carole felt sorry for him as he attempted to puzzle out the mystery that had been devastatingly related to him by two senior detectives. He reached for a glass of water; his hand shook uncontrollably, his pallor changed from the ruddy-faced gentleman they had encountered less than an hour ago to a sallow, almost pasty-faced man, his breathing increased rapidly as he reached in his pocket for an inhaler.

Tony, his attitude to the lawyer mellowing, looked at Carole for inspiration, hoping perhaps she could fathom out what was going on in the mind of Jordan Garnett. He assured the poor man that they would get to the bottom of this mystery.

"Can you tell me, Mr Garnett," asked Tony, "did anyone else ever visit Anna Leci on your behalf? Someone, I fear, has added to the document without your knowledge. From our understanding of events, Anna Leci was not the sweet lady you believed her to be, but a scheming mad woman. Did you really have no knowledge of the abduction of Lucy

Mears? It was on every news report in the country. The child was missing for ten weeks or more. Explain please how you missed that."

"No Detectives, I was quite sick. I had major surgery to my eyes and spent many weeks in recovery. I was not allowed to watch TV or read. It was a miserable time for me. I had to lie flat on my back. I was so drugged up that I had no energy or inclination to listen to news reports. It was touch-and-go as to whether or not I would lose my sight. My dear wife was distraught at my plight and visited me every day. We just held hands and listened to some music, and never spoke of world events. My nephew was in charge of the firm and updated me on occasions on essential events within the business, but never discussed anything outside of it. He was so focused, Detectives, and I have every confidence that he will be an excellent successor in my family business. I had asked him to to deliver some documents to Anna Leci for approval. He was to have them signed and put in the safe for my return to work. These very ones, I believe… Oh, no! It couldn't be Edward, surely not?"

Jordan Garnett was about to press the bell to summon the young man, when Harvey stopped him in his tracks.

"Let's hang on a bit, sir," he gently suggested. "We three need time to understand what we have uncovered here before we rush in. Let's think this through. Do you have a record of your visits to Anna Leci?"

The numb man rummaged in a safe and produced a pile of diaries.

"I keep these for several years in case I ever have reason to refer to dates. This one here should cover the times I called on Anna."

He passed the book to Carole Carr to examine. As she flicked through pages, Tony attempted to reassure the man that he was not in any way at fault.

"Here we have it, Tony. Look at this record of visits and expenses for the same, to Anna Leci. We have Mr. Garnett's entries and over here are several visits by Edward Garnett Jnr to Anna Leci."

"Several?" questioned the lawyer. "I sent him on only one occasion. He was to obtain a signature and return the document to the safe, that's all. I was to deal with it when I recovered from my illness."

"I'm sorry, sir, but it looks like your trusted nephew has colluded with a devious old lady and duped you. He must have worked with her on adding to the document but concealed it from you."

"I'm just a stupid trusting old man, Detective. Oh, and I passed that document on to Brenda Mears in good faith, not knowing the full contents of it. No wonder she looked at me as if I had no feelings about her poor child. Now I know why she was cold with me. I have to contact the lady and apologise for my behaviour on that day. She must have thought I had lost my mind."

Carole said, "Don't concern yourself at the moment, sir, about Brenda Mears. We will explain it all to her. Perhaps you can contact her later. Our priority is to resolve this upsetting discovery."

"Oh, but I have failed to carry out my work properly. I made a dreadful error in handing over documents to a client without even reading them. I trusted they were all in order. Oh, if this is true, and I suspect it is, I now have to reconsider Edward as my successor. Should we confront him now? I'm anxious to get to the bottom of this."

"Before you do that, Mr. Garnett, do you have a copy of Anna Leci's will? I would like to know if anything has been altered."

Once more the elderly gentleman shuffled over to the safe, where he retrieved a well-worn folder which he proffered to Superintendent Harvey who shook his head, saying, "I'd prefer you to look through it first, to ascertain if this document is the true document that you had compiled for her."

With his hand shaking even more markedly, the lawyer perused the document. The change in his expression and his rapid breathing told the detectives what they feared.

"This has been doctored! It's outrageous! But, Detectives, I am totally to blame here. I trusted Edward implicitly and I'm at fault for not checking the documents; a very serious breach of protocol on my part. Thank goodness I did not leave it with Brenda Mears to read. I've put that poor mother through so much lately."

"Tell us, sir, what has been altered?"

With shaking hands, the elderly man once more studied the document in front of him. His face was now red with rage and looking as if it had been badly burnt by the sun.

"Apart from generous bequeaths to her staff, Anna Leci's entire fortune was to be left to her great-niece, Lucy Mears, to be held in trust by my law firm until she reached the age of majority. That is what Anna Leci intended to happen, that and only that was her wish... but... but... oh, this is appalling... the changes made here... that monster of a nephew has altered this to allow Rita Hampton, Anna's nurse, residency of the estate for the duration of her life and total control over staffing. Edward, it seems, was to remain in financial control, the conservator of the estate. This is outrageous."

Harvey questioned the distraught man further, "Mr Garnett, I don't want to prolong this for you any longer than necessary, but what provision was made for the estate in the event of young Lucy's death?"

"I remember that quite clearly. In the event of the untimely death of Lucy Mears, the entire estate was to be placed in the hands of her mother, Brenda Mears."

Shuffling through pages, he was barely audible as he read from the fraudulently altered document.

"The name of Lucy Mears has been totally obliterated. She is not mentioned in this document."

Edward Garnett Jnr was called into his uncle's office and introduced to the visiting detectives.

CHAPTER 16

If Edward Garnett Jnr thought he was being summoned to his uncle's office for an introduction to potential clients the look on Jordan Garnett's face quickly put paid to that idea.

"Sir," he said, addressing his uncle, "are you all right Uncle? Is anything amiss?"

"Amiss?" hollered the elder lawyer. "Is anything amiss? You young whippersnapper! You are asking me if anything is amiss?"

He stood up as if to confront the younger man, his face as purple as the tie he wore, the veins on his neck pulsating rapidly, his whole demeanor menacing and health threatening. Sensing trouble, Carole Carr gently took the senior lawyer's arm and settled him back in his leather chair.

"Leave this to us, sir," she implored.

Superintendent Harvey took over and addressed the younger man who was visibly shaken by the change in his uncle's manner and felt an ominous sickly feeling in the pit of his stomach.

"We are here, sir, with regards to the last will and testament of Anna Leci. You had some dealings with her, I believe?"

Edward shifted from one foot to the other.

"Yes sir. I met the lady when Uncle was recovering from surgery. He asked me to have a document signed and placed in the safe for his return. I'm sure Uncle will confirm that," he said wistfully, looking towards the elder Garnett who was apoplectic with rage.

The elder man attempted to speak but was thwarted by Harvey who gestured to him to remain silent. Detective Carr took over the interview. Handing the young man a sheaf of documents she asked him to confirm if that was the document he had asked Anna Leci to sign.

"Yeah, umm, think so." He mumbled shifting yet again from one foot to the other.

"You think so?" questioned the detective. "Either it is or it isn't. What is it then? Is this the document you were to have Anna Leci sign for your uncle?"

Edward Garnett Jnr sifted through the papers in an attempt to stall the inevitable questions which were to follow.

"Yes, ma'am, it is."

"Please look carefully at these pages here and tell me if they were part of the original document given to you by Mr. Garnett here."

"Umm, yeah, well, perhaps not quite."

"Speak up man," screamed the angry lawyer at his nephew.

Knowing his fraud had been discovered Edward Garnett Jnr hung his head in shame, his face chalk-white with fear.

"We are waiting for an explanation," demanded Harvey.

"Get on with it Nephew, spit it out."

"We can do this here or at the precinct. Save your uncle any more distress and strain of travelling there in heavy traffic, and speak up now. At least you owe him that courtesy."

Edward Garnett Jnr lifted his head and shamefully spoke up, avoiding his uncle's eyes: "It was never meant to go so far, you have to believe me Uncle," he pleaded with his elderly relative who would not meet his eyes.

"After I had Anna Leci sign the document, she asked her nursing companion, Rita Hampton, to take me downstairs to have a meal before I returned home. Anna told me, 'Your uncle is a dear, sweet man. I hope you will be a credit to him when you take over the firm. He speaks very highly of you. I want you to return here, but do not let your uncle know. He has to conserve his energy and recover from his illness.'

"Sir, I returned as instructed. The lady wanted me to add more pages into the document that she had already signed. 'Make it look as if it's part of the original document, and ask no questions.' She gave me some handwritten pages that she asked Rita to witness. I was instructed to include it in the file and place them in the safe on my return to the office."

Harvey, enraged at the audacity of the man, roared at him, "So you were aware of what Anna Leci had added to the document?"

"Yes, sir," came the sheepish reply. "I read it over to the old lady as instructed."

"And Rita Hampton was in the room with you at this time?"

"Yes, sir, she was."

Detective Carr took over from her almost speechless boss. "So you were well aware of the whereabouts of Lucy Mears and her abductors? You knew the entire details of the abduction plot?"

"Well, yeah, I guess I did, ma'am."

Harvey exploded with rage, "You GUESS? You KNEW! You could have saved that child from enduring any more misery."

"But, but… sir… you have no idea how manipulative and powerful that woman was. I tell you, I was scared of her."

Detective Carr stood up: "And I suppose you were paid handsomely for your fear?"

She looked across at her superior to confirm what was to happen next. The senior man took charge; "Edward Garnett, we will continue this interview at the precinct. Cuff him."

Turning to the elderly partner, Harvey implored him to go home and rest.

"You will not be required at the precinct, sir. We won't put you through any more trauma. You will hear from us later. I'll call you in a few hours."

As they stood to leave, the elderly, shaking lawyer hollered at his nephew, "You disgust me. You are fired. I no longer have a nephew. Get out of here. Don't even stop to clear your office."

Shamefully, the errant young man had to suffer the indignity of walking through the main office, busy with legal secretaries and trainee lawyers who gasped in surprise as their senior colleague was led away in hand-cuffs, sobbing bitterly, his head bowed down as if hoping to avoid being seen.

As the shamed young lawyer was being locked up, Harvey turned to his deputy, "I had a gut feeling, Carole, that Rita Hampton was more involved than she let on. I'm not finished with that dame, and as for Anna Leci, even in death she continues to mock us."

While interviewing Edward Garnett Jnr, Superintendent Harvey became more and more furious as he took the young lawyer's statement, to the point that he had to leave the room, instructing another detective to continue recording the statement. Disgusted with what he had discovered, he stormed out of the interview room and almost bumped into his deputy who was coming out of her office.

"Hey, Tony, slow down. You need to cool it. You've let that creep get under your skin."

"I'm enraged, Carole; that creep as you refer to him, could have saved Lucy. Yeah, I'm uptight. I won't rest until he and that obnoxious woman are charged for this and get their just deserts. The death penalty is too good for them. He and Rita Hampton I'm sure were handsomely paid for their silence. We have to investigate where the money is and sequestrate those dollars. I'll contact our fraud squad and get things moving. As for Anna Leci, she completely fooled the elderly Garnett into believing that young Lucy's visit to her had been sanctioned by the child's mother. The poor man is in a state of shock. I gave him a call to check on him. I thought he was going to collapse on us. He has to rethink his retirement plans and consider the future of the firm. Poor guy. He so wanted to keep the law practice in the family."

Harvey sat in his office staring blankly out of the window over the busy city. He was staggered at the recent revelations. He was interrupted by an international call from DI Rab McKenzie from the Scottish squad who reported that his investigation into the possibility that the two American criminals had entered Scotland illegally via Scottish waters had no foundation in fact. Harvey had momentarily forgotten it was still under investigation, so caught up was he with events on his own patch.

"There's been a few drug smuggling incidents round our waters recently. A Colombian ship was searched, and three men arrested with class A drugs, but no illegal entry of people was reported. We're still working our way through CCTV from airports and harbours. The trouble is your two blokes could have arrived in the UK not long after you tracked them to Mexico. They could have slipped in unnoticed while your men were searching elsewhere.

"We were all presuming they came here recently. There's no proof either way, but we won't give up until we get the truth. I think we have to concentrate our enquiries around London where Barry Jones originated. I'm flying to the capital to speak with some London guys. I'll keep you informed of progress. I hate these unsolved cases on my patch and I'm determined to get to the bottom of it and bring some closure."

Sensing that all was not well with his Chicago friend, Rab McKenzie enquired: "Have I called at a bad time, Tony? You sound far away and I don't mean physically; is everything okay over there?"

Chicago's superintendent brought him up to speed.

"Things are moving rapidly over here, Rab, so rapidly that I haven't got back to you to update you. I have you top of my list to contact as soon as I catch my breath."

He related recent events to his stunned colleague and after some discussion the two men ended the call, promising to be in touch with any developments.

Well, that's a turn up for the books! thought Rab.

CHAPTER 17

Infuriated at the turn of events, Superintendent Harvey made yet another journey to interview Rita Hampton, this time accompanied by his deputy. His fists tightened on the steering wheel as they discussed the forthcoming interview. He parked erratically, lunging Carole forward as she held on to the side of the seat. She took a sharp intake of breath and refrained from commenting, knowing her boss was on a short fuse. He did not trust himself to be in the same room as Rita Hampton without losing control of his temper. Carole Carr conducted the interview as Tony, attempting to control his rage, watched from a one-way observation window of the interrogation room.

"I believe you have much more to tell us about Lucy Mears' abduction?"

"No, ma'am, I told Superintendent Harvey all I could remember."

"You omitted to mention Edward Garnett," said Carole, dropping the name and watching for a reaction from the prisoner.

"Who, ma'am? I can't seem to recall that name."

"Then let me cast your mind back to when Anna Leci had you witness her signature on a document which Edward

Garnett had rewritten, purporting to be her last will and testament and another document regarding the abduction of Lucy Mears."

"Ma'am, it was so long ago. I've been going mad in this place, my memory's not as good as it should be. I don't recall anything like that."

The scheming woman hoped to stall the flow of questions that she mistakenly took to be from a rather naïve officer whom she could easily deceive, by denying all knowledge of Edward Garnett.

Detective Carr was no pushover. She sat calmly staring at the prisoner in front of her, her stare disconcerting and menacing, a tactic often used by her to cause unease and agitation. She waited.

The silence seemed unending to the offender. Sweat formed on her brow, trickles of water ran down her face. She wiped her brow with her sleeve, her palms now hot and clammy; she felt uncomfortably hot. Carole waited.

When she could no longer stand the strain, Rita Hampton mumbled, "Edward Garnett? Well, ah, now I do seem to recall that name. Wasn't he a lawyer from Jordan Garnett's firm? Yeah, he did visit Anna when his uncle was ill... had to have some papers signed... yeah, maybe I did witness Anna's signature... "

Carole remained silent and waited knowing her tactics were working on the increasingly uncomfortable prisoner.

Outside the interrogation room, Tony Harvey whispered to himself, good girl, Carole, keep at it. He knew his partner's skills and trusted her implicitly to draw a confession from the errant internee. Silence makes people uncomfortable; a strong tool used as a power tactic disconcerting the other; it denotes control and inevitably elicits a response.

Rita Hampton felt her control slipping from her; her confidence shattered, she wanted a hole to appear to swallow her up, but her opponent waited. In silence.

She blubbered, "It all went too far. Anna's entire wealth was to go to a fifteen-year-old rich kid. It wasn't fair; she didn't need her aunt's mega riches. Eddie, umm, Edward came up with a plan to distribute it fairly. He added bits to the documents that Anna never knew about and got me to witness the signature."

Carole turned towards the one-way window, signalled to her superior that he was to join her.

Rita Hampton was surprised to see the superintendent from Chicago yet again on her case, believing Deputy Carr to be on her own.

"Sir," mumbled the flustered prisoner, "I am surprised to see you here. I hope you don't think I can give you any information about Anna Leci. I've told you and this officer here all I know."

"Stop there, lady. It's time to come clean. I have to tell you that your accomplice Edward Garnett Jnr has been arrested and has told us of your deceit."

At that she paled significantly, mumbled incoherently, and hung her head in shame.

"It's time to talk," hollered Harvey, having no compassion for the distressed prisoner. "Start talking, right now. Get your version in before Edward Garnett sings like a budgie and blames you for the entire deceit. May I remind you that five people are dead."

Harvey could be the gentlest, most understanding inquisitor when he felt a prisoner deserved it, or he could be ruthless and furious when necessary. Rita Hampton experienced the latter. His accusing demeanor took her aback.

"I... I... " She began through tears, "I'm so sorry. It was never meant to go so far, it was all a mistake. Wish to God I'd never set eyes on that lawyer."

"Go on," commanded Harvey with not a vestige of sympathy.

Carole Carr sat back and listened.

"It all happened so fast. Edward Garnett came to have Anna sign a document for his uncle, who was seriously ill in hospital. Anna said to me, 'Take that young man to the dining room and order a meal. You might as well stay and eat with him. I'm going to sleep now and won't need you for a while.' So I did that and we got talking. He asked me about Lucy Mears. 'I read from your employer's will that the kid is to inherit everything; this whole damn monstrosity of a place to go to a kid! What about you Rita? It looks like you'll be homeless when the old dear passes on. In my books, that's unfair.'

"Until then I knew nothing of the contents of Anna's will. Sir, he was so charming, such a smooth-talking guy and I fell under his charms. You have to understand, I'd been stuck in that place with little or no contact with people other than a few staff, and when he came along, well, he was a breath of fresh air. I'd never thought much about what would happen to me after Anna died. I'd a plan in mind to go to England and visit my cousin, but it was only a thought, and then Edward got me thinking about my future."

She stopped to wipe tears from her swollen eyes, but Harvey had no time for theatrics. "Get on with it."

Frightened by his brusque manner and aware of the silent detective still sitting in the room, never faltering in eye contact, she continued.

"Well, he then told me he could adjust the will to give me security and swore me to secrecy. At first I was shocked that a lawyer could be so deceitful, and then I guess his charms carried me away. 'If you breathe a word of this to anyone Rita, I'll deny everything and drop you right in it. I have the skill to discredit you in court so keep your mouth shut and listen up,' he told me. I have to say, I was mighty scared."

"And then?" demanded Harvey.

"Well, he came back on several occasions, supposedly to pay a courtesy call on Anna. He would sit with her and talk about everything and anything. Anna thought he was wonderful, but he was plotting all the time to gain her trust. It was all a game to him. The day after the incident that I told you about, sir, when I overheard Alf and Barclay talk about poor Les, Edward turned up at the house with flowers for Anna. He could see I was upset about something and, well, he was so concerned that I blurted it all out to him and told him that Alf and Barclay had planned to harm Les by fixing the plane. Detective, you have to understand how lonely I was and how kind that guy was to me, and I was real scared of those two guys and what they were planning to do."

"I don't have to understand anything but the truth," he snapped. "Continue."

In an attempt to distract him from more inquisitions and hoping for a whisker of sympathy, she asked for water, which Harvey sent a young officer to fetch, without taking his eyes from the distressed prisoner.

"And?"

Rita had no option but to proceed.

"'You leave everything to me, Rita, I'll deal with this,' he said after he finished his visit with Anna. I was in the kitchen clearing up after her lunch, not that she ate much, and I looked out to see Edward in conversation with Alf. They seemed to talk for ages and then shook hands. Edward slapped Alf on the back, you know the way men do, and I was scared they would see me looking at them, so I hid awhile before returning upstairs. I must have been away longer than I thought as I could hear Anna ringing her call bell. 'Where have you been? I need my pillows moved.' She could be quite demanding, sir, and I was real stressed."

Rita paused for breath and to sip some water. Realising there was to be no respite from Harvey's constant glare and no hope of sympathy; she continued to regale him with her confession.

"I didn't see him again for over a week, then he turned up one day with some documents for Anna to sign. 'Uncle has asked me to get your signature on this document, right here and here,' he said as he guided her shaky hand to where her signature was required. 'It's just a page he forgot to add, nothing really too important for you to concern yourself with. And how are you today, my dear? I have to say, you look a bit brighter.' He could be real charming."

"I'm not interested in his charm," barked Harvey. "What did he and Alf discuss?"

"I never found that out, sir; all I heard was a snippet of their conversation, something like, 'big bucks in it for you, you get my meaning?' but I moved away real quick like. Later that evening after dinner he said to me, 'Rita, don't you worry about a thing. Anna has changed her will; you have a home here for life and I'll be custodian of her money. Little Lucy will never inherit. What could a kid do with a place like this anyway? But you and me Rita, we could have a real good time here. Poor, sick Anna, she hadn't a clue what she signed, so remember, keep your mouth shut.' As I said, Detective, I was real scared of him by then."

Harvey stood up, thumped the table, and pushed the chair with such force that it landed across the room startling both the prisoner and attending officer.

"I'm sure you were real scared," he yelled at the top of his voice as he left the room in total disgust.

Rita collapsed onto the floor.

Harvey stood outside the interview room, head in hands as he tried to make sense of what he had just heard.

"Good God. It was Edward Garnett who set up the murder of Lucy and her companions. He colluded with Alfred Wysoki to prevent Lucy inheriting."

He shook his head as Carole approached.

"This has totally bowled me over. I'll have to inform our FBI guys. They had been searching for our two fugitives and know about the murders in Scotland but this takes it up a notch now that we have proof that the cause of the plane crash was a planned criminal act and the motive for the accident. They've been working closely with our own law enforcement agencies. I'll make the call."

When she recovered sufficiently in the prison medical centre, a senior detective read Rita her Miranda rights and passed on a verbal message from the superintendent of CPD to the effect that he would ensure she would never be freed from incarceration.

CHAPTER 18

Carole invited Tony over to her place for a meal and to talk things over. She knew he was angry at the turn of events after his visit to Rita Hampton and Anna Leci's lawyer, and thought a change of scene would bring him out of his morose state. She tried to reason with him that what was done was done, but he was outraged at the selfishness of the woman who could perhaps have saved Lucy from prolonged captivity. Her involvement in the treachery of scheming Edward Garnett Jnr had floored him.

"You're letting Rita Hampton get under your skin, Tony. Come on. Chill out a bit. Those two are safely incarcerated for forever and a day. Ted's opening a bottle of your favourite wine, so let's relax and enjoy my crazy kids. They haven't seen their Uncle Tony in a long time. Since we've got back from Scotland you never seem to have a minute. We never see you socially. Where are you hiding out? You're gonna burn yourself out. You need to chill and relax with folks who care about you. You spend too much time alone."

Tony squirmed with embarrassment; his face reddened as he bashfully revealed his secret.

"Well, I suppose I'd best tell you. I have been chilling out... with a lovely lady... for some time now. We wanted to keep it under wraps to see how it panned out but you've kinda put me in a corner."

Carole squealed with delight, bringing her husband rushing from the kitchen to see what the excitement was about.

"Who, Tony? Come on, spill the beans, who is she? I haven't spotted any signs, like you buying candy for your lady, or flowers. Hey, come to think of it, you have been spruced up a bit lately and yeah, look at those shoes! When did you ever clean your shoes before? Tony, I'm your part-ner and I haven't noticed anything!"

Tony threw his head back in raucous laughter.

"Flowers! That's one thing I'll never need to buy her, she has plenty!"

Carole digested this information before exclaiming: "Tony! It's Gina, isn't it? I thought you'd been going over there a lot. Wow! Tell me it is Gina!"

"Yeah, it is Gina. We got close after Lucy's death. When I went over to give her the tragic news, Abigail was bereft. I called by several times to check on them. I suppose it just grew into friendship then got more serious."

When he was able to entangle himself from Carole's hug and Ted's backslapping, he continued, "We took it easy to let Abigail get used to me being around. She's a great kid and we get on so well. She was devastated at Lucy's death. In fact, I don't think she is really over it yet even after all this time. Gina often finds her sobbing in her room.

"Gina's had a tough life; her husband deserted her when he found out Abigail was on the way. He didn't want kids but didn't think to let Gina know. She was shocked at the turn of events, but she sure is one strong lady and made a terrific job of bringing up Abigail and setting up her floral business. The two of them are close. Young Lucy envied them that closeness; she never had that from her own mother. Abigail is studying art at the School of Art Institute of Chicago now and has her own life ahead of her; she's pleased for her mom and me. She has become quite an independent young lady now, but will always be haunted by memories of Lucy."

"You've bowled me over! Wow, I'm so happy for you. What are your plans then?"

"As I said, we've been taking it a step at a time. And now, well, we've set a date for the wedding. I was going to tell you when I calmed down. Who knows what life has in store, so we've decided to take the plunge; we both realised how much we missed each other when I was in Scotland."

"And I wish you every happiness! Now I know why you were reluctant to have Gina and Abigail re-interviewed; you were protecting them and rightly so, Tony. I understand."

"Thanks Carole, that means a lot to me. Now, what I haven't shared with you or any of the squad was that I was engaged many years ago to a wonderful girl, but my darling Poppy died in my arms after two years of suffering from cancer. She was so brave. She told me, 'Tony, honey, after I'm gone, you have to find yourself a good woman. I don't want to think of you alone in the world'.

"I never wanted anyone else, Carole, so I immersed myself in work. When Gina entered my life I was bowled over at how I felt about her, and you know, I was a bit afraid; part of me thought I was betraying Poppy. I talked it over with Gina. She's such a level-headed person and she got me to see that it was okay to let go of my love for Poppy and was sure Poppy approved of our liaison. That's why I kept the news to myself until I was sure of my feelings."

He produced a photograph from his wallet, removed it carefully, and showed them his beloved Poppy.

"Oh, Tony, she is so beautiful."

***

While Tony enjoyed time at Carole's home, Gina and her daughter talked well into the night as they discussed the change about to happen in their lives.

"You're sure, honey, that you're okay with Tony and me?"

"Mom, I'm pleased for you both. Tony is a cool guy and I'm so happy that you will have someone with you when I'm off to college. I'm cool about it, Mom. Okay, there's a big age difference but what does that matter?"

Tony laughed when Gina related the conversation about the ten-year age gap.

"As long as she doesn't take to calling me 'Grand pappy'."

"What does age matter when love is involved?" whispered Gina as they finalised their wedding plans.

"You sure, honey, you want to take on an old guy like me?" laughed the groom-to-be, when he popped an engagement ring on his lady's finger. They were both aware of the poignancy of events which led them to find love: the abduction and death of young Lucy Mears led Tony as head of the Chicago investigation unit to interview Gina and her traumatised daughter, Abigail. Regular visits had been made to 'Gina's Floral Boutique' where Tony and his deputy Carole patiently questioned the distraught child on events leading up to the disappearance of her school friend.

***

Tony and Gina's wedding was a quiet affair, carefully choreographed and staged by Gina herself. The wedding took place in downtown Chicago. The hotel outdoor pool-deck offered the perfect setting for a romantic wedding. Abigail looked happier than she had been for many months and looked forward to having a stepfather. Several close friends were in attendance including Carole and Ted Carr. The bridal shower had been arranged by Carole and Abigail, the latter being chief bridesmaid. The couple had composed their own wedding vows which were said in unison.

"If Mom's happy, then I'm happy," she told Carole at the hotel where the reception took place. Since college was out for summer recess Abigail was to live with Carole and her family while the newlyweds honeymooned in Florida. Abigail often called around to spend time with Carole's two kids and the families had become close friends.

***

The Florida Keys, a thousand miles away, was the setting for another quiet wedding, that of Nora Kelly and her fiancé Peter. Molly, accompanied by Brenda, attended the quiet beach wedding. The once spritely lady was becoming too frail to travel alone. The events of the past years had aged her considerably. In spite of her being in her late sixties, her health was not good. She had become stooped and had lost her love of life; everything was an effort for her. She suffered attacks of angina, which she tried to shield from her daughter and from Brenda, but she continued to push herself to the limit in spite of being asked to slow down. The trip to Europe with Brenda was an awesome experience for her, but the strain was telling on her aging body.

"I look in that mirror, Brenda, and I see an old woman looking back at me. Who is she and where has my youth gone? Inside me I feel young and apart from a few health problems, I'm still me!" chuckled the incorrigible Molly.

"I don't want to miss my only child's wedding," she told Brenda, when the arrangements for the day were settled.

"The invite includes you, of course. Nora wants you, her lifelong friend, to be part of her special day. It's to be a quiet celebration as Peter has only his father and one sister left now. I'm looking forward to meeting my son-in-law. I've only ever spoken to him on the phone. The sweet man called to ask my permission to marry my daughter. Perhaps we can spend a few days in the area and see some sights after the celebrations are over. I'm a seasoned traveller now, you know!"

"As long as you don't drag me with you on those Disney rides, Molly Kelly!" laughed a more relaxed Brenda as they began arranging their trip.

"Now, we need to do some serious shopping; the mother of the bride must look the part," she said.

Nora's beach wedding was a beautiful occasion, perfect in every way. Mother and daughter had a long, emotional chat about the events which led Nora to this day.

"Mom, I'll never forget George, he was my first real love, but what's done is done, and Peter is a real good guy. I'm looking forward to spending my life with him. We plan to stay in this area and open our own small hotel; you know that was always my ambition and I keep thinking that maybe I put George under too much pressure about it and that led to his involvement with those scumbag loan sharks."

"Honey, don't beat yourself up about the past. George was an adult. He made the mistake, not you. No, you have to think of the future and maybe get me some grandkids before I get any older," laughed Molly as she helped her daughter adjust her dress.

"I've left it too late for that, Mom. Not that I wouldn't like to be a mom, I sure would, and Peter would be a good dad."

"Honey, lots of women are having babies later in life. You just never know! Hey, I had you just after my thirtieth birthday and we made out alright, now, didn't we?"

Nora, an ecstatic bride, looked more content then than she had been for several years. She and her new groom headed off for a vacation.

Molly and Brenda sat by the hotel pool reminiscing on life's events which led to this contented day. As the sun set, casting a spectacular glow over the area, they raised their glasses to toast the newlyweds.

"What an awesome day, Brenda. My girl is so happy and so am I. I couldn't be a happier mom."

Wistfully, Brenda turned to Molly and poured out her heart.

"I envy you, Molly Kelly. I'll never get to see my daughter as a beautiful bride. You are so lucky. Nora was stunning. I'm so happy for her. Peter is charming and they make a perfect couple."

Molly hugged her lifelong friend. "I know, honey. I was just thinking that as I helped Nora with her dress. You are still hurting real bad, aren't you?"

"Molly, dear, I have to face up to things. I know Lucy loved you and looked on you as her mama; I'm not blind to my neglect of her. It pains me so."

"It's not too late for you to get some professional help, some therapy. It might help ease things a little. But, listen to this old fool; I need therapy as much as you do. I think I managed to hide my grief from you, didn't want to make things worse when you were suffering so, but, I'm still having flashbacks at night, sleep evades me most nights, so let's fix it up when we get home; yeah, a bit of therapy will help us both. You were a good mom, despite what you think, so don't beat yourself up."

"That's sweet of you to say that, but I have to face up to the fact that I poured money and material things Lucy's way. She wanted for nothing except her mom's love. No, Molly, I know I was not as good a mom as I should have been and things might have been different if I'd given her my time and my love. She might still be alive."

"Brenda Mears, listen to me. Even if you had been the most loving mom in the world it would not have changed Anna Leci's despicable plot to take Lucy from you. Now, less of this talk and let's have a cocktail. I fancy a cool margarita. Don't you? Served by a handsome waiter like that one over there!"

***

A few days after the wedding, Brenda returned to the poolside after her swim to find Molly snoozing in the sunshine.

"Come on sleepy; let's head for lunch. Swimming always makes me ravenous. The food here is too good to waste."

As she gently shook Molly, she knew then that her darling lifetime friend and mentor would never know the joy of grandkids. Molly had simply slept away.

Brenda had the unenviable task of informing the honeymooners of the demise of Molly Kelly.

CHAPTER 19

Carole settled her young kids in her sedan ready to drop them off at school.

"Hang in there kids, I've left my cell phone, won't be a minute."

She returned to her car to find the kids staring out of the window.

"Mom, a man in a car stopped on our driveway and just stared at us. It was creepy. He made a sign with his fingers, like he was going to shoot us. He drove off when he saw you come out of the house."

At that moment, her husband Ted arrived home from his late-night shift.

"Hey, I had to swerve at the bottom of our street for some madman who was driving way too fast for here."

"Daddy, a man was staring at us from his car, just now."

Trying not to alarm her kids, Carole tried to make light of the incident. She was unsure how much information her seven and five-year-old children could understand without becoming afraid of every passing car or every stranger who smiled at them.

She whispered to Ted, "Honey, I'll drop the kids off and come right back. Try to remember all you saw of that car. I'll be back shortly."

En route to school, Carole gently reminded her kids of the rules about not talking to strangers or going in strange cars.

"Yeah Mom, we know all that, you're always telling us about good guys/bad guys."

"I know you do honey, but it doesn't do any harm to be reminded. You have to remind your friends too; will you do that for me? It's probably nothing to worry about, but just remember the rules; you must never take a ride from strangers."

"Sure Mom, but we all know these things."

Carole spoke to the school principal about the incident and reiterated her strict arrangements for collecting her kids from school.

"They must never be picked up by anyone but me or my husband. If we have to arrange for someone else, I'll call. Please be extra vigilant; this may be nothing, but I can't take chances, not in my line of work. Every day I meet all kinds of people; some harmless, others downright dangerous."

"I'll inform my staff right now, ma'am, and we'll make sure the CCTV cameras are constantly monitored. We do all we can here to keep the kids safe. As you know, we have an officer on the premises monitoring the school as part of the city 'safe zone policy'. I'll speak with him and make sure he keeps his eyes open for any untoward activity."

Back home, she and Ted discussed strategies for dropping off and picking up the kids. What they had in place worked well. They were meticulous in setting a strict routine for the kids' various activities.

"We just have to tighten up a bit," admitted Carole. "I'm guilty of running late at times but the kids know to hang around in school for me."

With the flexibility of Ted's job as an environmental officer and his ability to work from home when necessary, child minding had seldom been a problem. He could vary his work hours to fit in with his wife's shift pattern, allowing a plan of action to ensure the safety of his children. In the light of the morning's incident they rescheduled some dates to ensure watertight school runs.

"As for the car, all we have to go on is that it was black and driven by a creepy man. I'll call it in and ask our guys to patrol the area for a while. It may be nothing, just some guy out to terrify folk, but he sure as hell scared the kids."

"Well, whoever he was," commented Ted, "he sure sped off from here. Another few seconds and I'd have been in a head-on crash."

At work that day, Carole related the incident to her colleagues who arranged for a police car to patrol her street. With that in place, Carole attempted to concentrate on her work and put the incident to the back of her mind but she was unable to shake off the feeling of trepidation deep in her being.

Back home later that day, she was preparing dinner and attempting to control her unruly husband, kids and dog as they played around her feet, when she caught a glimpse of the mailman popping something into the mailbox.

"Ted, that's odd. We don't normally get mail at this time of day."

"I'll go fetch it," he said and was about to race his kids down the drive when Carole screamed.

"No!" She startled them all. "Ted, go by yourself, honey. Kids, stay here, go wash your hands before dinner."

She had almost forgotten the incident that morning but in true detective mode, had the presence of mind to be concerned at a late mail drop.

Her fear was justified as the envelope contained a picture of her kids playing in the schoolyard. Without causing alarm, the couple again discussed with their children the need for extra care when not with their parents. Some days later, the two youngsters were playing upstairs and alerted their mother with a scream so loud that Carole dropped the plate she was removing from the dishwasher and ran upstairs like an Olympic sprinter. A heavy stone had shattered the window. The children were unhurt but shaken. Carole, once more in detective mode, ushered the children to a safe corner of the room, donned nylon gloves, and bagged the offending stone. Only then did she spot the handwritten note wrapped around it. It read revenge.

Alarm bells rang. Colleagues were called to an incident room by Superintendent Tony Harvey, recently returned to work after his holiday. He took immediate charge of the investigation into the apparent harassment of his deputy and her family. Staff were briefed on events and helped plan strategies to locate and arrest the person who brought dread into the heart of their chief deputy detective.

Several more incidents occurred, adding fuel to the already tense situation. A few days after the stone incident, the vigilant caretaker spotted a black sedan circling the area around the school.

"Sorry, ma'am," he reported to the principal, "he was too quick for me to catch the number. It was a black Chevy, with darkened windows. That's all I can say. He drove around several times, too fast for here. Maybe Officer Karl will have something for us."

Sophisticated surveillance cameras had for some time been installed in several schools to provide a safe zone for the students and staff. The specially developed technology had been in operation across the city for several years and had proved a useful tool in deterring crime.

"I'm checking it out right now," said the portly officer, whose charismatic personality added to the sense of safety within the school. He was well liked by staff, adored by the kids who thought of him as a rather jolly Father Christmas type of person owing to his rotund frame that wobbled as he laughed and joked with them.

"Yeah, I've caught the black Chevy right here on camera, and the times it circled our premises, way too fast for a school zone and too darn fast for the number to be recognised. I'll send the film to our lab guys who might be able to retrieve it."

Several days after the caretaker had reported the incident, Officer Karl, viewing the area with a camera, identified the black Chevy as once more it cruised around the school perimeter. The recordings were carefully studied and sent to the lab but no more sightings were made of the black Chevy for many days.

Sitting in the family room at home some days later and engrossed in some paper work for his latest reports, Ted was alerted to the roar of a motorbike speeding up the driveway. He rushed outside in time to see the bike racing off down the drive and turn into the street beyond. He called Carole at work. She immediately asked patrols to be extra vigilant.

"Whoever it is has changed tactics. Who is trying to scare us?" she asked her husband after they settled the kids for the night. "It's unnerving. I'll get our guys to call over this way as often as they can. If the creep sees regular patrols it might frighten him off."

Meanwhile, the perpetrator of the crime returned to his apartment, stored a few groceries and locked himself in his den where he pinned his latest trophy to his collection. He congratulated himself on his achievement in photographing Carole Carr's kids and placing a copy in her mailbox, without being observed. The mailman uniform stored in his car was one of several disguises used by him in his conniving scheme. Among his props on his wall was a plan of her house. He made several silent phone calls and thought he could detect fear in the voice of Carole Carr.

Good, he thought, *that's what I like to hear: Fear.*

What he didn't perceive was that he was not hearing fear in the voice of Chicago's deputy chief, but anger, and an angry Carole Carr was a force to be reckoned with.

For the next few weeks all was quiet until cops on patrol in the area spotted a black Chevy once again creeping slowly towards Carole Carr's home. It took off at speed when the driver spotted the cop car, but despite their chase the vehicle was quickly out of sight. For several days cops in the area were extra attentive and were awarded for their patience when the black Chevy, unaware of the unmarked police car nearby, cruised around Detective Carr's street.

"Hey, we have the licence plate, caught it on our on-board camera from quite a distance. This thing is damned efficient."

"Call it in and run a search, Chuck," hollered his partner. "Let's find the creep who's been stalking Detective Carr and her kids."

A call came through to her: "Ma'am, we have the name of the owner of the black Chevy. Burt Kennedy. Does the name ring a bell with you?"

"Can't say it does. Let's get him checked out. So many cases come my way that it's impossible to remember them all; in fact, he may not have any connection with anything I've ever investigated. I'll do some research myself. Have you brought him in for questioning?"

"Two of our guys are chasing him up, ma'am. He's not at his last known address, and he seems to have moved. Our guys are making enquiries from the neighbours. Someone might know where he has gone."

"You looking for Burt, you say?" asked a former neighbour to the detective who came looking for the man.

"He moved on from here a few weeks ago, got a place downtown. Real nice, quiet guy keeps himself to himself mostly."

The chatty neighbour, lonely and inquisitive, was happy to spend time with the cops.

"Does he own a car, sir?"

"Yeah, a real nice Chevy: black tinted windows; his pride and joy. He washes it regularly too, takes real good care of it. He's one lucky guy; has a Suzuki Boulevard motorcycle, a real nice ride. That's why he moved downtown; got a place with secure garaging. Up here, it wasn't garaged and he worried about it. Hey, if you guys want to talk to him he eats out a lot in 'Mike's Diner' two blocks down, goes there most days. Told me he never liked cooking. He's a real cool guy, would do anything to help a neighbour. Sure when I was sick last few weeks he fetched groceries for me. Yip, Burt's a real good guy. Hey, I hope the guy ain't in no trouble."

"It's just routine, sir, and thanks for your help."

The helpful neighbour returned to his newspaper thinking he had done his duty as a good citizen and hoped Burt's motorcycle hadn't been stolen or damaged.

CHAPTER 20

Burt Kennedy did not show up on the system as having any criminal record. Who was he and what interest did he have with Detective Carr? One of their own was being targeted and the entire squad it seemed, worked relentlessly to locate the wanted man. Two young cops patrolling the area spotted the black Chevy parked at 'Mike's Diner'. They waited for the man to return to his car. The unsuspecting diner continued with his meal, watched some TV sport, and sauntered out.

"See you tomorrow then Burt," said Mike to his most regular customer. Like Burt he had failed to notice a cop car parked in a corner of the parking lot. Burt Kennedy returned to his car and satisfied with yet another good meal, smiled to himself as he thought of the plan he had in mind for Carole Carr. He was so engrossed in thought that he was unaware of the approach of two officers.

"Burt Kennedy?" they asked.

The stunned man spluttered and answered, "Yeah, that's me."

He was cuffed and arrested. As he sat in the back of a patrol car he appeared bemused that his foolproof plans had been discovered. At the precinct he waited in an interview room for a considerable time mulling over where his plan had gone wrong. Just as he thought he had been forgotten about, an irate Tony Harvey burst into the room, terrifying the detainee with his overpowering presence. The superintendent sat opposite him in total silence, never taking his eyes from the increasingly nervous man who wriggled uncomfortably in his seat, sweat beginning to form on his brow and palms of his hands, wanting to speak but finding his mouth dry and his brain confused as to what to say to break the unnerving silence.

After what seemed an intolerable length of time, Harvey launched into a vicious interview, not sparing the agitated prisoner from his verbal attack.

Despite his bravado at stalking Carole Carr, Burt Kennedy was nervous and excitable during the relentless questioning and with the possibility of imprisonment looming, came clean. He had been one of a number of people who lost their jobs when the newspaper company he worked for had been closed four years previously, following the scandal surrounding Ross S. Witherspoon, a presidential nominee. A rogue cop, Kip O'Rourke, a former colleague of Detective Carr and Superintendent Harvey, was responsible for passing on sensitive information to a newspaper reporter, Sonny Woods, during the investigation of the disappearance of Lucy Mears. Their scheming actions resulted in the suspension of the two detectives on suspicion that they, and not Kip O'Rourke, had disclosed information leading to the revelation that the man selected as a potential candidate for the office of President of the United States was the father of the missing girl. Uproar and mayhem had followed the exposé.

Burt Kennedy, by now scared witless at the thought of imprisonment, revealed his reason for stalking the detective and her family. He found his voice and talked incessantly, the words tumbling out like bullets ricocheting from a machine gun.

"Sir, I've never been in trouble in my life, not even a parking violation. This has all gotten out of hand. I worked with Sonny Woods at the newspaper and lost my job when the FBI closed down the outfit. Hey, I knew nothing about what was going on with Sonny and that cop, none of us did. It was a shock to find ourselves out on the street with no money and no prospect of work in the newspaper business. Other printing firms wouldn't look at any of us, tarred us all with the same brush."

Burt, now that he was able to unburden his feelings of guilt, continued his account.

Harvey menacingly stared at the uncomfortable man and listened in silence.

"I got me a job in a fast food place but it wasn't enough to live on. I visited Sonny in prison to find out if he had any contacts in the newspaper business, hoping he could help get me a better job. He owed me that at least. Sonny told me he knew some guys who might employ me, but he said, 'Burt, you don't get this for nothing. I've got a job for you, nothing dangerous like'.

"He explained that he and his accomplice cop friend, Kip O'Rourke, wanted revenge on the detective who caused their incarceration. 'Nothing too difficult, Burt' he told me, 'just do a bit of stalking, put the frighteners on her and her kids, but don't get too close so as to get caught. Just want them scared a bit so that she'll be watching over her shoulder for the longest time.'

"So that's what I did sir, wasn't too happy about it, but didn't see much harm in just driving around and scaring them some and I was promised a job with a guy Sonny knew in the business. Unfortunately, I was so bored with having no job that I threw myself into this scheme and got carried away with it. I have to confess, and I hope this gets me credit for honesty, I actually enjoyed it... didn't think there was any harm in scaring those guys, just for a short time."

"You are right. You didn't think," hollered Harvey thumping the table. "Have you any idea how scared those little kids were? They have nightmares. They can't sleep properly and when they do, they dream of a bad guy coming after them. And for their parents, constantly looking over their shoulders for a madman? Yeah, you didn't think but you'll have plenty time to think, where you're going."

The shamed man, aware now of the seriousness of his situation, attempted some sort of apology which was curtly dismissed.

"You say you had no job, no money, right? How come you could afford a Chevy and a motorcycle?"

"Sir, I've had that Chevy for twelve years. Bought it when I was employed. It's paid for and I look after it, do my own repairs and things, and it don't cost me much to run. The Suzuki belongs to my brother. He's in Mexico on business for three months and I get to look after his dream machine. I could never afford to buy a machine like that. I'm staying at his pad while he's away; he has secure garaging there."

"Let's rephrase that: you were staying at his pad."

A furious Harvey stormed out of the interview room leaving a junior colleague to elicit more details from the prisoner.

Burt Kennedy was held over to face charges.

***

Superintendent Harvey insisted that he go alone to interview Kip O'Rourke who still had many years of his sentence to serve.

"You stay here Carole. I don't want that lout gloating and thinking he has gotten under your skin. Leave him to me. I want to find out if there is any more to this Kennedy guy. I'm not finished with him yet. Stay out of the interview room; let your colleagues deal with Kennedy and O'Rourke.Take the rest of the day off, go shopping. Hey, give Gina a call; she may join you. I can't figure out what you gals get out of spending so much money, but, hey, I'm just a mere guy."

Carole smiled at her boss's attempt to defuse a stressful situation. Harvey made his way to where the bent cop was being held.

Before interviewing Kip O'Rourke, he met with the prison psychologist who had carried out an assessment in an attempt to shed more light on the wayward cop.

"O'Rourke," said the profiler, "was insecure, and had real low self-esteem. He desperately craved power and recognition. He suffered from a mental disorder, which we have only now identified in him as bipolar. Sufferers swing between depression to manic behaviour to being charming and plausible. I don't know how he managed to give us the slip and be accepted as a police officer, except that he was shrewd and manipulative and able to cover his deficiencies to the extent that he fooled us all. Being a cop gave him the power he so badly needed. He had a jealous streak and became almost paranoid when Detective Carr was promoted to a job he felt should be his. He holds on to that hatred to this day. He was astute enough to get Sonny

Woods to arrange for someone else to do the stalking, thinking it could never be traced back to him."

Kip O'Rourke faced a tough time in prison. Not many inmates had sympathy for a bent cop. He spent his time talking to the wardens, regaling them of his past glories at catching crooks and putting them behind bars, missing the irony of his own situation. Staff knew of his mental health problems and let him talk of his exploits. He was in the midst of such a conversation when a call came through to one of the wardens.

"Kip, get yourself tidied up, you have a visitor, a long-lost friend."

Seeing Superintendent Harvey in the interview room, his heart sank, the disappointment showing on his pale face, but being the master of deceit, he changed his stance to one of defiance. His first ploy was to congratulate Harvey on his promotion.

"I always knew, sir, that you would be superintendent some day. You're the best boss I ever worked for; it was a privilege to serve in your team. Glad to see you again, sir. I don't get many visitors… too far out for folks to travel, I suppose…"

Harvey sensed the crooked cop was gloating during his interview with him.

"You think this is some kind of game O'Rourke, do you? We have Burt Kennedy in custody and he sure is spilling the beans. This should get you a few more years in here."

Kip O' Rourke, visibly shaken at the thought of a longer jail term, attempted to blame Sonny Woods for arranging the stalking of his former colleague.

"Hey, I never meant it to go so far, just wanted her scared some. Sonny musta told that guy to scare her and the kids way too much. I ain't got nothing against her. Hell, I worked alongside her for years, got nothing but respect for the broad, sorry, the lady. Sure she got the promotion I'd set my mind to, but, hey, these things happen and the best person was appointed. Can't see how you blame me for all this. How's she getting along? Give her my best regards. I sure enjoyed working alongside her."

Harvey, like the police psychologist, wondered how such a disturbed man ever got himself accepted into the force. As he left the prisoner to mull over his impending fate, he was determined to tighten up recruitment procedures. *We want well-screened folks for the job, guys and gals who will be as honest and as uncomplicated as we can get.*

***

He then interviewed Sonny Woods, who, realising he had been rumbled by Burt Kennedy, came clean and admitted his role in setting up the stalking of Carole Carr, and hoped his confession would spare him more jail time. Harvey turned on him.

"Not bloody likely. We in the force look after our own. You have caused more than enough damage in the past and we sure as hell won't let you get away with any more interference in CPD. You've done the crime, so get on with doing the time. You and your buddy, Kip, can look forward to a few more years of imprisonment. We will throw the book at you for this latest incident."

Superintendent Harvey stormed out of the prison, leaving the former news reporter to ponder his fate.

CHAPTER 21

Thousands of miles from the problems facing Scottish and American crime officers, a young man faced his own seemingly insurmountable problems.

Sergei Bregovic, always alert, watching, remembering, studying his enemy, noted the guards as they paraded around the compound where he was held. For almost six years he had been held captive by hostile forces as the war in Bosnia continued around him. He, with others, was constantly moved from place to place under the cover of darkness and always on foot, sometimes returning to a spot previously used to hide the captured men. The alert young man was aware of this ploy: others might think they were being moved further and further from their homeland, but Sergei noted that they were at times being moved around in circles.

He was badly injured when first captured and suffered constant shoulder pain from a bullet fired randomly into the group of young men he was working with. Guards prodded the bedraggled captives with rifle butts to ensure they kept moving. Those who weakened were left where they fell, a bullet to the head ending their misery. The mercenaries were ruthless, callous, cruel, but they too showed signs of fatigue. Exhaustion breeds carelessness which young Sergei planned to use to his advantage. He studied their every move, their every inattentive action, and waited, waited for the right moment to make his move to escape from his hell of existence. Patience was something he had learned. He had attempted to escape before and was savagely beaten for his efforts. The pain and humiliation only served to increase his determination to flee, to return home to his only living family member, his sister Amila. Unknown to Sergei, she and her husband believed him to be dead.

He had little idea of his location, but listened out for clues from the guards who sat around the night fire smoking hash and drinking heavily. They became crude and raucous as the night wore on. They became careless. They entertained each other with tales of sexual bravado. One guard, inebriated, cold, and homesick for his woman, pointed to his village.

"Look, only twelve miles across those hills to my home, so near, a stone's throw from Sarajevo."

Sergei took his chance when the guards drifted off to sleep as they inevitably did each boring evening. Summoning strength that came from sheer determination to escape, Sergei ran like a wounded gazelle towards the direction the careless captor had stated was near the outskirts of Sarajevo. He left the compound totally undetected having previously checked for weakness in the flimsy fence which was meant to deter escape attempts. Sergei had cultivated the friendship of the guard dogs that trusted him to bring scraps of food, sometimes his own only source of sustenance. As the dogs ate, they ignored their friend as he clambered under the fence. He ran. He ran until he felt his heart pounding as if it would explode with exertion, paused briefly to catch his breath, and then fled to freedom. Night dangers lurked everywhere. He proceeded swiftly but cautiously into the darkness, using the stars as his only light. He listened for warning shots indicating that his absence had been noted. All was eerily silent in that troubled land.

Nothing would happen until morning, not before the break of dawn, and then, God have mercy on his fellow captives; they would suffer beatings and worse. Anger from the guards would explode like a raging inferno in uncontrollable savagery, like a demon released from the depths of hell. Sergei himself had been at the mercy of the sentries who, knowing harsh punishment awaited them for their carelessness, exacted inhumane vengeance on their weak and defenceless prisoners. "God forgive me for what I have done to them," whispered the gentle individual.

As dawn broke heralding a new day, hope of a new life filled his soul.

He reached Sarajevo and found a bombed-out building in which to hide as he recovered from his ordeal. He slept. His sleep was disturbed by memories of the horrors of the past years. He slept fitfully until wakened by some people who alerted by his nightmare screams, tended to the dishevelled boy, and carried him to hospital where he drifted in and out of consciousness, in and out of near death.

It was there, some days later, that he was recognised by elderly Doctor Josef, a former colleague of his sister, Amila. Doctor Josef was exhausted from the relentless work but refused to retire, as was his right. 'While my fellow citizens are in need of my help, I will remain here,' he told anyone who pleaded with him to rest.

"I know this young man. He is Sergei Bregovic. Most of his family was wiped out in the early days of the siege of our beloved city. His sister and brother-in-law believed him to be dead."

Doctor Josef examined the young man and assisted a nurse in dressing his horrific wounds.

"*Siroti, mladié*, you poor young boy. He has been whipped like a dog, within an inch of his life. He is on the verge of starvation. I must operate on this shoulder. He is in danger of losing his arm to infection. With God's help I can save it. Poor boy."

Sergei, recovering from surgery, lay in a strange bed in a strange room, not knowing where he was or what had happened to him. He drifted in and out of sleep. Painkillers helped ease the pain in his body but not the pain in his heart. He mumbled incoherently calling out for his family: "Amila, my sister, *moja sestra*, my sister, Amila."

Concerned staff, many of whom had lost family to the ravages of war, comforted him, hearts full of pity for the young man who not only faced a long physical recovery, but an even longer emotional one. As yet, he did not know of the whereabouts of his sister.

Later, when he felt his patient strong enough to comprehend what he had to relate to him, the elderly doctor took a deep breath, wiped the sweat off his hands and brow, and sat with Sergei. He gently explained what had happened to his family.

"It was not safe for your brother-in-law and his beloved Amila to remain in this war-torn city. I myself encouraged them to seek a new life in America. I had sent my own family to safety in Germany where we have relatives. My wife protested, but she saw for herself that the city was no place for the children and grandchildren to live in. 'I don't want to leave you here Josef, please come with us'. She pleaded with me Sergei, but I had taken an oath to help people in need, and where was most help needed but here in our beloved Sarajevo and I knew my family would be safe. Amila was caring and devoted, she tended to her patients as if they were here own family which in a way they were; we are all Sarajevo people, all sufferers in a cruel war. I persuaded them to leave here just as I had persuaded my own to go to safety. They were young. Amila and Nikol had a future ahead of them. They believed you to be dead and wept for you. Amila had miscarried her child; it was such a disappointment for them, in the midst of war and hardship. When she recovered sufficiently they left for Europe and hopefully, onwards to America. I have heard nothing from them, but letters seldom arrive here with any regularity, sometimes they come years later. I live in hope of some day hearing from them."

"Then that is where I must go. I must find my brother-in-law, my sister, my family."

"Then I will assist you in whatever way I can. I too am anxious to have news of them. But for now, you rest, you eat and you build strength. You have many months of recovery ahead of you. Your arm will heal through time, but your heart like my heart, will take a little longer. War, it eats into the heart of a man and how can we fix that? By hope, my young boy, by hope. You are so like dear Amila. She too has a gentle soul."

***

In her apartment in New York Donata Stojanovic relaxed with her usual morning coffee as she read the newspaper. The years had brought about a contentment which she never thought she would experience again. Her mind often dwelt on her homeland but she had no wish to return; *no, this is my home now, this is where I will live out my life.*

"Dragi, darling, who are you talking to? Have you turned into an old woman who talks to herself instead of her beloved husband?" laughed Marc as he looked at the skyline of New York. The view from their tiny apartment never failed to amaze him.

Donata chuckled and returned to her morning read. Something there caught her attention.

"Marc, dragi, darling," she called to her husband, "here is an enquiry from someone requesting information about Amila and Nikol Tanovic from Sarajevo. That was surely the names of our dear friends Zelda and Kristof? Do you remember they had to change their names when we were in transit camp in order to obtain forged documents to help them get out of the country?"

"You are correct, my dear. I recall those names. Let me read the enquiry. I remember them so well, the young couple with a new life ahead of them, and then to die in a plane crash; so tragic, so tragic."

Marc read the article and exclaimed, "There is a number here. We must call at once. The name is Sergei Bregovic. Surely that is the brother they feared had been killed. They wept so much for him, just as we did for our beloved son. Is it too much to expect that this boy has somehow survived the atrocities and has come to seek out his family?"

CHAPTER 22

Having established contact, Marc delayed answering the young man's many questions regarding the whereabouts of his relatives.

"It is best we meet face-to-face and I can tell you all you need to know."

Sergei had only recently arrived in New York, and was as yet unsure of his surroundings. The three agreed to meet at Grand Central Terminal. They sat in a coffee bar; the noise of trains, traffic and constant announcements went unheeded by the trio as they concentrated on the task in hand. Sergei, still pale from his illness and fearful of what he might hear from these kindly people, fixed his eyes on them ready to listen for any speck of hope in locating his family.

Donata was struck by the resemblance of the young man to his sister Amila. As gently as they could, the couple took it in turns to relate the tale of how they met with his relatives, how they travelled together across Europe, parted company, each going their own way, and the joyous reunion some time later in New York. Marc, holding the young man's hand, gave Sergei the devastating news of the deaths of his last remaining relatives. His heart went out to the boy as he watched the impact of what he had told him, his demeanor changing from hope to despondency in one short moment.

"They were aboard a flight to Chicago when their private airplane crashed on landing, killing everyone on board, including a young girl who had been abducted. The strange thing is, Sergei, that they, your brother-in-law and sister, were the abductors. We do not understand any of this."

"No, never. Ne, nikad, that could not be, not my family, not Amila, never, not my sister, moja sestra! No!"

Donata comforted the young man as she had similarly comforted his sister several years previously. She could feel every bone shaking in his thin body as he allowed his emotions to pour out like an unstoppable tap. People noticing them probably presumed a difficult parting was forthcoming for a traveller. Gently, she explained the change of names.

"They were known as Zelda and Kristof Djuric. The last we heard from them was when they left us to search for employment in another area of the city. We were surprised not to hear from them and had no means of contacting them. We longed to come across them somewhere in the city, but it is such an immense place, we were not hopeful."

Marc took up the story; "Then we heard of their deaths and involvement in the abduction of a child. Sergei, to this day we cannot believe such good people would ever do that. There must be more to it all. We are confused."

The couple offered Sergei a home with them until he had time to assimilate the news and make a decision about his future. Donata fussed over him and made his little room as comfortable and as welcoming as she could.

"It's small, Sergei, but clean and warm."

Marc assisted him in dressing, as his arm continued to cause pain.

"You are such kind people. I'm glad Amila and Nikol had friends like you to assist their journey from our war-torn city. I cannot leave things like this," he wept. "I must seek for the truth. Nikol and Amila would never do such a shameful deed. Ne, ne, nikad. And now I am totally alone in the world. I am a sad man."

Marc assisted the distraught man in an online search through past newspapers for any explanation which would lessen his sorrow.

"Together, we will find the truth."

They sat together in the library where a sympathetic librarian assisted them in their search. Reading of his relatives' involvement in a heinous crime distressed both Sergei and Marc. They found the names of the senior detective who was involved in the investigation.

"Here is where we begin, Sergei. We will call this person and get to the truth."

Marc put a call through to Chicago police headquarters to be told that the person in question, Tony Harvey, was now Chicago's superintendent of police and was presently out of town at a police conference. The young detective logged details of the call to be picked up by Harvey on his return.

Marc was surprised at the speed of response from Superintendent Harvey who spoke briefly to Sergei, stating he had too many details to give him and preferred to meet face-to-face. He arranged to come to New York as he was anxious for more background information on the deceased and wished also to speak to Donata and Marc Stojanovic whose involvement with the couple was, until then, not on record.

"It would sure help fill in a lot of gaps about this case," he said to no one in particular as he ended the call.

Once again, Harvey teamed up with Carole Carr and travelled to New York.

"Here we go again Carole, criss-crossing the country, this time with the mayor's approval and no one giving us grief about cost. Hopefully, we can get some more background information."

"These people might have info that would clarify a few things," said Carole. "We never did find any background on the couple on the plane. They were a total mystery."

"Yeah and all we know about them is what Rita Hampton told me and I find it difficult to believe one word that comes from that person's mouth. We know from Anna Leci's letter to her solicitor that they were illegal immigrants and were probably here on false documents. The abduction and death of young Lucy, even after all these years, leaves too many unanswered questions. I hate having loose ends. It riles me when cases go unsolved."

"You don't think they had anything to do with the Scottish murders, do you?"

"Let's keep an open mind until we have met them, Carole. Why are we only now, after four years, locating people who knew the abductors? Maybe they want to come clean. They may well be the ones who exacted revenge for the loss of their friends or put out a contract on them. Contract killers don't care who they eliminate and can name their price for the vile deed. Let's check these people out."

They had arranged to meet at the apartment of the couple and were surprised at how welcoming it was.

There's a good feel about this place, Carole thought as they made their introductions and drank tea and ate cake which the motherly Donata insisted they have.

"We don't often have visitors. Please help yourself."

Tony Harvey always prided himself in his discernment when it came to interviews. He was seldom wrong in his judgement of people and, being with the couple and Sergei, he was convinced of their non-involvement, of their honesty and, like him, of their desire for the truth. *We can rule them out of any suggestion of involvement in contract killing*, he thought to himself.

The couple spoke at length of their flight from Sarajevo and how they met and befriended Zelda and Kristof, of their flight from war-torn Bosnia until their arrival in Europe.

"Sir," explained Marc, "our son, Stefan, was taken at gunpoint along with other men from our village while working the fields. We waited for news but nothing came, until months later when we heard that the mercenaries had killed a group of young farmers. We prayed that Stefan would some day return to us but in our hearts we knew we would never see our son again. We made the decision to leave the war-torn city."

As they continued with their horrendous tale, Carole, usually the strong, unemotional detective, found it hard not to feel sorrow as they explained about Zelda's miscarriage and the carnage of their city, which wiped out their families.

"This young man," said Marc, pointing to Sergei, "was believed dead. How they wept for him. We cannot believe in our hearts that our friends, whom we grew close to, could have been involved in something as awful as child abduction. Something is not right, sir."

When they had finished relating the horrors which had befallen them, Superintendent Harvey took up the story of the involvement of Zelda and Kristof Djuric as they had come to think of the abductors.

"Sergei," he gently disclosed, "your brother-in-law and sister were innocent victims of a mad, scheming woman who threatened to have them deported if they did not follow her crazy instructions in the abduction of a young girl."

Detective Carr took up the story, "We can tell you that they were kind and considerate to their young charge, protected her from harm, and saw to her every need. They were good people. We have this from the woman who nursed the mad schemer. They were so afraid of the consequences should they disobey her orders. Until your phone call, Marc, we did not know the true identity of Zelda and Kristof Djuric. I will read you part of a letter from Anna Leci, the mad woman who caused such havoc for them. Sergei, it totally exonerates your relatives and explains her hold over them."

On completion of her task, Carole comforted the sobbing Donata, who, through tears, replied, "We knew they were good people and something must have happened for them to be involved in that horror. When we read of their deaths we were bereft and confused and we knew there was more to it. Thank you for explaining things to us."

Sergei remained silent throughout his time with the detectives, saddened at the loss of his family and distressed as he heard of their fate.

Harvey explained to the heartbroken trio, "It was all so unnecessary. Our country would not have deported them. We have schemes in place for genuine asylum seekers. Sadly, being unaware of that, they allowed themselves to fear the worst and were caught in a dreadful situation. Their worst nightmare was to be sent back to their warring homeland. That would not have happened.

"Before we return to Chicago, I would like to arrange for you all to accompany us there to meet and talk with Lucy's mother. It would perhaps help her with some closure to listen to your story and know that her daughter had been cared for by good people during her captivity and for yourselves too, to understand more about the child who spent her last few weeks with your family."

Marc was at first sceptical about taking up the offer. Somewhere in the recess of his brain was a fear of author- ities, borne of years of unrest and war, but he was a fair man who discerned goodness in the officers who were obviously affected by their story of their flight to freedom.

Harvey looked at the bemused trio and continued, "I have to make a few calls first to have the trip sanctioned and to speak with Brenda Mears."

Emotions were high in that little New York apartment as the stunned trio quickly packed for an unexpected jour- ney. Sergei, stomach churning with grief and a sadness he had not felt for some time, wondered at the wisdom of meeting the mother of the girl whose life was tragically entwined with his family.

The Chicago duo returned to HQ with more informa- tion than they had hoped to amass and with three extra passengers.

***

Brenda Mears paced up and down as the time approached for her to meet with some people that Superintendent Harvey thought might help her sorrow. She adjusted her dress, her hair and make-up, and looked out towards the long drive, impatient, nervous and wishing the visit was over. She welcomed the visitors to her home, a home no longer filled with music or laughter, but one that had taken on a more morbid aura. She showed them into the only room that was now in use, the others having been closed up since Molly's last cleaning frenzy. She had suffered so much loss and wondered at the wisdom of recalling painful memories by having these people visit. Detective Carr had persuaded her to meet with the group. She listened attentively to them as they recounted their story and warmed to the young man who attempted to apologise for his relatives' part in the abduction of her daughter.

"Sergei," she said, holding the hand of the youth, "you have nothing to apologise for. It was my relative, my own aunt, who brought this tragedy to our doors. We have all suffered such loss because of one mad woman."

Carole Carr noted how Brenda Mears had mellowed over the years since her daughter's death and thought *such a pity it took a tragedy for her to become a much nicer person*.

Before they left, Brenda asked Sergei about his future plans. She offered him employment with Mears Empire if he wished to consider a career in the publishing business. He thanked her for her offer but felt he had to return to his homeland.

"There is nothing for me now in your country. I must return to my homeland and build a life for myself. Perhaps I can help restore my beloved city to its former glory. My ambition is to be an architect. Perhaps I can work and pay my way through university and realise my dream. My injured arm is healing and is stronger now."

To the surprise of the group sitting in that room, their host offered to fund his university course. Sergei waved a hand in protest, but Brenda continued, "Sergei, I have more money than I'll ever need. I have set up several trust funds in memory of Lucy. You would be doing me a great honour if you accept my offer. It would keep her memory alive and of course, that of your sister and brother-in-law, whom I now realise in my heart, had only Lucy's best interest in theirs. We have all suffered loss, so let's build a lasting memory befitting to them, in the future career of a sincere and gentle young architect."

The visitors returned to New York, more at peace with the world and still reeling from the generosity of the one person they were afraid to encounter. It was agreed that Sergei remain with Donata and Marc until he was fully recovered from his traumatic few years.

The motherly Donata fussed over the young man, fed him well and together with Marc talked and wept for their shared loss. He remained with them for some months until his strength had returned and his injured arm ceased to be a problem. Feeling refreshed Sergei made the decision to return home to Sarajevo.

He was assured by his hosts that he would always have a home with them should he wish to return to New York, and a place in their hearts forever.

"Sergei, we are your new family now. You are our son."

All three wept together as they parted company.

On returning home, his first task was to seek out Doctor Josef to report the tragic demise of Nikol and Amila Tanovic.

CHAPTER 23

During their vacation, B-J and Fred continued their tour of London unaware that they had been followed for several days. Two Bryson brothers, Bobby and Joe, seldom let them out of their sight since the night Bobby spotted them in a pub and confirmed the identity with his brother.

"It is Barry Jones," said Joe; "definitely him. I'd know that brute anywhere. No amount of disguise could wipe out that creep's features. Mind you, he looks as if he's been living the high life. Did you notice that suit? Must have cost a pretty penny."

The brothers discreetly followed the unsuspecting tourists, who, after an evening drinking, parted company and headed to their separate hotels a few streets apart.

"Oh no, Bobby! They're staying in different hotels! Right, we take one each and stay close. Keep tabs on that nerd. We owe it to mum to sort him out. I'll take our old chum Barry and you stick with the other guy. Don't let him out of your sight."

"What about him, the other guy? We don't even know who he is. Should we even bother with him?"

"It's his bad luck to tie up with the bad guy. Can't afford to have him spot us. We need a plan. Let's collect our van and hole up near the corner here where we can see both hotels in case they leave."

The brothers settled down to their surveillance duties, taking turns on the watch until they were sure the two were unlikely to put in an appearance that night, then they themselves settled to sleep in their vehicle.

The tourist duo continued with their exploring, the Londoner almost euphoric as he pointed out landmarks to his friend from the top of the London Eye, from the comfort of a riverboat, from the banks of the Thames and from the top of Tower Bridge. They had no idea that they were being followed. They quickened their pace when the heavens opened with yet another torrential downpour.

"So, Fred, me lad, what do you think of London?" asked a jovial B-J, delighted at being back in his home territory and loving the rain after the searing heat of Rio.

"I sure like your Blighty place, sure do. It's awesome! But your English weather, hey, it's too cold for me, and all that rain! Makes me long for our beach back home. How soon can we go back? My bones are frozen like icicles."

"You gonna chicken out on me then?" laughed his buddy, knowing his friend longed to be gone from the miserable weather.

"We can go home anytime you like; separately again though. You've got your return tickets. You head off in the next few days if you've a mind to, and I'll follow next week. I'll go over travel arrangements with you and make sure you know exactly where to go. I'd sure like to stay longer and see a bit more, even pop down to the coast, but, hey, I understand you want to get home to the sun. Never took you for a tourist anyway!"

They had their collars up, heads down and tucked into their jackets. The rain was relentless. It stung at their faces like sharp needles, the wind whipping it around them. Their lightweight clothes afforded little protection from the elements. Fred shivered as he rubbed his hands together and stamped his feet in an effort to keep warm. His head felt cold, a coldness he had not experienced since he last lived through a Chicago winter. Little did he know then that the coldness he felt was a precursor to an even colder, sinister event about to change his life.

"Yeah, good idea. I'll head back to sun, sea and work. You can stay here and turn to ice if you like, but I'll be off as soon as possible."

The thought of home lifted his spirit. He imagined himself once more in casual beach clothes, warming his body from the heat of the sun, swimming in the sea and enjoying life to the full.

There was no prospect of any respite from the deluge. It was as if the weather had caught the sombre mood of the unhappy, nervous sightseer. The dark clouds mirrored the darkness in his heart. He longed to be gone from this miserable place. They dived into a dark alley to shelter from the worst of the rain. As they entered the garbage-strewn lane, Fred hunched his shoulders. He felt totally dejected. The stench from the shelter did nothing to improve his spirit.

Other people similarly avoiding the rain joined them.

"It's a real downpour this time," B-J said to the likewise soaked men who shared their shelter.

"It's on for the day."

"Yeah, Barry, it is that!"

He was taken aback to be addressed by name by one of the strangers.

"Hey, man, do we know each other?" he inquired as he stared at them, recognition slowly awakening in him memories of a time long forgotten.

"Oh, yeah, we do! You must remember us, and one and t'other. The Bryson bros! We go back a long time, don't we Barry? We must have a catch up and a cosy chat about old times. You'd like that, wouldn't you Barry?"

The colour drained from his face and he feared the implication of this encounter. Suddenly the terror and fear he had meted out to those brothers many years ago paled into a distant memory. The tables had turned. Odds were stacked against him. He felt trapped in the stinking alleyway as the two men blocked his escape from the shelter. His heart beat rapidly as he sought a way out of the impending doom.

There was no place to run to. While Fred was trying to figure out the cockney slang he had just heard, he suffered a sharp blow to the head and felt a rag, which smelt of something foul, placed over his mouth.

B-J screamed: "Hey, what you doing? Leave him alone, he ain't done nuffin'."

Bobby Bryson, his face contorted with rage, hollered, "He's a mate of yours, so that's good enough for us."

"Now, Barry, we'll have that chat, but in a little while!" said Joe as he secured the panic-stricken man's hands with strong rope and placed a similar gag in the mouth of his shocked foe.

The brothers groaned as they lifted the struggling men unceremoniously into a large waste container at the back of the alley, an alley strewn with litter, remains of food, and a few rats who relished the food discarded by untidy people among the capitals citizens and visitors. Water poured from broken gutters, hungry birds fed on remains of food. Through this lane, the brothers ran to retrieve their truck. Their heavy footsteps squelched on the cobbles as they hurried from the stinking alley.

"They won't be heard; no one in their right mind will come near that foul container, not in this weather. They'll be fine until we get back with the van," said Joe.

The brothers were keen anglers and often went on fishing trips for days on end using the van for overnight stays. It stank of fish, but the brothers never noticed. They returned to the alley, laughed as they threw their bruised and stunned victims into the van which they then stored in their garage in a secluded area, knowing it would be undisturbed until such time as they had formed a plan to dispose of their two unfortunate captives.

***

In his unruly youth, Barry Jones had committed petty crimes, spent time in detention, and always returned to his lawless ways on release from prison. His peers, who avoided him whenever possible, feared him. He was short in stature, with a stocky build and a menacing look which he used to the full should anyone dare cross his path. His swaggering gait and general demeanour ensured a path was cleared for him as he walked through the estate where he lived. Short of money, he entered a local shop where Peggy Bryson, a neighbour and friend of his mother, had worked for several years. She was friendly and popular in her community. The shop owner, Mr. Allison, had gone to the warehouse to fetch more provisions. She was alone in the shop.

"Hello, Barry, what can I do for you today?"

Peggy Bryson smiled at the young man who was well known to her. She was aware of his past history, but like his mother, she always hoped he would turn over a new leaf. Her sons, like others on the estate where they lived, avoided him, knowing that confrontation with the bully would not bode well for them.

"Never mind that, Ma Bryson; just empty the money into this bag, and make it quick!"

"Barry Jones, just you get off with you! Haven't you caused your poor mum enough trouble? She deserves better. Now, go away and I won't mention this to anyone; scarper!"

He, however, did not listen. Fuelled with drink or some other illicit substance, he lent over, pulled some cash from the till, and wrestled with the adamant woman. Peggy Bryson was a petite lady but was deceivingly strong. She fought back as hard as she could but was no match for the muscular youth. He pushed her so hard that she fell to the floor. He ran off clutching a handful of notes and turned the door sign to 'Closed for lunch'.

An hour later, Mr Allison returned to find Peggy slumped on a chair. She had attempted to go for help, but in doing so suffered a massive stroke.

Lying in her hospital bed, she tried to speak to her worried family. Her voice was weak, her speech slurred, her mind in turmoil. Her eldest son, Alex, who had been summoned by his brothers to be with his mother, held her hand: "Mum, who did this to you? Can you tell us?"

The boys listened carefully to what she tried to say. She was almost incoherent, but then, Bobby, determined to find the identity of the thug, put his ear closer and listened.

"Are you saying 'Barry,' Mum? It sounds like 'Barry'."

Peggy squeezed his hand, her face lit up in acknowledgement of his perseverance. She nodded.

"Well! What do you know! Barry Jones!" exclaimed Alex. "Don't worry Mum, we'll get him for this. You just concentrate on getting better."

Within hours, Barry Jones, rather bruised and battered and clutching a broken finger, was arrested and taken to the local police station. The arresting officer commented on his dishevelled appearance.

"Well, if it isn't our old mate, Barry Jones. Welcome back, sir. We didn't think it would be too long before you visited us again; can't seem to keep away from the place, eh? Would sir like his usual room? I'm not one for commenting on our guest's appearance, but, man, you look as if you've gone six rounds with Mike Tyson."

"Fell down some stairs, man; just missed my footing, that's all. It's no big deal."

After an uncomfortable night in a police cell, he appeared before the judge, who shook his head at the return of the well-known villain.

He was convicted and jailed for his villainy. As he was led away to begin his sentence, he looked towards the public gallery where the three brothers sat, smirked at them, and shouted: "How's your *finger and thumb* lads?"

The boys were enraged. His cockney reference to their mother did not go down well.

"With our crazy justice system, he'll be out in no time," said an angry Joe.

"And we'll be waiting for him. We owe it to Mum," said Bobby. "No one messes with the Bryson boys, and no one messes with our mum."

On release from prison and fearing reprisal from the Bryson brothers, Barry Jones changed his moniker to Barclay Ellis-Jones and headed for America where he hoped to start a new life with a new identity.

It was many years before Peggy's sons, still determined to avenge their mother's ordeal, could not believe their luck when their hated foe was spotted in a bar in London's East End.

CHAPTER 24

For days, the captives endured agonising incarceration in the stinking, almost airless van, while facing daily visits from either Bobby or Joe, and sometimes both.

"Drink up boys," yelled their captors as they poured water down their parched throat.

"Got to keep you guys alive for the main event."

"What's that you're saying Barry? Can't quite hear you, just like our poor mum. She couldn't make herself understood either. I'm sure you're keen to hear how she's doing? Eh? Well, she's making great progress in a good care home, the one in Great West Road; you know the one, 'GWR Care Home', the posh building near the park, paid for by Mr. Allison. Kind of him, wasn't it Barry? She's walking well now, gets lots of therapy and her speech is coming along nicely. She's made new friends in that home and seems quite content. We see her most days. Bobby, here, will visit tonight. He'll be sure to pass on your regards."

Fred, terror-stricken by his situation and terrified of the brothers, drifted in and out of consciousness.

Joe quipped, "Shame about your mate here, Barry. He ain't nuffin' to do with this, is he? But you gotta appreciate we can't have him going to the cops now, can we?"

Joe and Bobby waited to hear from their brother Alex to initiate the next part of the plan. Alex, the eldest, was the planner, the schemer, the quiet, ruthless man. He relayed clear instructions to his siblings by phone. They had the upmost respect and a modicum of fear for their elder sibling.

"This is what you do," began the elder brother...

And so, handcuffed to iron bars in the van that was normally used to store fishing gear, the two unfortunate tourists were thrown onto a grubby mattress and secured tightly as the sneering brothers set about checking the chains.

"We're going on a little trip, boys. Hope you'll be comfy here," smirked Bobby as he locked the van securely.

Joe laughed, "You're making it too snug for our guests with that sedative stuff. They'll sleep most of the way and miss all the bumps and potholes."

They sent off north on a marathon 500-mile journey, sharing the ten-hour drive. They avoided built-up areas by following country roads where possible. As they drove along they sang to the music and stopped occasionally to dispense water and insults to their prisoners.

***

Alex, the elder of the Bryson brothers, had moved from the rat-race existence he lived in London, to an idyllic part of Scotland after he married a local girl whom he met when in the area for a job interview. He loved the relative peace there and the sedate pace of life compared to the life he had known in the fast lane. His wife had encountered her two brothers-in-law on several occasions and loathed their coarse manners and negative influence on her husband, so much so that she discouraged visits from them. She had no inclination to become involved with her husband's family and had met her mother-in-law on one occasion, that of her wedding to Alex. He had called his brothers to say that Alice had gone for a week to one of her pottery courses. She ran a small pottery business from home, working in a converted garden shed where she could concentrate and indulge her passion for ceramics. Alex arranged to meet his brothers at a secluded spot known to them from previous fishing visits, several miles from his home, thus avoiding the vicinity of his house and village.

"Some nosey neighbour would be sure to spot you and tell Alice. That's all we need. For some reason unknown to herself, she can't quite take to you scruffs," laughed the jovial elder Bryson.

"We'll meet at the loch where we used to fish and where you camped last visit."

Arriving in Scotland, Bobby opened the van to introduce Alex to the cargo.

"My God, Bobby, what a stink! That's revolting!"

"Can't smell a thing, can you boys?" he said addressing the distraught captives.

Alex stood by the door and laughed.

"Well, well, if it isn't our old mate Barry Jones! Hope you had a comfortable ride, cos the next one won't be so cosy! We've been looking forward to this get-together for many years Barry; sorry we won't have time to hear your adventures since we last met, as we're a bit pushed for time. And your expensive suit! What a shame, it seems to be a bit of a mess now. Don't worry about it; you won't be needing a change of clothes where you're going."

Barry wriggled in fear, mumbled incoherently, his heart racing as he faced his nemesis. His companion, alerted from his coma-like state by the noise and sudden commotion, feared for his life, his worst nightmare not yet over. During the journey, in his semi-conscious state, he mistook a pair of fishing waders which were hanging there, for some kind of apparition, like a ghost determined to attack him and haunt his ever-waking moment. He closed his eyes but his dreams were of ghouls and vampires. His fate was dire, his mind befuddled, he did not know what had happened in B-J's life to merit such treatment from these bullyboys and was in no fit state to ask. On the journey he attempted to speak to B-J. He had something on his conscience that he wanted to offload but the words appeared stuck in his gravelly throat. He regretted ever having set foot outside his comfort zone of Rio.

***

Over many years there had been an increase in coal production in Scotland. Coal sourced from open-cast mining caused controversy. Apart from a blot on the landscape, the dust created problems for people living nearby, for farm animals and for food production. At best, it created employment in the area and less tonnage of coal was required to be imported. Restoration of the sites after use was mandatory. Companies were required to minimise danger and disruption. Some sites became creative works of art and enhanced the local community, transforming a former eyesore to a pleasant outdoor recreational park. The eldest of the Bryson boys enjoyed this type of restoration work.

"It's a million miles away from anything I've ever worked at in London," he told his workmates. "Good, clean fresh air in my lungs, instead of pollution from chemicals and traffic. Yeah, this is the life for me. London is too crowded now; it's changed so much over the years. Even in the estate I grew up in I used to know everyone. Now there are too many incomers, people hardly know their nearest neighbours."

Alex Bryson, employed in this outdoor restoration work, enjoyed hearing about mining practices from previous eras from his work colleagues whose lives and those of their relatives had centered on the coalmining industry for several generations. He was aware of the dangers of old mine shafts and was warned by his workmates to avoid them at all costs.

"They can cave in at any time," he was informed. "The ground around the shafts is unsafe for walking on; best to give them a wide berth if you are out and about walking."

His manager took him on a tour of the area. He had taken a liking to the new recruit and hoped he would settle in with the rest of the close-knit team. He was a firm believer in getting to know his workers in order to get the best out of them and wanted to help the burly Londoner feel at home.

"Come with me lad, I'll show you what we mean by these dangerous shafts. If you know what to look for, then you can avoid them."

They drove around the area, the happy-go-lucky boss enjoying showing the sights to the new worker, as they looked for pit shafts to avoid.

With this store of knowledge, Alex Bryson led his brothers to a disused pit shaft which he had earmarked for their nefarious scheme.

"There's an old shaft here that was closed down years ago. It's abandoned and the roof is shattered. This area is riddled with these old shaft things. Some are linked to tunnels under the River Forth. I've checked this one out; it's going to suit our purpose well," he laughed.

"We'll force open this cover here, should be easy enough to do, and dispose of Barry Jones once and for all. Be careful, cos the ground might be weak around your feet. We have to work quick like if we don't want to join Barry in the pit."

"Get it over with! This will give me creepy nightmares," stuttered Bobby as he looked in horror as the shaft cover was removed showing a dark pool of deep, stagnant water. He stepped as near as he dared; his whole body trembled at the thought of the terror that lay ahead. They struggled with the weight of the now heavily sedated Barry Jones and succeeded in lowering him into the open space where the iron bar he was handcuffed to, caught on a piece of metal. With their gruesome task complete they sealed the shaft with pieces of concrete block and moved back quickly from the scene.

"Should we say a prayer for his soul?" stammered the highly-strung younger brother.

"Don't waste your breath, Bobby. Barry Jones had no soul."

"What about the other guy? Who is he anyway?" asked Alex.

"We have no idea. He had the misfortune to keep bad company. What're we gonna do with him?"

"Same again then bros. I know where there's another one of these shafts a good few miles away from here, thirty or so. You up for it?"

Bobby shrugged his shoulders and resigned himself to another gruesome session.

"Do we have to do that again? He ain't done anything to us, has he? We could dump him somewhere else, don't put him in that hole-thing."

His brothers laughed at his discomfort.

"Always the wimp, our baby bro! Time to toughen up and man up! We can't risk his body being found, it will have our prints all over it. Sorry, bro, but we have no choice. In the hole he goes."

"Get it over with then."

After completing the second gruesome task, Alex took his brothers to a site where they burned the contents of the van.

"Get this cesspit of a van hosed down, inside and out, and get rid of the stink off yourselves too. You need to find somewhere far from here to hole up for a couple of nights before you make the journey south. Do you want to grab a bite to eat first? There's a place nearby that does food to go; serves good grub."

Bobby, emptying the contents of his stomach, interrupted him. Joe laughed.

"I think the answer to that is no!"

One look at Bobby told the brothers that their young sibling was not fit to travel the long distance home, nor was he in any state to help with the driving. Alex booked them into a cheap motel for a few nights.

"That should give him time to recover," he told Joe. "There's an outlet shopping place nearby where you can pick up fresh clothes and turn yourselves into human beings. No one at home will notice you're not around. Your neighbours will presume you've gone fishing. We can phone Mum's care home and let them know you're on a fishing trip. She will be content with that for a few days."

Despite their teasing of Bobby, his brothers were concerned about him. He was always a weakly child who succumbed to every ailment available, causing his mother endless nights of worry about her youngest son. Several bouts of depression dogged him all his life. Bobby was only months old when his father died in a horrific train accident that took the lives of twelve people. Compensation from the rail company was invested for Peggy's young boys and became available to each as they reached the age of majority.

As Bobby rested in the motel, his nightmares began; he slept during the day, leaving Joe free to purchase clothes and items necessary for further fishing trips from a second-hand store that he located nearby. He had discarded all vestige of gear that might have been handled when moving the two unfortunate prisoners. He spruced up the vehicle inside and out. No one would suspect it had been used as a makeshift prison. A few days later they were ready for home but Bobby had developed night terrors that were to last him the rest of his life.

"We'd best get on our way, got to let Mum know Barry Jones won't be bothering her again. We'll tell her he met with a bad accident," said Joe. "We have to keep silent about this trip, Bobby; not a word to anyone, got it? Never mention it to anyone or it will be the finish of us and we'd have Alex to face, so, make sure you keep your mouth shut."

Bobby nodded in resignation.

The two pit shafts lay undisturbed for many months until a curious dog sniffed too near the edge of the weakened ground, and a cyclist bumped against a boulder.

CHAPTER 25

Months later, with the mystery of the killing of two American villains still unsolved and with UK police on full alert to help resolve it, appeals to the public for help through media resulted in a hotel owner from London contacting the authorities to report that a male guest had not been seen for some time.

According to the owner, the guest was a polite and charming man.

"He kept himself to himself. He paid in advance for his room and only ever ate breakfast here. He seemed to be on a nostalgic trip home and planned to explore the capital and see the changes in the city. He told me he would probably take some time at the coast. When he didn't appear back, that's what I thought had happened. He had booked the room for a month and when he didn't return, well, my hotel is fully booked now, we're in the middle of the tourist season, and I needed the room. I wasn't unduly concerned about him until my wife saw the TV appeal. What a shock we got when we found out about his past. He was extremely plausible and to think he was under my roof. We could all have been killed in our beds. We boxed up his personal belongings; everything is here, including his passport and return tickets. Thank goodness my wife Cath spotted that news appeal or I would still be holding the room for him because he seemed such a nice person.

But Cath was adamant; 'We have to get rid of this stuff now that we know our guest won't be coming back,' she told me as she went about her usual methodical way of packing."

The passport picture was that of Barclay Jones, but all other details were false. "This is an excellent forgery!" exclaimed Brody Cameron, taking a satisfactory draw on his trusted pipe and blowing enough smoke in the direction of the others who were hoping to view the document before him. He had been invited to travel to London to assist in forensic matters."Whoever did this was damn good!"

London crime scene detectives working with colleagues from Police Scotland continued to probe the atrocities, checking and rechecking the area where Barclay Jones had stayed. At a nearby hotel it had been discovered that Alfred Wysoki too had been booked in for a month but had not been seen for some time. There too, the hotel owner spoke of a quiet, polite American.

"He seemed to me to be nervous about something, never really relaxed and didn't want to engage in conversation, so I left him alone. His room was booked and paid for and when he didn't return after that time had expired I left his things alone until I needed the room. All his stuff is here boxed up and untouched. I run a respectable establishment and don't want any fuss over this guest. I read about him in the newspapers and want his things out of my hotel. I hope guests aren't put off by this revelation. I've had his room thoroughly cleaned and refurbished. I don't want any trace left of him," said the hotel owner.

His housekeeper, annoyed at the extra work added, "Imagine us having a murderer under our roof; it makes me cringe at the thought, and he seemed such a nice man."

"Well, he obviously planned to return here. He wouldn't have gone off without his passport," said a cop.

"Or his shaving kit! A man likes to use the same kit for a good shave; well, I do," concluded a detective as he recorded and repacked the possessions of the deceased, before removing them for forensic analysis.

"Or his favourite pipe!" mumbled Brody Cameron to no one in particular as he used match after match to light up, puffing rings of smoke into the air.

Among the possessions were travel documents and an excellently forged passport.

Detectives examined the documents of both deceased men and put together what appeared to be their travel routes from Rio to UK.

"That was a clever plan," commented a senior officer as he gathered the team to assess the latest findings. "Whoever came up with this idea was no dummy. From those travel papers we should be able to find out how they arrived on our shores."

He continued, "These guys travelled separately, via different routes. We'll get our European colleagues to check out CCTV cameras; that is if they are still available after all this time although I doubt it. It would confirm our suspicions regarding their entry to Europe. These return tickets have no cut-off date, so our guys could have travelled home at any time. They must have had plenty of money to pay for their trip; it certainly wasn't cheap."

Enquiries showed a clear picture of Barclay Jones arriving at Charles de Gaulle airport and several days later, boarding a Eurostar train to London. Of his companion there appeared to be only a grainy picture of him exiting a cross-channel ferry.

"That could be anyone," commented a detective looking over the shoulder of the young technician whose task it was to perform miracles from hours of grainy films. "Can't we get it any clearer?"

"Not possible; we were lucky to be able to retrieve these shots at all. They are not usually kept for long before the films are re-used."

They concluded that they had enough proof from the torn boarding ticket found crumbled in the victim's passport pocket.

"A visual shot would have corroborated things, but we have enough to go on. Those nerds have given us a monumental task, but, that's what we guys do best: detect things."

Rab McKenzie spoke with Tony Harvey and updated him on events.

"My squad will continue with enquiries for another month or so, and then we'll slow down the investigation. We are concentrating on clubs and pubs near where your guys' hotels were located. They had to eat and drink somewhere. It's hard to break the distrust that people around here have of the police. No one will talk. Someone must have seen them; someone must remember serving food to them. They appeared to be well dressed and came across as polite Americans. They must have stood out from the crowd in these parts."

Police visiting clubs and bars in the area of London's East End in an attempt to find out more about the deceased men met with a wall of silence as few people were willing to be seen talking to the cops. Suspicion and dislike of the establishment were rife. Seeing the police enter the premises caused some customers to be unsettled. One man quickly drained his glass and headed for the gents' room, another ran for the back door, while others put their heads down as if deep in conversation while listening closely to questions being asked of the bar staff.

"What does it take to get people to trust us? Is no one prepared to help?" questioned one frustrated detective of his colleagues after hours of enquiries.

"We know when and how these guys came to the UK, but not how they ended up in Scotland," commented the senior officer to the team he had gathered to collate information. He chewed on the end of a pencil as if hoping for inspiration from the contents of the stump. "It's essential we get that information."

"Maybe they took a sightseeing trip there. We'd better investigate travel shops, airports, railways and bus depots," replied another, hastily scribbling notes of various possible venues. "This will be a marathon task as there's a limit to the time that details are kept. If these guys paid by card, we might have a chance of finding them somewhere on the system. If they paid cash, then we have a problem. Remember too, these guys have been dead for over a year now so it could be an almost impossible task to find the evidence we need."

"Okay, let's organise teams to start the ball rolling," concluded DI McKenzie as he shuffled papers around wishing he could throw them into his done-and-dusted file. He had considered assigning the case to the cold case where it would remain on hold to be re-examined should any further evidence surface.

"We'll give this a few more weeks and if nothing comes of the current investigation, I'll make a decision as to whether we go forward or not."

Reggie Allison, owner of a mini-market in Mile End Road, annoyed that television programmes had been postponed to accommodate yet another political debate, flicked through channels searching for something suitable. He chose to watch a crime alert programme where crimes were re-enacted in an attempt to jog the public's memory. He was about to flick channels again when a familiar face appeared on a wanted list.

Well then, if it isn't Barry Jones! I thought I'd heard the last of that rogue. They are calling him Barclay.

Police were asking for information about him. Reggie Allison wasted no time in calling the number on the screen and was immediately connected to a member of the squad currently investigating Barclay Jones and Alfred Wysoki.

"I'm not sure if I can help, Officer, but about a year ago, maybe more, I thought I saw him and another man, the one on the poster with him, in a bar near my home here in the East End. I thought I was imagining things as the guy looked right through me, no recognition at all; mind you, it's a long time since he's seen me and I have changed a tad, you know the thing, middle-age weight gain and hair loss," chuckled the shop owner. "As I was saying, he didn't know me and then I doubted my own judgement. He looked too posh to be Barry Jones; that's his name by the way, Barry, not Barclay. I never gave it another thought until tonight's programme."

The information was passed to a senior officer and before he could draw breath, Reggie Allison was invited to attend for a further chat. Looking through an album of photographs of known criminals, he identified Barry Jones.

"That's a good picture of him, just as I recall him in his younger days and, yes, I'm positive he was in the bar on Morgan Street last year." Reggie confirmed the identity when shown the criminals' up-to-date passports. "Yes, that's Barry Jones and that's the other man in the bar. I'll never forget that creep or forgive him for what he did to Peggy."

"Peggy?" inquired the alert detective. "Tell me about her."

"It's over ten years now since it happened but it stays in my mind. Peggy Bryson worked in my mini-market. It was a Monday. I remember it well. I always went to the bank and the warehouse on Mondays. A young girl, Michelle, came in on Mondays to give Peggy a hand, but on that particular day she called in sick. Peggy wouldn't hear tell of me staying on, 'you go about things, Mr. Allison, I'll manage fine here,' she told me. I was back after about two hours and found the shop locked, lights blazing and no sign of Peggy. I got in via the back door and found poor Peggy slumped on a chair in a real bad way. I called for an ambulance and police, then I noticed the till drawer lying open and empty. Peggy had been attacked and suffered a massive stroke. It was touch and go for her.

"Police found the culprit, Barry Jones, a bit battered and bruised as Peggy's lads had found him first, although that was never mentioned in court. That was an open secret around these parts. He was jailed for the assault and was never seen in the estate after his release from prison. Talk was that he had fled to America. Even his poor old mum didn't know where he was. We all knew she secretly feared him and was probably glad to be rid of him. She died about five years ago. As for Peggy, she's in a care home. It's a posh, private care home, excellent place, 'GWR' in Great West Road. I pay for her stay there; it's the least I could do for the lady. I used to visit, but sadly she developed dementia and doesn't know me any more, so I stopped visiting. Her sons keep in touch with me from time to time. I often wonder if things would have been different if Michelle had turned up for work that day, but I don't dwell on it; it could have been worse. Mind you, would that creep have backed off when he saw two women? Michelle's a big lass and can hold her own; you don't mess with her, that's why I was always glad when she was there with Peggy. Barry Jones was a bully to attack an elderly person like that."

Reggie's information was a breakthrough for detectives in providing background for the deceased Londoner.

***

After weeks of investigative research into the likelihood that the two American tourists had taken a trip to Scotland, and with no evidence forthcoming, DI McKenzie allocated the case to the cold case department to be resurrected when and if new evidence came to light. His associates in Chicago had put the case on hold at their end to await new evidence regarding how the victims had arrived in Scotland, since nothing new had come from the visit to Scotland. DI McKenzie talked to Harvey and briefed him on the decision.

"We won't give up, but we have to scale back the investigation for the moment. We have about 100 of these unsolved cases here in Scotland at the present time. This case has used up a hell of a lot of our budget and the big chief is bending my ear to either solve it or assign to the cold case department until further evidence is forthcoming, so that's what we've done."

"Same here, Rab. We can't give up on this but at the moment we're up against a brick wall. We have interviewed everyone involved in the four-year-old tragedy of young Lucy, looked at possible revenge links, but cannot find the perpetrators of your Scottish crimes. I hate to be beaten. Someone, somewhere wanted rid of those guys, but I'm damned if I know who loathed them so much as to give them such a gruesome end. I won't rest until we have answers. People aren't forthcoming in helping."

"It's endemic here Rab, folks just don't want to give us information for fear of reprisals or to spite us or something. We sure ain't the most loved of folks, that's the bottom line, until, that is, they need us, and then they come hollering and expect us to jump when they snap their fingers. But, hey, we can take it on the chin."

Harvey shared how one of his task team, set up during the enquiries into Lucy Mears' disappearance, had undercover cops mingling with customers in a bar, and had a successful result.

"It led us to the rogue money-lenders and eventually to the whereabouts of the kid, although, as you know, we were too late to save her. It takes the right kind of cops to carry it off, but it worked for us. It gave us a lead to the kid's abductors."

"Aye, we do that kind of thing here too. I'll run it past the squad and see what we come up with. If only people would talk to the police, someone must have seen your two guys around the area of their hotels. I'll speak to my top man and see if he agrees to offer a reward for information. Money talks, so they say, although I can't see him jumping for joy if I ask for even more funding."

CHAPTER 26

I don't recognise that person. Why is she in my bedroom? Who are you? I want to shout but the words seem to stick in my mouth and I can't find my teeth. I'm sure I put them in the dish like I always do. The lady in my room seems nice; she's speaking to me as if she knows me. 'Don't worry Peggy, we'll find your teeth', she says to me. So my name must be Peggy... yes, that's it, Peggy, Peggy Bryson. I remember now. It wasn't always Peggy Bryson; it was Peggy Symmons before I married my Jimmy. Where is Jimmy? I haven't seen him in ever such a long time. I'd ask that nice lady who's helping me look for my teeth, but the words are stuck. They are there somewhere in my head so why won't they come out? I'm sure the nice lady will know where Jimmy is.

Peggy Bryson had over some years developed dementia. Her older sons, Alex and Joe, accepted the deterioration in their mother's condition with sadness. Bobby, however, dependant on his mother's emotional support all his life, could not come to terms with the fact that the woman he visited daily was not the same mother he knew. His brothers attempted to explain the symptoms of dementia to him, but he was in denial.

"Bobby, the stroke she had all those years ago caused a bit of brain damage. She is very confused and can't remember things from one minute to the next. It's irreversible, we have to accept she's lost to us as our mum, but we still need to be here for her. The staff are good. This is a top-class care home and she is settled. Look at all the activities she's involved in; she loves the singing group who call over each week and the dance parties they have and the day trips. We need to be strong when we visit and make sure we don't upset her. The doctor has told us there might come a time when she no longer recognises us."

Since the disposal of Barry Jones and his friend in the pit shafts, Bobby had recurring nightmares. With each passing day he wanted to unburden his guilt to the only person he felt understood him. On a visit to his mother on one of Peggy's better, more lucid moments, she asked:

"Where's Alex? Why isn't he here with you?"

"Mum, Alex is married. He lives in Scotland now with his wife Alice."

"Alex, married? Who is Alice? Why was I not invited to the wedding?"

"Mum, you were there. Remember you got a lovely blue dress for the wedding?"

As he spoke, Peggy nodded off and woke with a start.

"Where's Alex?"

"Mum, I've just told you. He lives in Scotland now."

Peggy looked at the stranger in front of her, a glazed look in her eyes as she rubbed her palms together on her pretty frock. *Who is that sad young man in my room? I'll ask him why he is so sad. He looks familiar, but why is he crying?*

Peggy lifted her head up a little and asked, "Where's Alex?"

The conversation was repeated ad nauseam to the point that Bobby could no longer cope. He cried as he looked at his vacant-looking mother and could not accept her deterioration. In his distress, and needing to unburden his soul, he blurted out about the killing of Barry Jones and his mate, telling of the disposal of the bodies in the pit shafts. He did not stop until every detail of the macabre deed was offloaded to the poor woman, who smiled, nodded her head and fell asleep. Bobby left the place in tears. A staff member, seeing the distraught man, did not approach him but thought to herself, *poor man, he finds it so hard to accept his mother's condition*. Bobby did not tell his brothers about his exposé.

On Joe's next visit, his mother asked: "Where's Barry Jones? Why was I not invited to his wedding? I have a lovely blue dress. I think Jimmy was here. He looked sad. Do you know where Jimmy is?"

Joe panicked at the mention of the name Barry Jones, and realised that his feeble brother had broken his resolve to keep quiet about their crime. He tried to hold his mother's hand, but she clenched her fists and pulled away.

"Mum, it's me, Joe. You remember me, don't you?"

What have you done, Bobby? he thought as he sat with his head in his hands as if all the troubles of the world had suddenly fallen on his broad shoulders. Peggy had fallen asleep.

Senior Nurse Lydia waited in her office with the door ajar so that she could spot Peggy's son before he left the building. *This is going to be difficult, but it has to be.*

Sensing there was no reason to wait any longer, Joe headed for the front door, only to be called into the office by Lydia. Staff were on good terms with Peggy's sons and admired their faithful visits and concern for their mother.

Joe, feeling stressed and angry, experienced more of the same when Lydia reported how Mrs. Bryson's condition was deteriorating rapidly to the point that she was disturbing other patients with her constant calling out and wandering into other residents' rooms, demanding they leave what she thinks is *her front room.*

"She shouts out about Alex being in a hole in the ground and is extremely upset and disturbed. She needs to see all her sons to be reassured of their safety. And who is Barry? Is he a relative? She wants to go to his wedding. She was very upset and became even more confused after Bobby's last visit. I don't know what transpired, but the poor man left in tears. We are all quite concerned for her."

Sensing Joe's anxiety, but knowing she had to be open about his mother's situation, she continued as gently as she could.

"I know this is not what you want to hear but I have to be honest with you. Peggy is becoming more and more confused and frustrated and I'm afraid, quite aggressive. Aggressiveness is part of her condition but she is unaware of it and can't control it. We find her wandering aimlessly, crying out all the time and sitting in other residents' rooms. It upsets them. Doctor Wallace has given her a strong sedative which calms her down for a time, but I'm afraid we might have to consider a more specialised establishment. She needs more nursing care than we can offer here. Also, part of her illness is loss of taste for food, and food Peggy once loved is left untouched. She won't let any of us help feed her and I'm afraid she tosses her food at other residents. We're concerned about her weight loss.

"I think you need to talk this over with your brothers. In the end we want what is best for Peggy. The doctor will speak to a specialist in charge of the elderly in the local hospital and we may have to consider a move there. I understand your anxiety, but if we leave things any longer she could become a danger to herself and to the other patients. Already she has poured tea over one of the kitchen staff. I know this is upsetting, Joe."

Joe held back tears of frustration and anger as he quietly left the premises, frustration at his lack of control over his mother's mental state and anger at the foolishness of his brother. He returned home, emotionally exhausted. He berated his younger brother for his foolhardiness and related what had been said to him by Lydia.

"Due to your stupidity, Bobby, Mum might have to be moved to a more secure place. GWR has been her home now for years and we will have to uproot her. You bloody idiot! She will hate being in hospital in a ward full of other people when she's been used to her own room and privacy. The staff here are so good with her. She loves the activities, the singing group, the crafts, and the different events, all that will be lost to her if she is moved. GWR has been her security since her stroke, it's her home, and look what you've gone and done."

"I can't cope, Joe. It's doing my head in. I can't sleep and every time I close my eyes I see those guys in the shafts. Why did we have to do that?"

"Yeah, so you've forgotten that when Barry Jones attacked mum her whole life was changed? She lost out on the good life that she had with us. If you go about spouting forth and blubbering, Alex and I will give you something to have nightmares about."

Joe left the room in anger. It took all of his willpower not to strike out at his brother. In frustration, he left home to drown his sorrows at the local pub where he called Alex to update him on events.

"Calm down, Joe. Take it easy, right, tell me from the beginning."

"I'm worried now about Bobby's mental health as well as worrying about mum. Wish you lived nearer, Alex. I feel it's all fallen on my shoulders."

Joe sobbed as the effects of his drinking loosened his emotions and he unburdened his fears to his elder brother.

"I can't reason with him, Alex. He can't take in the fact that mum's health is deteriorating and that she's not going to get better."

Bobby's stress levels by now had affected his mental well-being. The young Bobby had always suffered from low self-esteem and anxiety. His saving grace as he grew up was the security of knowing his brothers would protect him from being bullied. He attempted to emulate their toughness and bravado, but was not comfortable in doing so. He was basically a gentle person who avoided confrontation at all costs. Now, his sleep was disturbed by the recurring nightmares, as Joe who slept in the next room was well aware. His brothers realised he needed professional help, but knew that to go down the route of counselling would lead Bobby to unburden his guilt to a stranger and inevitably involve them in unwanted police enquiries.

Joe continued, "I can't risk him going to see the GP. I just know he will break down and tell the doctor what we've done, especially if it's Doc Chambers who always asks after Mum. It would be the finish of us."

Things came to a head after a recommendation was made by the medical doctor to move Peggy Bryson from her privately run care home to a state hospital. Joe visited it as suggested and was appalled at the crowded conditions that his mother would have to live in compared to her present situation. He told his older brother how he met some kind staff but how exhausted they looked.

'There just aren't enough of us,' he was told. 'We do our best but the old folks need more time than we are allowed to give them. It's rush, rush, rush. We'll take care of your mother sir, but without more hands on deck, she won't get the same amount of care as Great West gave her. Sorry, but that's the way of it here. We need more funding but the likelihood of that coming our way is practically nil.'

He and Alex decided that something had to be done. For the time being, the youngest sibling had to be kept away from their mother.

"We need to come up with a plan for them both before next month when Mum is due to move."

CHAPTER 27

At Great West Road Care Home, a Yamaha V-Star Cruiser glided carefully into a space used regularly by the rider. Skillfully controlled, it gleamed like a mirror reflecting the helmet-clad owner's love for the vehicle. A man tending a flowerbed stopped his work to admire both machine and rider.

"Morning Sam and how's your baby today?"

Patting the motorcycle affectionately, the rider dismounted like a proud jockey after a successful race.

"Baby's fine, Liam, runs like a dream after the garage sorted the sluggishness. I can't wait to finish today and take her for a spin. Am I still okay to park here? Won't be in your way, will I?"

"You're fine right there. I'll be over by the rose garden for most of the morning. Baby will be safe here," he laughed at the affectionate name for the motorcycle.

"I best get started then. See you later."

As the rider made to head for the building, something niggled.

"Hey, Liam, are you okay? You seem a bit nervous this morning."

"No, Sam, I'm fine… think I might be coming down with a cold; nothing to worry about. You enjoy your visit."

Each week the residents of the care home had a visit from a lively, enthusiastic hair stylist. Sam's time with them was special; they looked forward with anticipation to seeing her colourful outfits and weird hairstyle, her ever-increasing tattoos and body piercing. The charismatic girl brightened their day with her chat about her latest boyfriend, her dog, and her passion for motorcycles and cooking. But her real skill was her rapport with the elderly. She had a genuine interest in the tales they told her of their life before old age took such a hold, and had endless patience when they repeated their stories week after week. She was indeed a tonic and often stayed longer than her allotted time and joined in an impromptu sing-a-long session. Staff too adored her.

"Sam's a breath of fresh air," commented one staff member, "a real find."

"That's you for another week Sal, we'll go and have a cup of tea and I'll collect Peggy, she's next on the list," said the stylist as she finished cutting Sal's hair. She held Sal's arm and guided her towards her place at the tea bar where staff fussed over her hairstyle as they served her morning tea and biscuit.

"Here's your favourite, Sal, lots of chocolate for you this morning."

Peggy was not in her usual place for morning tea break. Sam went off to fetch her from her room thinking perhaps she had nodded off, but the frail lady was not there.

"Anyone seen Peggy?" she called as she returned to the tea lounge. No one recalled seeing her since breakfast. The residents often had hospital appointments and such like so Sam was not unduly concerned. A member of staff announced that Peggy had earlier gone for a walk in the grounds with her son.

"It's a lovely sunny day. Joe came for her; perhaps they are sitting in the garden or gone for a stroll to Great West Road to the ice cream shop. Joe often takes his mum there. Peggy likes her ice cream. I'll pop out and see if they are sitting in the garden. Peggy won't want to miss having her hair and nails done."

GWR was an excellent care home that had recently been visited by inspectors from the Care Quality Commission, the body responsible for regulating such residential establishments. It had been commended for the high standards of care it offered the elderly, its good leadership and security of residents. It sat in a large estate on a corner site, a haven of peace where the trees provided quietness from traffic from the nearby road. It met all standards of care. The home had a strict policy of signing in and out of the building.

"I'll check the book," said a staff member. "If Peggy is out, her son will have recorded it in the book; her family is faithful at using our security system. Ah, yes, it says here that Peggy went out at 10:15 with Joe for a walk in the garden and they returned at 10:35. That's about normal. Peggy gets agitated now if she is out for any length of time. She must be in the building somewhere. Sam, come and help me look, Peggy's getting a bit confused, and she could be sitting in another room."

Peggy Bryson could not be located anywhere in the building. A search was made of the garden. Liam, the head gardener, helped the distraught staff in the search of the garden and outhouses.

"I spoke to her and Joe around 10:20. We chatted about the flowers and the weather. They were heading for Great West Road, probably going to the ice cream parlour. I can't recall seeing them after that, but I was busy over by the rose garden."

Panic was beginning to set in. All available staff were called to help search for Peggy Bryson. Someone went to the ice cream cafe, but Peggy had not been there. Sam abandoned her planned motorbike ride and remained to help with the search.

A call was made to her son, Joe. Unusually, his phone was switched off.

"Maybe he's taken his mum for a drive," began a member of staff who quickly changed her mind. "No, he signed her back in, so she has to be here. Joe might be driving and has his phone off."

Every area of the house and gardens was searched, outhouses, garden shed and greenhouses, nothing was missed in the search for the missing resident. After several attempts at trying to contact Joe, the senior nurse put a call through to Bobby. He did not pick up. Lydia had no option but to call Alex Bryson in Scotland, only to be be told by his wife that he was unavailable.

"Alex's gone for the weekend on a team-building course with the firm he works for, to a remote mountainous area. They are very strict about phone calls; calls can't be made until evening, and even then the signal isn't always relia-ble. If I get through I'll let him know later about his mother. I'm sure there's a simple enough explanation. Have the boys dropped her off at a friend for the day? If they aren't answering they may well have gone fishing. Alex seldom manages to make contact with them as there's no signal where they fish."

Alex Bryson was not, as his wife thought, at a team-build-ing weekend. He had flown to London and joined his brothers to discuss his plan for their mother.

"It's a crazy idea," said Bobby when he finished listening to the senior Bryson.

"Not half as crazy as your stupid idea to tell her about Barry Jones; it's tipped her over the edge and we have to take her away from GWR. There's no way she is going to that hospital. I'm sure the staff do their best but there are not nearly enough of them. Mum will be even more confused. Now, here is what we do... listen up both of you."

Bobby hung his head in total despair. "I'm scared Alex, I'm bloody scared."

"Get over it, bro. Man up."

CHAPTER 28

Joe, quietly, and virtually unnoticed by busy staff, had collected his mother from her care home. He packed a few essential items in her handbag and his pockets. *The rest will just have to stay until we send for it.*

"Let's have a walk in the garden, Mum. Wrap up well."

He signed out in his usual way and casually escorted Peggy out of the building. So as not to arouse suspicion he stopped from time to time to allow her to admire the flowers. He met Liam at a prearranged spot in the garden and handed him an envelope. He had confided in the gardener whom he had got to know well over many years of visiting.

"You know what to do. Just pop in and sign her back in when the place is quiet. We are grateful for your help, Liam; we have to do this for our mum."

"You can rely on me. I'll miss the old dear and you guys too; always enjoyed a bit of banter with you and they will have to drag information from me. I'll play dumb. Can't fault you for not wanting her to go to the hospital, she wouldn't like it, not after here. Good luck, Joe."

Peggy, totally oblivious of the escape plan for her, held her son's arm, her fingers never relaxing as she felt the smooth material on his jacket, and strolled to the back of the garden shed where Alex and Bobby waited patiently in a car, ready to whisk their mother as far as they could from the threat of hospital admission.

"What kept you Joe?" cried the nervous Bobby. "We thought you were never coming."

"Patience, bro, Mum walks very slowly, as you will be finding out for yourself."

As they drove away, Liam, who did not require permission to be in the building, signed the book stating that Peggy Bryson returned from her walk at 10:35 a.m. No one paid any attention to him. Residents and staff were used to him popping in and out to refresh flowers.

"We're going on holiday Mum, to the seaside. You'll like that, won't you?"

Peggy smiled and promptly nodded off. Bobby sat beside her, clasping her withered hand, willing that human contact would help restore her to her former self. Her hand felt as cold as ice. Every vein protruded from the transparent skin.

"Stop sniffling Bobby. How can I concentrate with you sobbing?"

After several hours they stopped to change drivers and pick up coffee. A plaintive voice from the back whispered: "I need to go to the bathroom."

"Oh heck, who is going to take her?"

When no one volunteered, Alex escorted his mother to the area of the garage bathroom, instructed Joe to fetch the coffee and Bobby to sit still. A woman entering the bathroom and aware of the man's predicament, offered to take Peggy with her. She returned to Alex.

"Sorry, but she seems to have had an accident; does she have clean underwear?"

"I think so, in her bag. Look, I'm really grateful to you, you don't have to do this you know."

"It's no problem. I care for my elderly aunt. I saw you were uncomfortable about this. She'll be sorted in a minute. What's her name, by the way?"

"Peggy, her name is Peggy."

"Hello Peggy, I'm Rebecca."

Peggy went willingly with her and was soon ready for the remainder of the journey. It slowly dawned on Alex that perhaps he and the others had taken on a bit more than they could cope with.

"We will just have to make the best of it," he reported to his brothers as they took off on the next part of their journey. "There won't always be a kind Rebecca around to help out."

Alex had rented a holiday cottage by the sea. It was midsummer, the area was busy with holidaymakers; families played on the beach, children screamed in delight as they ran into the sea attempting to jump over waves without being knocked down, couples strolled arm in arm along the promenade, sea-front cafes were busy, making the most of the season. The scene unfolding in front of them belied the anxiety felt by Peggy's sons. The family sat in the car, eating fish and chips, cajoling their mother to eat and savouring the sea air. Peggy had no interest in food. The boys hoped to merge in with the holidaymakers. The world looked normal but in Peggy Bryson's life, normality had long been lost.

"You're enjoying this Mum, aren't you? You always like the seaside," commented Bobby.

Peggy Bryson could have been anywhere; she was totally unaware of her surroundings.

***

Peggy Bryson was indeed missing.

Several hours had passed since Peggy had last been seen. There was no reply from any of her sons. Panic spread through the care home. Where was Peggy? *Nothing like this had happened before.* Staff, due to go off duty, remained to help search every corner of the building and grounds. Sam cancelled her plans for the day and remained to help. A search of her room showed nothing was missing. The staff member who saw her go off with Joe remembered she was dressed in her warm coat and had her handbag over her arm as usual. 'Peggy, you are just like the Queen,' the staff would comment to the elderly woman who always carried her bag with her as if it held treasured memories.

"There was nothing out of the ordinary. They didn't see me; I was in the office and glanced up just as they left the building. If we don't hear from her sons within the next hour, I'm calling in the police."

Alice Bryson, Alex's wife, eventually made contact with her husband, still believing him to be in a remote mountain area with his workmates. He did not enlighten her. She told of the care home's concern for Peggy and insisted he phone them at once.

"You know I don't like to be contacted about anything to do with your family. I was in the middle of an important ceramic plate for a customer when I was interrupted; most inconvenient for me, Alex. Get things sorted with your mother, once and for all."

He assured her he would deal with it immediately. "I'll be home Sunday evening, as planned," said the scheming man as his wife ended the call. He sighed as he thought how much easier life would be if his wife was not so adamant about contacting her in-laws. *I'll never change her attitude to them.*

The boys settled their mother for the night and sat together on the sun deck drinking beer and discussing their next move. There was a calmness about the beach now that it was empty apart from the occasional couple strolling by the water's edge, a calmness that none of the boys were experiencing at that moment. Alex's plan seemed to fly in the face of logic.

"I'm going home tomorrow evening. You guys have to take care of Mum and never leave her alone. It won't be easy as we saw today, but there's no alternative. I don't know when I can get back down. I'll phone every day. If it gets too much for you, we'll have to regroup and rethink."

Bobby piped up, "They must be panicking at GWR. I thought you said you would phone and tell them she's safe. They are nice folks and we don't want them to worry anymore than necessary or get into trouble over this."

He promised to call the care home immediately.

"I'll do it now," said the elder brother as he walked down by the shore to a private spot, where he spoke to Lydia. He could hear the relief in her voice.

"Mum's safe with us. We couldn't have her put in that hospital so we'll look after her ourselves. She won't be coming back to GWR."

The senior staff nurse berated Alex for his thoughtless actions.

"We could have discussed this more. There was no need to do that. How are you boys going to cope with her personal needs, her medication, and her confusion? She requires medication which can only be prescribed by a doctor. Are you sure you have thought this all out? It would be better all round if you brought her back here and we will have a rethink about her placement. Nothing is set in stone, Alex."

Alex was silent for a moment knowing full well he had acted from the heart and not the head.

"She'll be okay with her family. We will cope. She's our mum. We have some medication here. We'll follow the instructions."

"And when you run out of it, what will you do? Alex, I have to tell you, the police are now involved. We held off contacting them until we heard from you or your brothers, and when that didn't happen, I called in the police an hour ago. They are interviewing staff as we speak. Where are you?"

Lydia realised she was speaking to herself. Alex had ended the call.

***

Alex checked in in time for his flight north.

"We are experiencing a slight delay, sir, for this flight, due to fog. We will keep you informed. Check the departure board for updates."

Alex groaned inwardly. This was the last available flight that evening and if he was delayed it would be disastrous for him. Alice still believed him to be with his workmates and expected him home soon. He became anxious knowing that he would be late for work next day and his wife would discover that he had lied to her. He took himself off to the bar hoping a few drinks might calm him down; instead, he became more agitated. An announcement was made that no further flights would depart that evening.

There was nothing for it but to phone home and come clean. He held the phone some distance from his ear as his irate wife berated his foolishness. He would have to listen to it all again when he returned home. He spent a restless night in the departure lounge, cursing the weather, cursing his youngest brother, and generally feeling out of sorts with the world.

"I'd no choice, Alice; they were going to send Mum to hospital, to a ward for patients with dementia. She would be away from everyone and everything she's known for the past decade, it would not be fair to her."

"And you think you've done her some kind of favour by doing exactly that, taking her out of her comfort zone to an unfamiliar holiday place? What's the next part of your crazy plan, or haven't you boys thought beyond the present day?"

"We'll work something out, she needs us Alice. I don't suppose she could come…"

"Don't even go there, Alex, we've had this conversation before. There is no way your mother can come here to live. It is out of the question. Get her back to the care home where she can be looked after properly. They know what's best for her, and if it has to be hospital, surely that won't be the end of the world. Anyway, from what you tell me, she won't know where she is."

"But Alice, they tell me that routine and familiar surroundings are essential for people with dementia."

"Like the seaside you've taken her to, you blind fool. What's familiar about that?" For all his bravado in settling scores with people who crossed his path, Alex Bryson was no match for his wiry Scottish wife who dominated him and kept him from straying back to what she often referred to as, 'his old London ways'.

"You live here now in a respectable area, so wise up," was the mantra of his resolute wife.

CHAPTER 29

At GWR care home, the head gardener, Liam, was becoming more and more uncomfortable as police interviewed members of staff. He was basically an honest man, a hard-working chap who was nearing retirement. He succumbed to the temptation of accepting cash from Peggy's family for what he thought was easy money for a few minutes of work. He was worried sick in case they searched him and found him with a wad of money. With the frenzy of staff running here and there all day, he had no time to think about a safe place to conceal it. Spotting Sam's motorcycle, he quickly placed the large envelope in one of the panniers. When called for interview he was unable to conceal his extreme nervousness: he was excitable and sweated profusely; his forehead and neck and his palms became moist, his heart raced. He felt ill. Suddenly, the enormity of the enquiry struck him; the stupidity and recklessness of Peggy's sons' action and his own part in it took on a more serious note. The detective interviewing him had many years of experience in police work and spotted the nervous man's demeanour.

"You seem a bit worried sir, are you feeling up to answering some questions?"

"I'm fine, Detective; it's been a long day. We are all worried about Peggy. She's never been missing before."

"I hear you spoke to her and one of her sons this morning? That makes you the last person to see Peggy."

Liam reddened, his body language spoke volumes. "I suppose I must have been," he stuttered.

"Do you think she has wandered off and got lost?" asked the detective never taking his eyes from the edgy man who remained motionless and silent as if struck dumb by fear.

"Sir," continued the detective, "I have to remind you that this is a serious enquiry. A vulnerable woman is missing; she could have wandered off and got herself lost. We have to find her. If you can shed any light on her disappearance, please help us here. The staff are upset, they are frantic with worry, and you can see that for yourself. Her sons are not answering their mobiles. It seems a bit strange to me that all three are unobtainable at the same time. I have a feeling, Liam, that you know more than you are telling me. Am I correct in my assumption that you are hiding vital information?"

Unable to stand the strain any longer, Liam wiped his sweaty palms on his gardening overall, cleared his throat which seemed as rough as sandpaper and told the detective all he knew of Peggy Bryson's disappearance. He did not know of her whereabouts.

"They didn't tell me where they were taking her, and I didn't ask. I should never have got involved in this, but they were desperate men. They didn't want their mother moved from GWR. I didn't think I was doing any harm to anyone."

The immediate search was called off. Staff were informed that Peggy's sons had removed her to a place of safety, and that no further search of the care home was necessary. Staff were astounded to hear of their trusted gardener's involvement. He was taken to police headquarters for further interview. Although he was not the principal offender, he was liable under law to be charged with an offence.

While Liam was being interviewed, Senior Nurse Lydia was ending the conversation with Alex Bryson. She rushed to the interview room to relate events to the detective only to discover the gardener's involvement in Peggy's disappearance.

"Thank God she is safe. That's what matters most at the moment. We can deal with everything else later."

Relieved care staff who had held on to help search for Peggy began leaving for home, having been thanked by senior staff for their time and concern for one of their most loved residents. Among them was Sam who had donned her bike gear ready for a spin in the countryside. One of the young police officers, an avid bike fan, chatted with her as only people with a similar passion can do. Together they examined the vehicle. Sam opened the pannier to show the storage space and found the envelope deposited earlier by the gardener.

"What's this?" she gasped as she spotted the contents.

Resuming immediate police mode the officer took charge of the situation. A quick glance told him there were several hundred pounds in the grubby envelope.

"Can you account for this cash, ma'am? It seems a lot to carry around."

A flummoxed Sam seeing the rapid change in him, one moment taking on the role of a fellow bike enthusiast, now that of a suspicious policeman, retorted sharply, "Well, I assure you it's not mine. Someone must have put it there.

Oh no, not Liam. How could he involve me?" She was spitting mad.

She was asked to return to the house while the eager young officer searched for his superior to relate the find of the cash.

"I just knew, sir, that someone must have colluded with the lady's sons in this kidnap. I think we have found our source. Incidentally sir, one of the staff told me she saw the gardener chatting to the biker at the time Peggy was being spirited away."

Knowing the young man's keenness to solve the world's crimes, he asked him to slow down with his assumption of guilt.

"Remember your training Constable; gather evidence, question the suspect before you jump to conclusions. The gardener has already confessed to receiving cash and to hiding it in the pannier, not to frame the hairstylist in any way, but in a moment of panic. I'll talk to her and assure her she is free to go. And, by the way, the elderly lady was not spirited away... curb your enthusiasm. Now I'll explain things to the hairstylist."

A rather shamefaced young cop asked Sam to accept his apology for his haste. The look on her face told him that if he wasn't an officer of the law he might have been going home with a bruised face.

***

Liam Norris was held in custody overnight and appeared in the morning before the magistrate, Karen Stevenson, a wise and perceptive woman who had a reputation for fairness beneath her severe facade. She glanced down at him, fixing a stare that would do justice to a rabbit caught in headlights and spoke to the errant man.

"Liam Norris, you have acted irresponsibly in colluding with Joseph Bryson in a foolish act which caused unnecessary worry to the good people at GWR care home, not to mention the time wasted spent looking for the missing resident, time which was needed to tend to others in their charge. You are a man of exemplary character, or so I am told, but in a moment of weakness, or greed, you took money from Mr Joseph Bryson. As this is your first appearance in this court I intend to be lenient with you as I can see you have shown remorse and appreciate how your action has affected so many others. I intend making use of your gardening skills and sentence you to 100 hours of community work, where you will be supervised as you tend to gardening projects set for you. What happens now to your future employment I leave in the hands of your employers."

Next day, the shamed gardener appeared before a discipline committee at GWR. Dora Martin, the owner of the business who oversaw all appointments, interviewing each person who applied for work to ensure they were fully aware of her high standards, headed it.

"It goes without saying, Mr. Norris that I am extremely shocked and bemused at your involvement with Mr. Bryson. I accept that you acted in a rash moment, thinking that a few more pounds would help your retirement plans. The committee agrees with me that to dismiss you at this stage of your working life would be a blot on an otherwise excellent working life, and while we do not condone your actions, we appreciate your years of service here and so will not dismiss you. You will resume work here on Monday."

Liam Norris' troubles were not yet over. His wife and family who had accompanied him to the hearing were vocal in their condemnation.

"Dad, how could you embarrass us like that? It's in the local newspaper. All my friends will know about it, this is awful," chided Trish his daughter, brows furrowed as she tossed her long chestnut hair in a gesture of defiance.

Son Jon chimed in, "My colleagues at school and the kids I teach will be laughing up their sleeves at me, the supposedly upstanding teacher of religious and moral education. I'll never live it down."

Moira, his wife, took his arm and walked alongside him.

"Okay, you two, that's enough. Leave your father alone. He knows he's done wrong and is paying for it. Liam, you were a complete fool. Now let's put this behind us and go home for a nice meal. You have only three months until you retire, so keep your head down and your hands clean."

"That might prove difficult Mum, since he's a gardener," laughed Jon, attempting to diffuse the tense situation.

Still laughing, and feeling suitably chastised and forgiven, Liam linked arms with his family and said, "Now, what about that special dinner?"

CHAPTER 30

Miles from the troubles of Liam Norris and Peggy Bryson's sons, Brenda Mears, saddened beyond belief at the sudden death of Molly and experiencing a loneliness she had never encountered before, considered a move from her house in Lincoln Park, which had almost become a mausoleum with even more areas closed off and no longer required. Molly's apartment lay empty and eerily quiet. Nora spurned any suggestion of visiting her former home to deal with her mother's possessions and requested Brenda send her personal items and dispose of everything else. Her own smaller apartment, once a happy home that she had shared with her fiancé George, remained empty too, as if in mourning for a lost love, a lost promise, and a lost future together. Together with Lucy's suite of rooms which Brenda had virtually turned into a shrine for her lost child, the mansion stood as if mocking the spirit of its former residents. It was not a comfortable place to reside. Apart from a poignant visit from the detectives with the Bosnian visitors, and that of her loyal executive staff, she seldom entertained anyone. Her depression was deep, her thoughts jumbled, and her heart broken. Even a talk with the elderly Jordan Garnett did not seem to ease her pain. He had called to explain his rather odd behaviour.

"You must have thought me a silly old fool, not knowing about your dear daughter's abduction. I can't apologise enough, my dear."

"Let's put it all behind us, Mr Garnett. Superintendent Harvey explained to me about the situation. You have enough to worry about now with your own troubles. My aunt has caused pain and sorrow for us both. I for one am glad she has gone to meet her Maker."

As he hung up, the gentle man whispered to himself, "and so am I."

She sat on the floor in almost semi-darkness in her father's office, surrounded by a mountain of paperwork, unable to settle to the task she had always promised she would attend to when she found time. She felt the spirit of her parent as she reflected on the many hours she spent in that room as a child, then as an adult, as her father explained the running of Mears Empire and awakening in her an enthusiasm for business matters which was to become her life's work and first love. She took a deep breath and began the monumental job of sifting through her father's meticulous filing system. It was then she came across some personal documents she had never seen before: her parents' marriage certificate, her own birth details and poignantly, her mother's death certificate, stating cause of death to be postpartum hemorrhage. *I never knew what caused my mother to die just hours after my birth... How sad!* She held the paper tightly in her hand for some time as if by doing so she could feel connected to the mother she never knew. This discovery motivated her to investigate more of her family's medical background. She spent many hours researching records from national archives and was curious to learn more about her maternal ancestors. Anna

Leci, in her letter to Lucy, had drawn a veil over her own parents' death, a mere mention of something sinister. This intrigued Brenda.

Online death certificates for her maternal grandparents revealed their deaths were confirmed as suicide caused by mental illness. Brenda discovered that suicide is the tenth leading cause of death among adults in the USA. Her grandfather had a terminal illness. His wife, mentally incapable of caring for him due to bipolar disorder, wavered in mood swings from manic highs to depression. Life was becoming intolerable for them both. In a lucid moment they made the decision to end their lives together. A shocked housemaid found the couple dead in bed with empty pill bottles nearby.

Brenda found the report disturbing and questioned the possibility of the disorder being the cause of what she termed, 'Anna's madness'. She had now some insight into the obsessive protection of Anna towards her young, vulnerable sibling. In her own grief Anna attempted to become both mother and father to the young Francesca. Brenda's fact-finding led her to some understanding of the need for ongoing research into hereditary bipolar disorder. She was anxious to discover the potential risk, if any, of herself inheriting the disease. She donated a generous sum to research studies. *At least, I owe it to Lucy. Perhaps if Anna had been treated for the disorder Lucy would still be alive.* Knowing how unusually and highly talented both her mother and Lucy had been, Brenda ruminated over the likelihood that as they were so creative, they too may have manifested some degree of psychotic illness in later life. *The dark side of their musical talent*, thought Brenda as she continued clearing her vast mansion of unwanted items.

***

Back in Rio at 'Les's Bar' some regular customers perched on wooden stools at the rustic bar and drinking cool beer were pouring over an old discarded newspaper.

"Hey, look at this! It's our B-J and Fred. They are in the news."

"What have they gone and done? Let's have a look and see."

Some tugging of the newspaper followed before someone took control and began to read, much to the frustration of the others who felt aggrieved.

"Oh man, they've just got themselves murdered in that England place they went to visit."

"Give the paper to Dan," suggested a drinker. "He can read good, sure you can read good, Dan?"

Dan, in charge of the bar during the owner's absence, read the newspaper report silently at first, while the others gathered around him waiting as he read every word. They watched as his face changed from concern to bewilderment.

"What does it say then? What happened over there in England?"

Dan looked at his buddies, and with hands shaking, told of the demise of their friends.

"It wasn't England, it was Scotland, it's nearby," said Dan shaking his head as he digested the horror unfolding in front of him.

"Do you guys remember some years ago, a big-shot politician had to stand down from being elected as a presidential nominee because he got found out that he was the pa of that missing kid, Lucy Mears?"

"Sure we do Dan. It was big news and then the kid was killed in an airplane crash," replied one drinker.

Another chipped in, "Yeah, I remember that. My sister lives in Chicago, it was a big scandal there, and the politician guy came from nearby. Everyone knew him."

"Hey," continued Dan, "you guys ready for this? Wow, it turns out that it was our buddies B-J and Fred who killed her, seems like they were involved in the kid's kidnapping and sabotage of the plane that was bringing her home to her folks. They hotfooted it to Mexico and changed names and appearances then ended up here in Rio. We've been served by cold-blooded murderers and to think I took on the responsibility of this crap bar for them, working every hour to make a healthy profit for them."

"Man, you think you know people," said a customer. "We've sure been fooled. Come to think of it, I asked Fred about them scars on his face, told me he had some plastic work done cos he'd been burnt as a kid but they looked kinda fresh to me."

Dan continued, "It was a hell of a death they got though; listen to this guys: they were thrown into a sinkhole kind of place, still alive, an old pit shaft it was, filled with water and junk and left to die. It gives me the shivers to think about it."

"Got all they deserve, that's my opinion," commented the guy whose sister lived in Chicago.

"I agree there. They sure did. But that poor kid. How could they do that to a kid?"

Discussions took place over many hours, drinks were consumed in great quantities, no one felt any guilt when Dan declared the drinks were on the house and everyone voiced their opinion as the enormity of the event sunk in.

"Guess it was revenge then for what they did. Someone must have found where they were hiding out over there and finished them off. Strange how they were killed in Scotland. They must have been followed. Kinda weird, ain't it?"

"Maybe there was a contract put out on them, that's my take on it," contributed Dan who by now had relinquished responsibility of running the bar.

The customers of 'Les's Bar' spent many hours pondering and digesting the news of their former friends. Dan, enraged at the whole scenario, announced, "Well, they won't be coming back here, that's a cert, so let's drink up. The drinks are on the house until we empty this bar."

Some days later a fierce fire engulfed a beach bar in Rio reducing it to ruins. Mysteriously, no bottles of alcohol were found among the debris.

CHAPTER 31

After the departure of Alex for home, Joe and Bobby Bryson spent a restless night at the beach holiday home. Their mother, unsure of her surroundings, became agitated and did not settle for long. She wandered from room to room as if searching for familiar things, her mind confused by her surroundings. The noise emanating from her was not unlike that of a whimpering puppy. She wrung her hands together as she looked around the strange place.

I can't find Jimmy anywhere. Where are you Jimmy? Have I been here before? I'm not sure, maybe I should ask these men, and they look kind but why are they in my house? Barry might know, yes I'll ask Barry.

The boys took it in turns to sit with her in an attempt to soothe her anxiety. While Bobby eventually slept from exhaustion, Joe continued his watch until he too gave way to sleep.

Oh dear, they've fallen asleep. I'll not wake them to ask... what was it I wanted to ask? I hear water, lots of water... I like water...

Peggy managed to open the main door and headed out of the house.

Bobby woke to the noise of holidaymakers beginning their beach activities. Children squealed with delight as the cold sea, as yet to be warmed by the sun, swirled around their feet.

"Mum's gone! Joe, get up. Mum's gone! The door is wide open. Oh hell no! Where is she? She had only a flimsy nightdress on and slippers. Joe, wake up, man."

Bobby was frantic with worry as he shook Joe's shoulder. Joe slept deeply. Bobby ran from room to room to make sure she wasn't in a corner or cupboard or had slipped and fallen, all the time yelling at Joe to wake up.

Joe eventually woke with a start at the screaming coming from his brother.

"Not another bloody nightmare Bobby. I can't sleep for you screaming."

"Joe, Mum's gone; get up, she's gone."

Search of the immediate surroundings did not locate the absent woman. The brothers frantically ran around the resort and made enquiries from people they met but Peggy was nowhere in sight. Joe's worst fear was that their mother may have wandered into the sea. They ran to the shore. Others, hearing of their plight, joined with them in searching the shoreline. Holidaymakers ran along the shoreline searching, calling her name, and reporting back to the fraught brothers. Some used binoculars in at attempt to spot the missing lady. A few good swimmers dived into the sea and swam up and down covering as much of the area as they could.

"I'm scared Bobby. I'm bloody terrified she's drowned."

Joe ran along the length of the bay while Bobby sat on the sand, head in hands rocking back and forward and crying out for his mother. Some people tried to comfort the distressed man. After an hour of fruitless search, Joe held his brother in his arms, something he had never done in his life, and cried with his younger sibling.

"There's nothing else for it, Bobby, we have to contact the police and the coastguards."

At the local police office not far from the beach area, Geoff Nolan, a senior detective took the brothers to an interview room and assured them their mother was safe and was being looked after.

"A member of the public on an early dog walk came across the distressed woman and called us for assistance. She was cold and very confused and I have to say, quite aggressive. Our WPC had great difficulty in calming her down."

"Where is she, Detective?" asked Joe. "Can we see her and take her back to get on with her holiday?"

The relief they felt was overwhelming.

"I'm afraid not, sir. You see, because of her distressed state she was unable to tell us who she was. She kept muttering that Barry was in a hole in a blue dress. Is one of you Barry?"

"No, no idea who that is. Someone in her imagination, I expect," replied Joe. "She has dementia and gets mixed up."

"Yeah, no idea," added the tense Bobby whose face was smeared with tears and sand, his clothes not yet dried by the sun. They stuck to his skin as if painted onto his slim frame. His restless manner did not go unnoticed by the detective.

"So," continued Joe, "can we see her now?"

"As I was saying sir, the lady was very confused, and we had no way of finding out who she was. We made enquiries at the two local care homes in the area, but they knew nothing about her. The social welfare department was summoned and has her safe with them until a decision is made about her future."

"Well, we're here now, so we'll collect her and take her home."

"That I'm afraid is out of the question. We have to follow procedure when someone as vulnerable as this lady comes to our attention. I'll give you the name of the social worker dealing with her and you can contact the department. You will have to deal directly with them. Now, we need some details from you. There are some questions to be answered."

The brothers looked at each other in total bewilderment. Bobby mumbled, "I don't understand why we can't just take her home with us."

"I have to get some details from you both, sir. Don't worry about your mother, she is being looked after."

The detective, a senior figure in his district's police department, towered over them. His superior manner spoke volumes. No one in his or her right mind would dare challenge him. He was a man used to having respect. Many hardened criminals crumbled under his interrogation. He escorted the brothers to separate interview rooms, and aware of their damp, distressed state, arranged for hot drinks to be provided.

They spent several hours being questioned about their mother. Joe, well aware of his brother's emotional state, feared that he would be easy meat for the rather overpowering officer and reveal more than he should about taking their mother from GWR. In the end, the astute detective easily elicited from the edgy Bobby, the entire events leading to their mother's removal from GWR.

"We couldn't have her put in that hospital," said Bobby. "It was too crowded and there was not enough staff. It wasn't right for her. We wanted to spare her that."

He, along with his brother, were held over until further investigation could be made. Both boys were stunned at the turn of events.

While stating he understood their reasons for removing their mother, the detective explained that it was now a police matter.

"This may amount to an offence. You will both be held over until a ruling is made. The Crown Prosecutor will make a decision and a solicitor will be allocated to you in order to explain what charges, if any, will be made against you. In effect you removed a person without permission and this has to be investigated further. I appreciate your concern for your mother's welfare but I'm afraid it has clouded your judgement. We are in touch with GWR and assure you your mother's best interest is top priority."

"As it is with us officer," replied Joe.

Joe was flummoxed as to how having only his mother's best interest at heart he had ended up in a police cell. *This could tip Bobby over the edge,* he thought as he tried to settle on an uncomfortable bed, the stench of which told of several occupants of unclean habits. A pigsty would smell cleaner than this. His own clothes smelt of sea, his hair was tousled and full of sand, his stomach churned with nervous anticipation of his fate. He was miserable.

Several weary hours passed before he was summoned once more to the interview room where a dishevelled Bobby waited patiently for his sibling to join him.

"I see you have an elder brother who was also with you when Mrs Bryson was taken from the home," began the officer. "He is being interviewed in Scotland, as we speak. GWR has related the events surrounding your mother's abduction. They have had a major drain on their time over this, but only want what is best for her. Senior staff there will liaise with a senior social worker from this area and a decision will be made based on our Care Home Law which regulates the provision of care home services throughout the country. When a patient is incapable of making a decision at a particular time, as in the case of your mother, the matter can be referred to the Court of Protection for a ruling. The doctor in charge of elderly care in this area will then most likely liaise with GWR will assess your mother. Let me assure you both again that she is being cared for."

Bobby began to moan quietly, withdrew his handkerchief from his pocket and blew his nose with such force that Joe momentarily forgetting where he was, kicked him in the shins, and admonished him for making a racket. The interviewing officer stopped what he was doing and turning to Bobby, asked, "Are you able to continue this interview sir, do you need anything?"

Shaking his head, Bobby signalled that he was fine.

Joe interrupted, "My brother doesn't have the best of health, sir, and this is putting a strain on him."

"As soon as we can," continued the officer, "we will inform you of our ruling. Meanwhile, I'll arrange for a medical doctor to check you over sir," he said, addressing Bobby directly. "As for you both and Mr Alexander Bryson, I require more time to decide with the court if charges are to be brought. Your brother is being brought here for further interview."

Some time passed before the numbed brothers were allocated a solicitor who had looked into the background of the case.

"I have secured bail for you and a decision will be made regarding your brother after I speak to him. You will return here at a later date to learn your fate and that of your mother. Please remain in the area."

Joe and Bobby, reeling in shock from the events of the past hours, returned to their temporary beach home, showered and changed and took stock of their situation while awaiting the arrival of their elder brother. Bobby had refused assistance from a doctor stating he felt fine.

"My brother fusses too much."

"We're in real trouble now Joe. What are we going to do?"

"We do nothing, repeat, nothing. Sit it out and wait for Alex to join us. They're sure to give him bail too. Just remember to keep your mouth shut about Barry Jones. We've never heard of him. OK?"

"It ain't easy, hell I still have nightmares about those pit shafts... I..."

"Bobby, shut up, just shut up. You're not helping anyone if you lose control. Did you have to tell that cop about GWR? We could have just said we were on holiday with her and she got lost, nothing else was needed."

"He scared me, Joe, never took those eyes off me, and made me feel uncomfortable."

"You'll be less uncomfortable when Alex gets here. Stop sniffling, go and take your calming-down pills. In fact, take two and go to bed."

CHAPTER 32

Alex Bryson, escorted by a police detective, sat uncomfortably in an interview room, unaware of where either his mother or brothers were. He had suffered the wrath of his wife and feared his marriage was doomed. Emotionally drained and exhausted from travelling, he waited to hear his fate. The same senior detective, Geoff Nolan, spoke to him, reassuring him his mother was safe and well cared for.

"I see you live and work in Scotland, Mr Bryson. I was up in your part of the world not long ago with some of my colleagues. You may have heard of the incidents we were investigating almost on your doorstep, so to speak; two bodies were found in some pit shafts; an unpleasant time for the guys who were dealing with it, not to mention the victims. Did you hear about it?"

"Yeah, yeah, I vaguely recall hearing something like that."

"Coincidence, isn't it? You coming from that area. Now about your mother, you must be anxious to hear what is to happen to her."

A solicitor joined them and explained as he had done so earlier to the others, the procedure for a ruling about his mother's placement.

"A meeting has been set to resolve this. You and your brothers will be invited to attend at a later date to be informed of the findings of the care protection people. It appears likely that Mrs Bryson will be given a place in this area. There is an exceptionally good care home for patients with dementia, similar to the high standard of the home she was removed from. Staff are trained in nursing such patients and we hear good reports about them. For the moment, sir, you will be bailed to be with your brothers until a decision is made regarding whether or not you have committed an offence of abduction. Remain in the area in order to be contacted by either myself or a colleague."

Alex arrived at the beach house, much to the relief of his siblings. His anger was fierce.

"I couldn't leave you two in charge for one night, could I? You damn fools to let Mum wander away. Anything could have happened to her and now we can't even get to see her. God knows where it will all end. We could be facing a jail sentence thanks to your incompetence. We might be done for abduction. Alice is furious with me. I don't think she will take me back if things go wrong for us."

No amount of explanation was required or would have been listened to by the elder brother, his mood menacing and vitriolic. His siblings had witnessed his rage on several occasions and knew the best course of action was to say nothing, knowing that he would eventually calm down. They waited at their holiday home for several anxious days, void of any holiday feelings. Beach life went on around them, families soaked up the last of the summer sun, and the place was alive with laughter and fun filled days. The brothers stayed indoors, getting on each other's nerves as they waited to be summoned to hear their fate.

Bobby's stress level increased, his horrendous nightmares disturbing his siblings and adding to the tiredness felt by all. It was not a happy family holiday.

"It's so unfair of them not to let us see Mum. She'll be worried about us," muttered Bobby with monotonous regularity which only served to fuel the anger of his brothers who despaired at his inability to accept their mother's health issues. Alex now understood something of Joe's concern for the youngest Bryson and the responsibility it placed on his shoulders.

"He really needs professional help," he told Joe when Bobby had gone for a sleep. "In hindsight we shouldn't have taken him to Scotland with us. It's blown his mind dealing with Barry Jones and his mate but we can't trust him not to tell all if he sees a psychiatrist, which is what he really needs. It's a mess. Damn you, Barry Jones. He's haunting us even in death."

After what seemed an eternity for the brothers, they were summoned to hear the outcome from the Crown Prosecutor, who spoke to them individually before summoning them together for a final briefing.

"As you have each been informed, the removal of your mother from her care home without permission from staff does not, in my opinion, amount to an offence in law. Had she been abducted while under a court order preventing her removal, things may have been very different for you. The local authority has now issued a guardianship order that includes power to place her in a suitable place of safety. These orders are set when a person, as in the case of your mother, has impaired judgement and is liable to become disorientated and wander off. You are free to go, but I advise you to reflect on the stupidity of your actions.

A recommendation has been made about your mother and officials are waiting to inform you of that."

They were then called before a group of people to have the result of deliberation on their mother's fate.

"A ruling has been made to place Peggy Bryson in Strand Bay Care Home for the elderly, here in our district. The home caters solely for patients with dementia and is well staffed by highly skilled people. Reports from the Care Commission are excellent. It is on a par with GWR. Now that we have a ruling from the Crown Prosecutor, you will be taken to visit your mother and shown around the home. Her safety and personal care and medical supervision will now be catered for, here in this area."

The Bryson brothers had no choice but to accept the ruling, relieved in a way that Peggy was safe. Alex said, "Well, I suppose in the end we have saved Mum from hospital admission. It's been a nightmare, not knowing where she was or if we were going to prison. This is a nice area with the beach nearby. I'm sure they will take her there at times."

***

Strand Bay Care Home stood in magnificent grounds that had once belonged to a wealthy businessman, James R. Strand who had willed it to the people of the town on condition that it was used in some capacity for the care of the elderly. The grounds were well tended with colourful flowerbeds and baskets. Seating was in plentiful supply in sheltered spots and a few summer houses adorned the spacious gardens. Ornate garden statues and sculptures from classic to contemporary decorated the area and spoke of a splendid and opulent history.

"Liam would love to tend these gardens," remarked Joe.

At the mention of his name, Alex remembered how they had asked Liam for help.

"I hope he hasn't got into trouble on our behalf."

Joe took up the conversation, "He won't say a word to anyone. Liam's an okay guy. I'll get in touch with him when we get back to London. He'll want to know how Mum is."

Here, at Strand Bay, Peggy Bryson was reunited with her sons whom she hadn't seen since the fateful day she had wandered from their holiday home. A social worker and senior nursing sister from Peggy's new home explained to the brothers that they were free to visit their mother at any time, but that an appointment must be made beforehand. They would not be allowed to take her from the building.

"I'm looking forward to seeing Mum again. She'll be so pleased to see us," enthused the excitable Bobby clutching a bouquet of flowers, as they waited in a tastefully decorated sitting room while a staff member fetched Peggy.

The reunion did not go well. The boys were shocked at the deterioration in their mother in the few days since they had seen her. Her ordeal had taken its toll. While she was clean and tidy and sported a new hairstyle, her eyes were vacant. She looked at her sons and saw them as strangers. She felt threatened and let out an ear-piercing scream. *Who are these people? Why don't they go away? I want to find my Barry and tell him these men have come to put me in a hole...*

"It's us, Mum, me and Joe and Alex. It's only us."

Bobby attempted to hug his mother, only to cause the confused lady to scream all the louder I don't want to go in a hole in the ground. Where's my blue dress? His brothers pulled him away.

"It's no use, Bobby. She no longer knows us. You're upsetting her. Let her go."

Two nurses escorted the hysterical patient back to her room where they remained until Peggy fell into a sporadic sleep. The trio was asked to leave.

"It's best you don't all visit at once," suggested a senior nurse. "Three men towering over her overwhelmed Peggy. She was obviously frightened. I'm sorry, but that's the way her illness has progressed since you last saw her."

There was no alternative but for the brothers to return to their homes: Alex to Scotland to face his nemesis, Joe and Bobby to their London home where they picked up the threads of their lives as best they could. The whole episode had a detrimental effect on Bobby's well-being. Joe felt guilty at not allowing his disturbed brother access to professional help.

Alex took charge of visiting arrangements and set out a roster. Before flying home he called the care home and was reassured that his mother was calm and resting peacefully.

CHAPTER 33

Geoff Nolan, the senior police detective who had interviewed all three Bryson brothers was not one to let gut feelings beat him. Something bothered him and he was determined to investigate the niggling feeling that there was more to the Peggy Bryson incident than first thought. He loved a challenge and was determined to explore all avenues before he rubber-stamped the case as being done and dusted. He sat at his desk and turned his chair to face out towards the sea. He took this position when he needed to think. He chewed on the end of a pen, scratched his head as if trying to find answers and thought. Mulling over events of the past few weeks since the discovery of a distraught elderly lady wandering along the beach, he thought long and hard. He preferred to work things out by himself, involving colleagues only when he was sure of his findings. Then, as if struck by a light bulb moment of clarity, grabbed a marker and set to working on a whiteboard. He listed his suspicions and explored his thoughts:

It doesn't take a genius to join these dots…

Alex Bryson lives in the area in Scotland where two bodies were found in pit shafts…he lowered his eyes and avoided mine when I mentioned the incident… he works in the mining industry…

Barry Jones, one of the victims originally came from East End of London…

Alex Bryson, his brothers and mother also came from there…

Peggy Bryson calls out for Barry and shouts about him being in a hole in the ground…

She was attacked by Barry Jones who was jailed for the offence and vanished on release from prison…her boys threatened to get him…

Reggie Allison, shop owner confirms this…

Aha! I have enough here to suggest we rethink this case which has been puzzling colleagues here and in the USA.

***

DI Rab McKenzie, working in his office, received a call from his friend and colleague, Geoff Nolan with exciting information. He and Geoff had worked together when the two bodies were found in Scotland. They also knew each other from previous cases that involved Scottish-English collaboration.

"Rab, I think we can safely re–open the case of the two American villains found in your Scottish pit shafts. I have a theory here to explore with you. Listen up, man."

As he listed his thoughts, he was more and more convinced he was on the right track.

"Geoff, man, you may be on to a winner here. Send all the data you have and I'll contact the Chicago guys as soon as their time zone allows. I owe you big time, Geoff; looks like we might be able to put this case to bed before too long."

An impatient Detective McKenzie waited until he knew his Chicago colleagues would be up and running. *Blooming time zone; gets in the way of proper communications.*

In the absence of Tony Harvey from the office, his deputy, Carole Carr received the welcome news of the re-opening of the Scottish murders.

"That sounds awesome. I hate when we have to leave a case unsolved. It goes against everything we train for. It's as if we've allowed the bad guys to get away with murder and the like. Have you plans for us to meet or do we do this through the wonders of technology? Should I dust down my passport again?"

Rab McKenzie laughed.

"I thought you would be on the first plane over here! I think the best plan for the moment would be to let my guys do some more investigating at this end. We need to work with our colleagues in the London area, as well as doing a bit of footwork up here. We won't rush this, Carole. We need to make some discreet enquiries without alerting the suspects. My mate Geoff has some leads to follow up. It goes without saying that we'll keep you up to date with what we discover. Now, lass, you give our best to Tony and his wife."

Carole Carr signed off and thought how much the case had taken over the lives of her boss and herself. *On a positive note,* she thought, *we have made such good friends overseas. That counts for something.*

***

Forensic scientists come into their own when it comes to re-examining evidence of unsolved crimes. Often new methods are put in place as the science is continually developing. Doctor Brody Cameron was not surprised when told of developments in the case of the two American victims.

He firmly believed that good police work would, through time, bring criminals to face their nemesis.

"Passage of time, Rab, doesn't give criminals the right to think we won't come knocking on their door. The past always catches up with them. No one should escape justice, despite what cause they feel they are putting to right: in the case of those London guys, looking for revenge for their mother being attacked all those years ago. These new leads from your buddy down south look hopeful. Let's get our heads together mate and bring these villains to court and to justice."

As he signed off, Rab could hear the tap-tapping of Brody's pipe on the table; "The sign of a contented man," he laughed.

Geoff Nolan wasted no time in correlating his findings, which he discussed at length with his colleagues. His first task was to investigate Barry Jones whose name, according to Peggy's care home staff, was constantly being shouted out by the distressed lady.

"We have to research the court case involving Barry Jones and confirm what the shopkeeper has told us about the attack on Peggy Bryson."

Hours of research paid dividends for the determined detective. He soon found the link between the two.

Eureka!

He called a retired colleague in London whose name appeared on a police report from many years ago.

"Hey, mate! Got a favour to ask: I see you were involved with a case I'm interested in; an East End villain, by the name of Barry Jones."

"Jonesy! Well, there's a blast from the past. A real rogue was that one. Would steal the sugar out of your tea and come back for the spoon... so, what's he nicked for now?"

"He won't be nicked for anything else ever."

Geoff regaled his colleague with events in Scotland where Barry Jones had been dumped in a pit shaft.

"I'm trying to confirm a link between him and an elderly lady by the name of Peggy Bryson. I have some information here, but need your good self to assure me I've got the facts correct. I'll read what I have."

His former colleague listened as Geoff read; memories came flooding back to the retired cop, adrenaline pumping as he recalled the search and arrest for the notorious villain who terrorised his patch. He thought that on retirement he had put all memories of police cases to bed, but hearing the name of Barry Jones reawakened in the elderly man his love of a career that spanned his lifetime.

"Well, that brings back memories of that brute. There you have it Geoff. The thug beat the poor woman to a pulp in a botched robbery. She never really recovered from it. I remember the case well as there was an outcry at the leniency of his sentence. He went off the radar after his release. The thinking was that he had somehow evaded the authorities and got himself out of the country pretty sharply. He must have known the Bryson boys would be waiting for him. They're a close-knit family and very protective of their mother. It was well known that Peggy's sons were not going to let things go with Barry Jones."

Geoff spent some time relating events from the Scottish deaths and the involvement of the Chicago PD and concluded that he could now safely send all relevant data to the USA to be shared by both teams.

"Great to talk to you, Eddie, you've been a great help. Man, we need to meet up for old times' sake. I owe you a pint."

"I'd like that Geoff; you'll find me on the golf course most days though. Good luck with the investigation."

***

Joe and Bobby Bryson continued with their life in London, unaware that local detectives were making discreet enquiries about them. Their regular haunts were noted, as were their fishing trips. Undercover police regularly drank in the local pub frequented by the brothers, and were able to pass themselves off as building workers from a nearby construction project, thus avoiding suspicion. They succeeded in picking up snippets of conversation from the brothers, especially when Bobby, who was often drunk, became louder and argumentative with Joe. His rants were always about their mother being abandoned in a care home, many miles from them.

"Bobby, I keep telling you, she's okay. I phone regularly and the staff assure me she's settled and is even joining in some of the activities. She's made friends with a lady from Poland. The nurse told me they wander about the place arm in arm. The Polish lady doesn't speak English, Mum can't speak Polish, but they chatter to each other anyway. She's got company, Bobby. They take her to the beach regularly; she seems to be happy as far as anyone can tell. Alex is going to visit her next weekend and he'll call in and stay a night or two with us. I think he needs to get away from Alice; she's overpowering."

"Yeah, right, but I miss Mum. Why won't you and Alex let me visit? I could go with Alex."

"Bobby, we've been over this time and time again. You get too emotional and you know what you're like for putting your foot in it. If it wasn't for you shouting your mouth off about what we did in Scotland we wouldn't be in this mess. Anyway, they only allow one of us to visit at a time."

"That's right. Blame me," shouted the younger brother as he stormed out of the pub. "It's always my fault."

The undercover cops recorded these outbursts. One of them, while buying a drink from the bar, stood near Joe who was now discussing fishing with the barman.

"Sorry to interrupt," said the cop, introducing himself as Bert, "couldn't help but hear you mention fishing. Me and my mate here are looking for somewhere to fish. Can you recommend anywhere around here? We've got some time off from the construction job. We're both away from home with not much to do when our shift ends."

And so began a pseudo friendship resulting in Joe inviting his two new friends to join Bobby and him on a fishing trip. Bobby was not enamoured at the thought of strangers sharing their outing but soon warmed to the friendly guys especially when he found himself giving fishing advice to them. He relished the opportunity to share his knowledge and skills. Angling was something he excelled at and he often caught more fish than his brothers did. He enjoyed Bert's company and regaled him with advice for fly fishing.

"I use a number 5 line with this fly rod. It's 8 foot 6 inches and suits me fine. Got a bargain, got it for £50. Here, try it yourself."

His new mate was an easy-going, friendly guy who inspired trust, and before long the unsuspecting Bobby relaxed as they fished together.

"That's some van you guys have," initiated Bert, "ideal for fishing trips."

"Yeah, we often go away for days at a time. It's got everything we need."

"I could see that. Home from home, then? What's the mileage on it then?" quizzed the cop. "Must be high with all those fishing trips you do."

"Quite high, but we look after it. Joe's good at servicing it. Even went up to Scotland in it and only had to do an oil change and buy two new tyres; apart from buying fuel, that is."

"Scotland, eh? Never been up there. What's it like?"

"Don't much like it. It's a bit quiet for me after the noise of London, but my brother lives there and we visit him now and again and go fishing with him. Must say the scenery is lovely if you like that kind of thing. There are loads of lochs and rivers up there and good fishing. I caught a brown trout once, a real beauty about 16 inches long. We tried salmon fishing but didn't have much luck."

As he fished, the memory of his last trip invaded his mind and reawakened the horrors of past events. He lost his concentration. He dropped his fishing rod, swore, and waded in to retrieve it.

"Be careful, Bobby. Let me give you a hand."

As he dried off in the sun, Bobby and his new friend sat drinking beer.

"You gave me a scare there, man. You went a bit pale. Sure you feel okay?"

The more he drank, the more morose Bobby became and began blubbering like a baby. The medication he was prescribed for his mental health clearly stated 'no alcohol' which Bobby had chosen to ignore.

"Hey, mate, you sure you're okay? Want me to fetch Joe?"

Joe was further upstream with the other undercover cop.

"Hell, no, mate. Joe's got no patience when I get upset. It's just, well, I got things on my mind. I've not been in the best of health recently, get upset easily and to make things worse our mum is in a home miles from here at the coast. We don't see her very often."

He did not enlighten Bert as to the reason for that.

"Well, if you need to talk mate, I'm a good listener. Sometimes it's good to get things off your chest. Sorry about your mum, that's too bad, she must miss you."

"Unfortunately she doesn't know any of us now."

Bobby regained his composure and thanked Bert for his concern.

"I really mean that Bobby, if you ever need to talk you know I'll be in the local pub most nights."

Back at base the undercover cops reported their findings on the surveillance of Joe and Bobby Bryson to their superior officer.

"Good work chaps. We're a step nearer nailing these guys."

CHAPTER 34

With the intelligence gathered from the undercover cops, the detectives working on the cold case of the deaths of the American villains had enough data to investigate further the Bryson brothers' trip to Scotland.

"What we need is evidence that they were in the area around the dates we suspect the guys were deposited in the shafts. They must have stopped off for fuel and food and we know they renewed tyres, so let's get the work done up north. Bonnie Scotland, here we come."

Detective Geoff Nolan gathered a team around the crowded whiteboard and explained the evidence that had been found to link the Bryson brothers with the death of the American villains.

"Here's what we know to date: Barry Jones was well known to Peggy Bryson and her sons. They lived on the same estate and the guys went to the same school. Jones was a regular offender, in and out of prison, well known to the authorities. He was convicted and jailed for the robbery and mugging that took place when Peggy Bryson worked in a local shop near their East End home. He served his sentence and went off radar. We now know that he went to the States under an assumed name, Barclay Ellis-Jones;

more on that later. The Bryson boys threatened to 'get him' for their mother's mugging, that resulted in her suffering a severe stroke and having to live in a care home from that time on. We know this threat was real as they were overheard talking about it in the bars and clubs near their home. Our undercover cops did a marvellous job in gathering this and other evidence, which, when put together, paints a dire picture. Bobby, the youngest one, was particularly vocal when sounding off about revenge. He's a bit of a wimp in my opinion, and wouldn't be much of a threat to anyone by himself; a different matter altogether when in the company of his thuggish brothers. They seem to be his crutch.

"We come to this character here," continued Geoff Nolan, pointing to the name Alex Bryson. "Alarm bells rang in my head when I heard that he lived and worked in the area in Scotland where the two bodies were found in pit shafts. Then I discovered he worked in the open-cast mining industry up there, so he would have knowledge of pit shafts. It didn't take much to join the dots, but evidence is crucial. Here's where you lads come in.

"A squad will go up north and split up. We need evidence of Alex Bryson's time away from work to link it with the rough timescale we have from forensics, as to when they think the bodies were placed in the shafts. Doctor Brody Cameron will be on hand to assist. We believe Joe and Bobby Bryson stayed in a hotel somewhere in the area and had their van valeted, purchased new tyres and fuel and the like, so you'll be searching for that info. This has to be done discreetly. We know Alex Bryson is still living and working in the area. He must not get wind of these enquiries that would ruin the entire investigation.

"Now, according to GWR care home where Peggy Bryson was resident for over ten years, she often called out for Barry, mumbled something about his wedding, a blue dress, someone in a hole in the ground. We can't interview the dear lady as she suffers now from Alzheimer's, but linking these up, we could be onto some good evidence. The care home staff will verify what she has said. That brings me to the abduction of the lady in question from GWR that brought her to our patch and to my attention. Her sons removed her without permission, drove her here to our area, booked a holiday chalet but the old dear wandered off. Thanks to that, our enquiries led us to the Bryson lads and putting two and two together, we more than likely are looking at the murderers of the two American victims from the pit shafts. Good police work always gets us our man, or in this case, our men."

***

At home in Scotland, Julie continued with her writing. Unaware of the drama unfolding since his traumatic find in the pit shaft, Scamper, now fully recovered from his ordeal, sat at Julie's feet, his brown eyes pleading with her for a walk. The other two dogs slept peacefully under her desk, engrossed in contented dreams and oblivious to Scamper's plea.

"Five more minutes Scamper and we'll go. I'm just finishing this section."

Mary's Scotland and Elizabeth's England were intrinsically bound. Two Queens. Cousins who never met. One, Elizabeth I of England, the other Mary, Queen of Scots. Both redheads. Both wilful, highly intelligent and passionate. The relationship was fraught with suspicion, intrigue and fear...

"Scamper, stop whining. Oh, I give up. Let's go, but, no falling down holes please. I have enough drama to write about. Come on boys! Walks!"

Two sleepy heads looked up, reluctantly shook themselves free from their sleep, and joined Scamper at the door.

Not far from where Julie lived and worked, discreet enquires were being made in an attempt to gather enough evidence to bring the consequences of Scamper's find to a satisfactory conclusion. Detectives checked CCTV of petrol stations within a reasonable radius of both crime sites. Results were disappointing, as most recordings had been erased. Two detectives booked into a hotel, which unknown to them at that time, was the one used by the Bryson brothers. Using the excuse of a flat tyre they enquired about the nearest repair lot and were directed to a nearby garage. There, they found the evidence they needed as a garage owner remembered the politely-spoken Englishman who spent some time valeting his van.

"I remember the guy. He told me he was an angler and used his van for fishing trips but wanted to sell it on and needed to clear it out. He went to a lot of trouble to spruce it up, even had it spray-painted. I let him use the space around the back here. He bought tyres. I remember that, and some other stuff. He bought some metal bars to fit on the inside where some had come loose and got misplaced. Gave me a good tip for my troubles. He stayed in that hotel over there, told me his brother was with him but had caught a bug or something and was resting."

"Don't suppose you know what kind of metal bars they were?"

"As a matter of fact I have a piece of it over here. It was left over and I never throw things out as you can see from the state of the place."

Collating information about Alex Bryson's working time proved more difficult. He lived in a small village where a stranger, especially one asking questions, would stand out from the crowd. One of the detectives posing as a reporter for a magazine, and another, a photographer, sought out and were successful in obtaining access to Alex's place of work and interviewed the site manager.

"So, you want to find out about open-cast mining then?" said the gruff boss. "For a magazine you say? Well, it would be good to put our work in the public eye. Not everyone agrees with what we do. Some say it's a blot on the landscape, but we pride ourselves in restoring the ground, as per government regulations. Our site here speaks for itself. I've a squad of gardeners who restore the area to a very high standard. I'll get one of the lads to show you around and you can get your pictures. Be sure to send us a copy. Here's the very person you need," he said, as he introduced the photographer to Bill. "Bill here has been with us longer than the others. He will show you around and answer any questions you might have."

During their tour of the site with talkative Bill, the covert detectives enquired about the workforce and their work practices.

"Do you guys work here in all weathers?"

"We can be flexible as long as we complete the work in time. If the weather is too bad we have our glasshouse where we bring on plants and shrubs. There's always something needing done. We have a good system going here; flexi-time we call it. And some of the lads job share. We can usually work our hours to suit ourselves as long as we arrange with the boys to be on duty when we need time off. It works well for some of the family men who need time off during the school holidays and for one of our guys whose mother is in care down in the south of England. It allows him to gather time off to visit her. We're a good team. We look after our mates."

While photographing the site, the officer elicited more information about Alex. Bill posed proudly while he was photographed among the various parts of the site.

"You'll have to send me copies of these," he said. "Imagine me being in a magazine; the wife will be pleased as punch."

"Sounds a good firm to work with then, especially for the likes of that guy who has to go miles to visit his parent. Does he do that often?"

"Quite a lot; he's very good to his mother is Alex. Here, come over to the office and I'll show you the work sheet, just to give you an idea of the kind of folks we are up here. Have a look at that while I make us a brew."

The detective discreetly photographed the work roster showing Alex Bryson's time off.

***

Gathering reports from undercover cops, Geoff Nolan, delighted with the work of his team, planned the arrest of the Bryson brothers with precision. He carefully studied the evidence he would need; making sure nothing was left to chance. Satisfied that all was in order, two officers were assigned to detain Alex Bryson at his place of work and escort him to HQ, where detectives were waiting to charge the eldest brother with two counts of murder. DI Rab McKenzie from Police Scotland eagerly awaited the arrival of the first prisoner, having worked closely with Geoff Nolan and keen to bring the sorry mess to a conclusion.

Simultaneous arrests were arranged for Joe Bryson and his brother Bobby.

"This must be carried out with meticulous timing. It's essential that these men do not have contact with each other. Remove phones immediately, separate the London brothers. They will be held in different locations."

Officers were allocated to arrest Bobby Bryson. Intelligence reported the routine of the younger sibling.

"He jogs around the park near his home at a set time in the morning before collecting his newspaper. Nab him as he finishes his run. You can set your watch by him. While Bobby is being detained his brother Joe will be picked up at his home. Timing is essential in these arrests. Hopefully the sands of time are running out for the Bryson boys."

Alex Bryson, working outside on a flower patch, was unaware of the approaching officers who had located him after speaking to the site manager, who was slightly bemused when he recognised the photographer and reporter who had visited the site some weeks earlier.

"Weren't you here a month or so ago?" he began, but refrained from saying any more on being shown the officers' identification tags.

"Alex Bryson," called one of the arresting detectives, "stop what you are doing."

He turned pale and fear overcame him. He had never fully relaxed after the killing of his foe and the unknown man whose fate was sealed simply by being with Barry Jones. The discovery of the two bodies and resulting talk in the area about the horrific finds brought him out in a cold sweat. He was in denial that he and his brothers could ever be traced as the perpetrators of the crime, thinking he had covered their tracks well and had outwitted the authorities.

The disclosure of his victims as the killers of Lucy Mears and those on the plane with her, gave him a feeling of exoneration, a feeling that he had exacted revenge, not only for his mother's suffering, but also for the loss of the victims of the sabotaged plane. He was complacent. Until now.

Alex's workmates, thinking at first that the police wanted to speak to him with perhaps news about his frail mother, stopped work ready to commiserate with their colleague and were stunned when they saw him being handcuffed and led away.

While this was happening, Alice Bryson was being informed by detectives of her husband's arrest. She was shocked and acutely embarrassed at hearing of his horrific offence.

"I knew he would never fully leave his past life behind. His family had such a hold over him. I hoped that by living here in this quiet place he would leave old ways behind, but no, it doesn't seem like it. But murder! Detectives, are you certain about this? Maybe you are mixing him up with his brothers. I wouldn't put anything past them. If this is true, how can I continue to live here? This is so humiliating for me. What will the neighbours say? I hope this doesn't reach the newspapers. I have a business to run and a reputation to maintain and I can't afford scandal. What will become of all this? I'll have to leave the area for a while until things calm down. I'll head for my sister's place until this dies down. How can I go on living in this area, and who will want to do business with the wife of a double murderer? I can't take it in that he was involved in that dreadful find in the pit shaft. It was the talk of the place when those poor men were found there. What was it all about? I should have listened to my mother who had bad vibes about Alex. This is awful."

The detectives noted that she showed little concern for her husband's plight and thought only of herself.

Alice Bryson's rant was not yet over: "If there's any truth in this, I'll divorce him and revert to my maiden name. I don't intend to be associated with him or his family. I met Alex in the local bar when he came up here for a job interview and we just seemed to click. He was a charmer and a gentleman and I truly believed he wanted to change his life for the better. I didn't warm to his family. I'm no snob, detectives, but they were not in my league, a bit low-life, if you see what I mean."

She refused an offer to accompany her husband to the police station where he would be formally charged.

"He's made his bed and he can lie on it. I'm going to pack and get out of here before the gossipmongers start. I don't want any fingers pointing at me. This is a nightmare for me."

The detectives sensed their prisoner would be left to his fate.

CHAPTER 35

Unaware of his brother's plight, Joe Bryson lounged on the sofa at home reading an angling magazine while awaiting the return of Bobby. They intended to go fishing later in the day. Hearing a knock at the door he presumed his brother had forgotten his key and shouted, "Door's unlocked Bobby, come in."

Turning around, his demeanour changed when he saw two police officers standing in his sitting room.

"What the...? Who? Is it my mother? Is she ill? What's wrong?"

"Joseph Bryson, you are under arrest for the murders of Barry Jones and Alfred Wysoki."

Before he had time to assimilate what was happening, the detective read him his rights, handcuffed him, and escorted him to a police vehicle. Unknown to them, Bobby had returned early from his run having forgotten to take money for his newspaper and overheard the conversation from the safety of the kitchen.

He hid until the trio had departed, quickly changed his clothes, and ran. Inquisitive neighbours watching the activity at the front of the house were unaware of Bobby leaving by the back. He took off, boarded the first bus that came along and sat sweating and panting while he recovered from the bombshell of seeing his brother taken into custody. He put his head in his hands and thought. He was unused to making major decisions and panicked as he attempted to understand what his next move should be. His breathing became laboured; his head hurt and his heart raced. He felt as if it would explode.

His only solution was to turn to his mother, his life-long emotional crutch. He had no idea how to reach her by public transport and spent time studying destination information, not wanting to draw attention to himself by making enquiries.

He arrived unannounced several hours later at the care home. He was hungry, exhausted, and fearful and was reminded of arrangements for visiting.

"I was in the area on business," he lied, "and thought I'd pop in for five minutes."

His dishevelled appearance did not go unnoticed.

If he thought he would find solace or comfort from his mother, he was soon facing the reality of the deterioration in Peggy's illness as she sat rocking in a chair and show-ing no sign of recognition of her youngest son. He held her hand and sobbed as he begged her, "Come back Mum, come back to how you were, I need you."

Perhaps his plaintive voice triggered a memory for her, for she sat upright for a few seconds and made eye contact with her tearful son and smiled.

"Bobby," she whispered.

The distraught man hugged her, held onto her as if he wanted to hold onto that lucid moment forever.

"Oh Mum! Yes, it's Bobby! You've come back to us; you're cured! Oh Mum, I don't know what to do. Joe's been arrested and I don't know where Alex is. Help me Mum; I don't know what to do. Tell me what to do."

But Peggy had once more retreated into a private world, a world where no one could enter and few understood. She had a vacant look once more. Bobby, totally unable to cope with the trauma he was involved in, held her hand, lifted her chin gently until their eyes met. Peggy smiled and whispered, "Hello, Barry."

Bobby stood up and screamed at her: "No Mum. I'm Bobby, your own son. Forget bloody Barry. Barry Jones is dead. We fucking killed him," and ran out of the care home almost bumping into an elderly gentleman who was walking slowly along the corridor. He ran towards the seashore; past the beach house where he and his brothers had attempted to conceal their mother. Across the sand and fully clothed he ran into the sea. Bemused holidaymakers soaking up the last of the summer's sun, watched as the drama unfolded in front of them. He felt the sea close in on him. He stopped struggling against the force of the water and let himself go… down, down deeper into the warmth and contentment that his troubled soul had long searched for and had eluded him. He felt at peace.

Some quick-thinking swimmers dragged him from the sea. He struggled and tried to fend them off, but was over-powered by the lifeguards who had run to assist the holidaymakers. Someone had called for the coastguards. Soon an ambulance, escorted by a police vehicle, removed Bobby Bryson to hospital where he was placed under guard in a secure area while being checked over by medical staff.

Officers who had been searching for him around his home had alerted other forces to be on the lookout for the wanted man. The staff nurse, who had overheard his rant at Peggy, quickly called the authorities and reported what Bobby Bryson had said.

"You heard him say that?" enquired a detective. "He actually said they had killed Barry Jones?"

"Yes Detective, that's what he said. He was actually screaming at his mother, that's why I heard it."

***

Alex Bryson sat with his head in his hands, pondering his fate. *How did it come to this? I thought we'd outwitted the cops* .The police vehicle he was travelling in was most uncomfortable. He was a tall man. Leg room was tight and the seats hard. Before long he felt cramp and it took all his willpower not to shout out. He had been told he was to be transported to police headquarters to face charges. Hours in this van will be hell, he thought. He now understood something of the discomfort he had put his victims through on their arduous journey north. Other prisoners were picked up from various police stations, the detours making the journey even longer and more difficult to bear. The noise from some of the prisoners became unbearable as the journey progressed. Arguments started and voices were raised in protest about the vehicle's lack of comfort. One of the escort guards mocked his passengers: "So sorry, gentlemen, about the discomfort; our other vehicle was unavailable. Had we known how refined you gentlemen were we would have provided a top-of-the-range Mercedes for you. As it is, put up and shut up. We have a long drive ahead of us to pick up a few more innocent bad guys. Sit back, enjoy the scenery, and on-board entertainment."

He laughed as he turned up the radio in an attempt to drown the racket from the men.

Alex was miserable. His body ached from the tossing of the vehicle; there was no room to stretch. He attempted to sleep but the blare from the radio and the rowdiness from his fellow travellers became unbearable. *I have to get out of this*, he thought to himself.

A stop was made at a police station to pick up two more prisoners.

"We'll make this a comfort stop gentlemen. The plan is that you will be escorted to the bathroom, one at a time. Make the most of the fresh air," he again mocked the prisoners as they moved from the confines of the van to the nearby building.

As Alex stepped from the vehicle, a prisoner let out an ear-piercing scream; he was having a seizure. The guard rushed to assist him and was unaware that he had dropped a set of keys. Alex saw his chance and scarpered. He ran onto the road and into a nearby park. He ran to put as much distance between himself and the police. His absence had not as yet been noticed. Exiting the park at the opposite end, he flagged down a lorry and begged a lift: "I have to get to my mother as soon as I can, she's been taken ill. Can I hitch with you? I'm heading north."

The friendly, unsuspecting driver, bored from hours of driving was delighted to have company for part of his journey.

"I'm not supposed to pick up hitch-hikers, but this sounds like a real emergency to me. I can only take you to the other end of town. Drop you near the station, son?"

"Thanks. That's great. In the rush, I've dropped my phone somewhere. I really appreciate your kindness."

Alex, always the courteous gentleman when he wanted to be, gave nothing away of his flight to freedom and chatted amicably to his companion.

After being dropped off, Alex headed back to his home. While his mobile phone had been taken from him he still had his wallet with him and was able to purchase a train ticket. He slept for most of the journey. Once home, he hid nearby and waited until dark before going to his house. He shivered as the night grew colder, pulled his flimsy jacket closer to his shaking body as if attempting to generate some heat. The night was silent; a sliver of moon kept him company in the otherwise dark world he now inhabited. When he was sure that no one was about, he crept quietly towards his house and removed his shoes. He was aware that the crunching of his shoes could be heard on the gravel path which Alice had insisted they must have to alert them to anyone who might be lurking there. The irony was not lost to him. He did not want to be seen by anyone. Alice, he suspected, would not be at home and he knew she would probably never return to the village to face the gossipmongers. What a mess I've made, he pondered as he hid behind some bushes, awaiting the right moment to locate the spare key that was hidden in the garden to be used in emergencies.

His hunch had been right. Alice's wardrobes and cupboards were completely empty and nothing remained of her possessions. *She didn't hang around for long.* He settled himself at home, carefully avoiding using lights, or making noise which might alert neighbours of his presence. He was totally exhausted, emotionally and physically. He kept a low profile while planning his future strategy. As far as anyone was concerned, Alex Bryson was in prison and well away from the area. *At least she's left food in the fridge,* he mumbled to himself as he quietly settled himself for his last night at home.

CHAPTER 36

Detectives searching for Alex Bryson visited his place of work to interview his workmates who were shocked to hear of their colleague's involvement in the double murder of two Americans. Bill, the site foreman who had shown the undercover cops around the site, spoke up: "I feel bad about this, Detective. When Alex came here to work I was his mentor and showed him around the area. He was a pleasant man, quiet and unassuming, a keen worker who wanted to learn everything about the job. I talked nineteen to the dozen at him, told him about the old mine workings here, and warned him not to go too close to the old pit shafts in case of cave-in. I even showed him where some of them were. I feel so guilty now."

His statement was recorded and he was assured he had nothing to blame himself for. The man was distraught. He shook his head as if attempting to rid himself of that memory.

"And to think we were all talking about the horrible deaths those two guys had, and Alex Bryson joined in the conversation, giving nothing away. Well, I for one never suspected a thing."

Detectives entering the home of Alice and Alex Bryson saw evidence of recent occupancy. Clothes which Alex

Bryson was last seen wearing were found in a wash basket and with the remains of food and cigarette ends, provided enough DNA evidence to prove the fugitive's presence there after he absconded from police custody. The net widened to locate the missing prisoner. His wife, staying with her sister, was interviewed and cleared of any involvement in her husband's flight from justice. She was outraged at having to accompany detectives to her home in order to ascertain if any of Alex's personal belongings had been removed from the premises.

"Oh no! What if the neighbours spot me? This is embarrassing. Can't you park your police car somewhere else and walk to my house?"

Detectives had no time to pander to the wishes of the selfish woman. She had to suffer the indignity of curious neighbours, one of whom called to her: "Is everything okay with you, Alice, we have all been wondering about you?"

"I bet you have," she retorted sharply.

Once inside, Alice quickly closed blinds and curtains plunging the house into darkness, and the neighbours into curiosity mode. Detectives accompanied her as she toured the house, noting anything amiss. She was disgusted at the remains of a meal festering in the kitchen.

"He might at least have cleared up after himself before he took off," muttered the furious wife as she set about placing the crockery in the dishwasher.

"Stop!" screamed an officer. "That is evidence; evidence of his presence here."

She continued from room to room. Obsessed with having a pristine home, she quickly spotted anything that was out of place.

"Oh! No!" she screamed. "He has taken my cash that I had ready to take to the bank. With everything that's been going on, I didn't manage to deposit it. That money was from my ceramic business. I have to pay my suppliers!"

As she moved from room to room, she reported that nothing else appeared to be out of place. Then she called out, "He has taken his passport and left his bank card."

As investigations continued into the search for the absentee prisoner, media appeals for information resulted in the truck driver who had given a ride to the escapee shortly after he had run from police custody, contacting them to make a statement. After giving this to police he returned home to face the wrath of his wife, Edith.

"What have I told you about picking up hitch-hikers? You never know who you might have in your cab, and look at what happened: a double murderer! You could have been killed."

"But," he interrupted, "it's a lonely life in the cab; hours and hours of driving is boring so having company for a few hours makes all the difference. He was a pleasant chap, easy to talk to, very polite and grateful for the lift."

"So you say, Jack, but he was a killer, a double murderer! I'll not sleep now for worrying every time you go to work. Don't ever think of picking anyone up ever again. Don't be an idiot."

***

Lawyers preparing the case for trial of the Bryson brothers had a monumental task ahead of them. Evidence of Bobby Bryson's state of mind at the time of the abduction and killing of the American villains had to be collated, not an easy task when the accused, recovering from his attempt at drowning, refused to cooperate with investigating detectives. After a risk assessment carried out concluded that he was liable to abscond or self-harm, he lay in the prison hospital handcuffed to the bed. He struggled with staff, refused medication, and was abusive to psychiatric consultants who were attempting to assess his mental state.

Meanwhile, his brother Joe was evasive when questioned by detectives.

"I'll talk when my brothers are here," he told the solicitor who advised him to think of his own defence.

"Until Alex hands himself in or is apprehended and Bobby's hospital assessment is complete, you are on your own. A decision will be made by the court whether or not to go ahead with the trial at High Court, in absentia. Joe, that means we can go to trial without your brothers being present. I advise you to start cooperating. The working of the court is very complicated."

CHAPTER 37

Carole Carr interrupted a team meeting to take a call from DI Rab McKenzie of Police Scotland with news that both sets of colleagues were waiting to hear. She was informed of the arrests of the three Bryson brothers, being aware of their part in the macabre crime from regular updates from her overseas colleagues.

"Hey, that's awesome news. I can't wait to tell Tony, he's out of town at the moment. Now tell me all."

"Well, Carole, it's not all good news. In spite of our plan to arrest these people at the same time, we've been outwitted by the eldest one, who somehow or other managed to escape from police custody while being transferred and is holed up somewhere. We will pull out all the stops to bring him in and have him face justice. I've ordered an enquiry into how he was able to escape and a few of my guys will have their rears kicked over this. The younger brother attempted to drown himself and is currently in hospital under twenty-four-hour guard. He will be assessed and a decision made about whether to contain him in prison or prison hospital. Expert witnesses will be needed for a medical assessment for him. As for the middle brother, Joe, he has been transferred here and has appeared in court charged with both murder and abduction of your two American mobsters and held over pending further investigation. His case will now go to the High Court. It takes so long to bring these complicated cases to trial with all the background stuff that has to be done, but at least two of the miscreants are under lock and key and we will stop at nothing to apprehend the other one. It will be a long, involved case with three people facing court. I don't envy the solicitors who will be dealing with it. They have a hard task in front of them."

"I guess then we will be called to give evidence," said Carole. "I want closure on this as do the rest of our guys here. Things are moving forward here too with new evidence coming in about the part played by Anna Leci's nurse and a young lawyer dealing with her affairs. I've never seen Tony so enraged about any case and I've worked with him for many years. So it's beginning to look as if the murder in your Scottish pit shafts was not revenge on anyone's part over here. It had nothing to do with Lucy Mears' abduction."

"Yep, it appears to be unrelated; just a trio of angry brothers out to get even with a thug. Unfortunately his mate, Alfred Wysoki, was innocently caught up in the mayhem. There's a lot more to come out of all this, but I can see light at the end of the tunnel for us all."

***

Over time, Bobby Bryson calmed down sufficiently to allow medics to carry out a full assessment of his mental state. He was diagnosed as schizophrenic. This was more serious than first thought, much more serious than the bouts of depression that had dogged him all his life. His depressive episodes were never fully understood, nor was his withdrawal from any social life apart from that with his family. His challenging disorder made it difficult for him at times to distinguish between fantasy and reality. The loss of his mother's emotional support and his involvement in the horrific killing of the American villains tipped him over the edge and highlighted his strange behaviour culminating in his failed attempt to end his life in the sea. This was noted by the court and a decision was made based on the report, that Bobby Bryson was unfit to plead. His solicitor told the court that his client was at present unable to understand court procedure or the consequences of his plea. Nor would he able to challenge the jury, as was his right.

"His mental state at this time is unlikely to improve in time for the trial," he reported. "He has deteriorated since the time of the offence. It would be inhumane to expect him to stand trial and would serve no purpose. I believe he genuinely, at this moment in time, does not understand the charges made against him."

Bobby Bryson was placed in a hospital psychiatric unit for treatment. His brother Joe was given the news, that with Bobby in hospital for an unforeseen time, and his brother Alex still at large, it was likely that the trial would go ahead in their absence and that he alone would be standing in the dock.

***

Julie Sinclair continued with her writing:

Mary had no control over events in her life when ill health prevented her from condemning the murder of Lord Darnley. She could not comprehend how those close to her could have perpetrated such an atrocious act. Her trust in people became her downfall. Had she been more cautious of those around her, and less politically naive, she may have avoided becoming a victim, a victim wrongly accused of initiating her husband's murder. That Mary was involved in the atrocity was neither proven nor disproven; that she had condoned his killing would never be known. A secret taken to the grave. Her cousin Elizabeth, a woman who lacked compassion, condemned her cousin to death...

As Julie wrote, she was interrupted by her dogs barking furiously as someone approached her house. Annoyed at the interruption, she stood up smartly to attend to the caller, hoping this was not going to take long. She was given a citation to appear in court to give evidence at the murder trial of the three Bryson brothers.

That's all I need, she thought as she read the instructions enclosed in the letter.

"Oh, Scamper, look what you've got me into, you and your find."

CHAPTER 38

Thousands of miles from Scamper's find, evidence was being prepared for the trial of Edward Garnett Jnr and Rita Hampton. Both had admitted their guilt while continuing to blame each other. Written evidence from law records from Jordan Garnett's office overwhelmingly laid the plot to kill Lucy Mears and her travelling companions at the feet of his nephew, Edward Garnett Jnr. That he had colluded in this with Alfred Wysoki was admitted by the convict and confirmed by Rita Hampton who had chosen in federal court to turn state's evidence in the hope of being offered a plea, a lesser form of immunity, 'use' immunity, whereby her testimony could not be given in any subsequent prosecution. Interest in the case was closely followed by the public and media. The story of Lucy Mears was not yet over.

At home, on a rare evening off for Tony, he, Gina and Abigail, who was at home from a college break, finished off one of his special dishes. Abigail had taken to calling it 'Tony's surprise… guess the dish tonight' which he took in good heart knowing his culinary skills left a lot to be desired. As she rose to tidy up, her mother said, "Leave that for the moment sweetie and sit by us."

Gina announced the news of her advanced pregnancy to her excited daughter who squealed with delight as she hugged her mother and stepfather.

"Wow! I'm so happy for you both. I noticed you had put on a bit of weight, but I thought it was Tony's cooking that caused that. I'm going to be an older sister! I've always wanted to have a kid brother or sister. I can't wait! Oh, Mom and Tony, if it's a girl, could we call her Lucy? Please?" pleaded Abigail.

"Honey, Tony, and I have agreed that boy or girl we want you to choose the name. Now go and call Carole, we want you to give her the news."

Tony and Gina smiled as they heard the squeals of delight from both Carole and Abigail. Their decision to involve the youngster as much as possible appeared to be paying dividends.

"You are a wise man, Tony Harvey," said his wife as they listened to Abigail relay the news to all and sundry. "It will give her something good to focus on for a change."

***

When his trial eventually came to court, Edward Garnett Jnr, on being told that his accomplice had confessed all and realising there was no alternative for him but to admit his part in the fraud, asked to make a statement. He hoped by doing so he would be leniently treated by the court. His hopes were unfounded.

An elderly gentleman sat at the back of the federal court listening to proceedings. His shrunken appearance showed how he had aged considerably over many months since the discovery of his nephew's deceit. He had spent many years at the Bar and was familiar with court procedure. Today he was not a participant but was there as a citizen, albeit with an interest in the case in question. His wife held his hand as together they listened to the case against Edward Garnett Jnr. It was painful for him to have the good name of his firm so cruelly and ignominiously pulled to shreds. He thought of the years of hard work by his grandfather, his father and latterly himself that had gone into building a well-respected law firm, now about to become a source of ridicule and gossip. To discover his once beloved nephew had fraudulently altered documents was painful enough, but to discover his relative's involvement in the death of Anna's great-niece and her travelling companions was almost unbearable. His wife worried about his health: "After all he's been through with the threat of losing his sight and now this, I don't think he will ever recover from the shock and humiliation," she confided to a friend.

He took no comfort in hearing the sentence handed down to Edward Garnett Jnr regarding the ill-fated plane crash.

Life imprisonment without parole on five counts of murder, that of Lucy Mears, Les Soubry, Zelda Djuric, Kristof Djuric and George North and life without parole for fraud. He was aware that the death penalty there had been abolished a few years earlier but drew no comfort from that.

As he was led away to begin his sentence in a high-security prison, all hopes of taking charge of his family law firm evaporated in a moment of deceit. He glanced back at the public benches hoping to find a glimmer of comfort from his relatives. It was not to be. Jordan Garnett and his wife had left the courthouse.

CHAPTER 39

The trial of Alex Bryson was scheduled to go ahead *in absentia*. He had wilfully evaded the police. No trace had been found of him after his fleeting visit home when he collected his passport before going underground. All attempts to locate and return the prisoner to a place of security had so far met with failure. Staff at Peggy's care home were put on full alert should the missing villain attempt to visit his mother. Staff were fearful, having learned of his vicious ways. Security measures were put in place. A discreet police presence at the home went some way to calm the nervousness of care workers.

"Peggy must be closely watched," they were told. "There's no saying when or if her eldest son might turn up. We have to remain alert."

Back at Peggy's former care home, staff at GWR were astounded at hearing of the background of Peggy Bryson's sons. Senior Nurse Lydia voiced the thoughts of the others.

"To think that we trusted and respected those three men who were in and out of our care home and applauded their commitment to visiting their mother. They pulled the wool over our eyes; that's for sure."

"Yes, but credit where it's due, they loved their mother and wanted the best for her, otherwise they wouldn't have taken her away from here when things got tough," said another.

In her new home, after tucking Peggy in for the night, two nurses discussed the events which had shaken them all.

"She's such a dear, sweet lady, so trusting and loving now she has settled here with us. It's probably just as well she is unaware of what her sons have done. Thankfully, she doesn't pine for visits from them."

"And to think they were only out to revenge her attacker from all those years ago; probably meant to give the guy a beating, but it got totally out of hand. That's misguided loyalty."

"It must have been festering away in them like an abscess ready to burst. It gives me the shivers to think of the death they gave those American chaps regardless of what they had done. Let's go and have a cup of tea and try to think of something else. Tell me about the plans for your daughter's wedding…"

***

In a cell underneath the High Court, Joe Bryson awaited news of his sentence. After his first court appearance his case was referred to the High Court for trial. The tense atmosphere in the courtroom, the stern judge and the dark-cloaked lawyers, put him in a state of alarm as he awaited his fate. The whispering of those in authority and their occasional glances at him before proceedings began scared him so much that he felt his face twitching with stress. He held his sweaty hand to his face as if to control the uncontrollable. He had never felt so isolated and alone in his life. He glanced at the public gallery, longing to make contact with a friendly face, as if hoping to ease his fear and alienation. It was not to be. He was alone. In frustration at being left to carry the burden of guilt without support from his brothers, he had changed his plea to guilty thus saving many people the ordeal of appearing in court, a daunting task for some. He was commended for this by the judge but told not to expect any leniency. He was remanded in custody to await his fate.

Bloody brothers, leaving me to face this on my own. Trust Alex to chicken out and abscond, and him the big man, or so he always told us. Some brother he turned out to be, ran off at the first sign of trouble. Where the heck is he?

He sat with his head in his hands, wishing, so wishing he could turn the clock back.

Damn you Bobby for spotting Barry Jones in that pub. Life was good enough before then… and now you and your damn mental problems…getting off with a cosy hospital stay and me left to face years in a stinking hell hole of a prison. Poor Mum, wonder if she understands any of this… hope not…

His thoughts were interrupted by a visit from his counsel who informed him that the High Court Judge had deferred sentence until a later date.

"Joe, it could take up to four weeks before we have a decision. You will be transferred to a nearby prison until then. I'll put in a plea of mitigation since you've been left to carry the can. The judge might look kindly on you for pleading guilty, he alone will make the decision on length of sentence, but don't hold out too much hope. We're looking at a long prison sentence for abduction and double murder. Alex will be found, mark my word. The police will stop at nothing to find him. The guys who were escorting him have egg on their faces and have to redeem themselves somehow or other. It will bode hard for him when he's found."

Some weeks later, Joe Bryson learned of his fate. He was escorted to court by wardens and met there with his counsel.

"Prepare yourself for the worst, Joe," he said as he patted the prisoner on the shoulder. "I've done all that I could for you, the rest is up to the judge now."

Standing in the dock, cuffed between two burly wardens, Joe Bryson learned his fate: "Life without parole," announced the judge to the distraught man who felt tears stream down his face and was unable to wipe them away. He barely heard the judge's condemnation of his crimes. His mind was in turmoil. Anger would come later.

***

A ruling had been made that due to Bobby's mental disorder and diminished responsibility he would be held in a secure psychiatric prison wing without limit of time.

***

Alex Bryson remained at large with APW, all ports warning, an alert system which was hopeful of tracing the wanted man.

***

Some time later, Tony and the heavily pregnant Gina sat with Carole and Ted enjoying a quiet meal together. They were thoughtful and subdued.

"You know, I don't feel like celebrating the ending of this case. We got our man in the end but I feel numb now. Knowing Rita Hampton has been sentenced to life without parole doesn't make me want to shout from the rooftops. I don't think I'll ever forgive myself for not saving Lucy. If only..."

"Tony," said Carole, "I feel the same. The events of the past few years have taken over our lives. It has left scars for us all. All those lives lost…"

She never got to finish. A cry from a smiling Gina told them a new life was about to enter their world.

CHAPTER 40

Some of the team from Harvey's squad gathered around to talk via Skype with their Scottish colleagues and detective Geoff Nolan who had come from London for the trial of Joe Bryson.

"Good results all round then guys, on both sides of the pond," began Tony, looking more relaxed than he had for some time. "In the end, justice has been served."

"Yes, sir," responded Detective McKenzie, with a mock salute to his American friends. "Our trio of bad brothers led us a merry dance. We were all convinced your two thugs had been targeted by someone from your end of the world in revenge for young Lucy's death and all the time the Bryson boys were seeking out Barry Jones for a ten-year-old assault on their mother."

"It's sure been a roller coaster of a ride," commented Carole. "I for one am glad the ride has stopped. It's been great working with you guys and learning the difference in our judiciary systems and the different terminology."

Rab McKenzie picked up the theme, "Yes, it is different, but we got our men in the end, well apart from the one who has gone AWOL and he is sure to be picked up soon. He can't hide forever.

"Do you guys know that Scotland has its own system of law, quite separate from the rest of the UK, have had for centuries? We have three verdicts here; guilty, not guilty, and not proven."

Geoff Nolan piped in, "The crazy Scots have to be different now, don't you? Causes all sorts of confusion. I thought I was on another planet when I sat in your High Court. Why can't you be civilised and refer to it as the Crown Court, like normal people? And they don't use the word 'defendant' either up here; they talk about the 'accused'. Don't get me started on the rest!"

His remarks caused laughter among the friends who had bonded well over the many months of investigation.

"Yeah," said Tony, "I read about the different systems. Hey, in the end we're all reading from the same hymn sheet; okay, maybe from different pages, but we get the result in the end. If your guys had been tried over here, they could possibly be facing the death penalty."

"I'll be sure to tell the Bryson boy when I see him, he'll be really cheered up to know that!" said Rab.

Before signing off, Tony said, "We need to get together in the future and have a discussion about all this over a meal and a drink. I hope we will meet up again. I plan to visit Scotland some day with my wife and family when my son is a bit older."

"We heard you'd got yourself a wife and settled down to wedded bliss! And you have a son! Congratulations to you both. What did you call the wee man?"

"My step-daughter Abigail made the choice for us. His name is Lucian."

***

Julie, relieved at not having to appear in court, had concentrated on publishing her book. She finished a successful book-signing session, packed up her remaining books, pleased with the turnout for the event. She enjoyed talking to people about her work, enthused with those who, like her, loved history, and met some interesting people and answered questions with courtesy and professionalism.

"Would you ever consider writing in another genre?" she was asked by an enthusiastic book reader.

"I've only ever written historical fiction, but it's not outwith the realm of possibility. Perhaps in the future!"

***

As always, her mind wandered to the next book tucked somewhere in the deep recess of her brain.

"Maybe I do need a change of genre," she commented as she relaxed at home with her friend Liz and three lively pets who fussed around the visitor in the hope that her large pocket contained some biscuits. They were not disappointed.

"A mystery thriller perhaps," suggested Liz, "with an international flavour and a missing killer. Yes, the very thing. Perhaps Scamper could find that escaped prisoner, Alex Bryson, the guy who took flight from a rendezvous with justice. You could call the book, *Scamper's Find*."

ABOUT THE AUTHOR

Terry H Watson qualified in D.C.E. and Dip.Sp.Ed. from Notre Dame College Glasgow and Bearsden, and obtained a B.A. degree from Open University Scotland.

A retired special needs teacher, who recently began writing, Terry has three books published: *Call Mama*, of which Scamper's Find is the sequel. There is a third book in the trilogy called *The Leci Legacy*. She has also written a novella called *A Case for Julie* and a book of short stories called *A Tale or Two and a Few More*: Coming soon is a prequel to The Lucy Trilogy, *Before Lucy* , and a second short story compilation, *A Few More Tales To Tell'*

Contact
e-mail: Terryhwatson@yahoo.co.uk
Twitter: @TerryHWatson1
Website: www.terryhwatson.com

Printed in June 2019
by Rotomail Italia S.p.A., Vignate (MI) - Italy